USA TODAY BESTSELLING AUTHOR
DALE MAYER

Weapon in the Watermelon

Lovely Lethal Gardens
REWIND 04

WEAPON IN THE WATERMELON: LOVELY LETHAL GARDENS REWIND, BOOK 4
Beverly Dale Mayer
Valley Publishing Ltd.

ISBN-13: 978-1-778866-95-1
Print Edition

Books in This Series:

About This Book

When a young couple is attacked while prepping for a catering job, it seems like the family is dealing with a long-running curse—one that ends in murder. ... Doreen can't stop meddling, so, when she finds out that that the young woman's mother is an unsolved murder case, Doreen has her cold case to work her way into Mack's current investigation.

But, like all her cases, nothing is quite so simple. While Mack is dealing with the death of the dead chef, Doreen is working behind the scenes to sort out all the different family factions. Meanwhile she must also sort out a gift for Nan's birthday. Somehow Doreen manages to mix the two together.

Now if only things would go smoothly from here on in—but of course not they don't. With the animals involved, the chaos is even wilder.

Sign up to be notified of all Dale's releases here!
https://geni.us/DaleNews

Chapter 1

SEVERAL NIGHTS LATER, as Mack and Doreen were cuddling together after dinner when his phone rang. "Hello, Captain. … Yeah, I'm here with Doreen now. … I know. I know. We've just been discussing it. It's pretty sad."

The captain spoke for several minutes, the smile falling off Mack's face.

"Right, another murder," he muttered, turning all business. "No, I'm coming. … Yeah, I'll head down to the office. What do we know?"

Doreen leaned in to hear, but he hopped to his feet and glared at her.

"Right, sorry," she whispered.

"Okay. … Oh, okay." He frowned. "No, I'll be there in just a few minutes." He reached out a hand and helped Doreen to her feet, as he ended the call. "I've got to go," he said.

"A new case?" she asked, watching him sideways. "Any details?"

"No," he declared, glaring at her. "No details, specifically none for you."

"Why not?" she wailed.

"Because it's not a cold case. And, besides, you've got to work on yours. The senator's daughter, remember?"

"Sure, and I will, but I can't believe you've already got another one."

"I do, but it doesn't sound like a whole lot of fun though."

"Why is that?"

"A restaurant kitchen is the crime scene," he replied. "A man and a woman were working on a catering job. Apparently the man's been stabbed."

"Oh, wow," Doreen muttered, as she stared at him. "What was the weapon?"

"Don't know for sure. … They think it was a knife from the kitchen."

"Ah."

Mack groaned.

"What?" she asked.

"You won't believe it."

"But I do believe it."

He winced. "I think the captain mentioned they found the knife in a … watermelon."

"Watermelon?" she repeated, looking at him in shock. "Oh, cutting up the watermelon itself?"

"Maybe. I think so," he said, "but, until I get there, I won't know the details."

"Just remember to keep me posted," Doreen stated, with a bright smile.

"No way," he replied. "It's got nothing to do with you. It's a current case. *My* current case."

"It could involve me though."

"No, it can't. It's an active case."

"It's an active case, *but* …" She beamed.

"What?" he asked, frowning at her.

"It's a *Weapon in the Watermelon.*"

He closed his eyes, swore under his breath, and muttered, "Okay, I'll give you that one, but it's still my case, and you stay out of it."

Then he leaned over, kissed her hard, and headed for his truck.

Chapter 2

THE NEXT MORNING Doreen was up early, not sleeping well, her mind consumed with Mack's latest murder case. She had a quick shower and a quicker breakfast, plus fed her animals and let the four-legged ones outside for a bit. With the bitter cold weather here, they would want back inside soon.

Meanwhile, she sat at her kitchen table, haphazardly doodling notes on the pad of paper in front of her. And now she heard scratching at the door. That didn't take long. Doreen got up and let in Mugs and Goliath. She sat again at her kitchen table, before her notepad. Her mind just couldn't understand a scenario in which a weapon was found in a watermelon. But the phrase kept playing over and over in her head. She didn't even know if it was true because Mack, of course, hadn't seen the actual crime scene yet. Plus, he wasn't sharing much about his latest case. She couldn't blame him, yet it was frustrating because he was dishing out little teasing tidbits, as if leading her to an end—an end she wasn't allowed to participate in.

Groaning, she sat back, wishing she had a police scanner to be a fly on the wall in their office, allowing her to get the extra bits and pieces to satisfy her curiosity. In this case, she would only figure out what was going on if and when Mack got around to telling her. It was an active case, and that meant his case.

As she sighed, she thought about all the cases she had worked on recently. She'd been involved in so many different cases, and it was great. It really was, and she'd had a grand old time with all of them. By rights, she should welcome a break, a chance to sit back, relax, and just do nothing. However, as she stared around the house, the walls started to shrink in on her, confining her, making her realize that she needed spring to arrive more quickly than it would actually come. Either that or she needed something to keep herself busy. A hobby of some kind.

Mugs gave a *woof.* Doreen chuckled, as it seemed her trusty basset hound was reading her mind. She had to shake her head at that. Yet Mugs had been with her for years, helping her survive her abusive marriage to Mathew. In fact, Doreen wondered why he had even allowed her to have Mugs in the house and not relegated him to the outside. In truth, he'd probably preferred to have no animals within miles of him.

Doreen shook her head and couldn't imagine her life without her animals. Doreen checked on Thaddeus, Nan's African grey that Doreen now looked after. He was asleep on his roost in the living room. And she spied Goliath—also Nan's but now Doreen's to keep—asleep by her feet on the kitchen floor. He was a huge Maine coon. How boring and sad her life would be without them and her grandmother— and Mack. She glanced at her engagement ring and smiled.

When Nan called a little bit later, she was slightly cross and out of sorts herself.

"I figured that maybe you had something fun and exciting to help us along," she grumbled. "We're all bored."

Doreen groaned. "Mack does, but I don't."

At that, Nan asked, "You can't get anything out of him?"

"Not right now. He was very clear and a little too smug when he left as it was," she shared, with a groan.

"I know you don't want to discuss it, but we could always sort out more wedding details."

Doreen winced. "You mean, those details that I haven't even started thinking about?"

"Yes, those," Nan agreed. "I know that you're being … not overtly difficult about it, but maybe a little."

She stared down at her phone and frowned. "I don't mean to be difficult about it," she declared, "but I really don't want to get pushed into doing something that I'm not ready to do, Nan."

After a long pause on the other end, her grandmother sighed. "On that note, I guess I've just been told to back off completely."

"At least for a little while," Doreen murmured. "I just don't want to feel pressured."

"Of course not, but you realize that, for us, this is big. It's fun, and it's exciting, and we all want rather desperately to get little tidbits of information to keep us going because it'll be a big deal for all the Rosemoor residents."

"If all of them want to attend, where could we possibly have a reception?" Doreen exclaimed. "There won't be enough room there. I did talk to the manager at Rosemoor recently about the possibility of maybe doing two receptions. That way, everybody there at the home, … if they couldn't travel to the wedding and its reception, they could attend a second one there."

Nan cried out in joy, "That's a wonderful idea."

"But is it?" Doreen asked. "I'm sure some people won't want anything to do with my wedding and all the rest, while others will have a little involvement, with some all in."

"One of the biggest lessons in life that you have to learn, child, is that you can't make everybody happy all the time."

"It would be nice if I could make some people happy some of the time though," she noted.

Nan laughed. "Good luck with that."

"People always have wants and wishes, and they're not necessarily the same as yours." Doreen pointed out and waited for her grandmother's reaction. When Nan pealed with laughter, Doreen smiled. "I was afraid of upsetting you."

"No, I see that you're trying to be considerate and all, but feelings of frustration will arise every once in a while," she shared. "I just don't want you to go half crazy and cancel the whole thing because you can't see a way to move forward."

"I wouldn't do that to Mack," Doreen stated.

"If you *do* want to, it's better to do it to Mack now, before you drag this out more."

"No, I'm not uncertain about marrying him. It's just the push for an expedited time frame on the formal ceremony. I really need to be ready emotionally and mentally to connect fully. I don't want to feel pushed into it. Everybody keeps asking me, particularly Millicent." She mentioned Mack's mom, who had been more insistent with every visit. "And I know she sees time as an issue, but ..."

"You have to remember that Millicent is older than I am, and I'm sure she is looking forward to seeing *both* her sons happily married. She had those kids very late in life, and I wouldn't be at all surprised if she's looking to get this settled before she goes."

"Maybe," Doreen conceded. "Millicent is definitely pressuring Nick and Mack to get married soon. Although Nick did thank me the last time we talked, as my engagement to Mack seems to have relieved some pressure on Nick to find a woman and get engaged and married."

"Yes, and I think one of the things that has infuriated her to no end is that her sons have refused to get married and to give her grandkids for so long," Nan added pointedly. "So, even if you do tie the knot while she's alive, you can bet that then the push will be on for the next generation."

Doreen gasped and closed her eyes.

"I understand," Nan noted. "I'm not pushing for that, but I'm sure Millicent will."

Doreen winced. "I think you're right. She probably is looking for grandkids."

"It will be enough for the moment to know that Mack is happy. She just wants him to be happy."

"I hope so," she muttered. "And I hope she thinks he'll be happy with me because there are times when he's completely infuriated with me."

Nan burst into laughter. "I am certain he is, but I'm not sure that's a bad thing. You can't let them get complacent and think they know everything about us."

"But you never married," Doreen pointed out, "so, it's not as if anybody was hassling you to tie the knot."

"Oh, I went through the same thing, child. I basically just told my family to forget it. I wasn't going there, wasn't interested in going there, and, if they didn't like it, it was too darn bad."

"Ah, so now I know what to tell you." Doreen chuckled.

"If you want me to back off," she replied, "I'll try. No guarantees though because … it is definitely something I want to see happen before I die. Since moving here last April, you've had quite a busy life in Kelowna, and Mack has been there with you every step of the way," she noted.

Doreen modded. "Believe me that I do know how truly blessed I am to have him in my life."

"As much as he needs to know that," Nan admitted, "don't tell him too often. We don't want any more insufferable overinflated male egos."

"Mack's ego is hardly overinflated, is it?" she asked.

"It still isn't good to give him too much self-confidence," Nan muttered, then let out a gasp as a knock came at her apartment. "*Uh-oh.* I've got people at my door. I think I've forgotten an appointment. Got to go." Nan ended the call.

Doreen shook her head, reminded of how her grandmother had a way-more-active life than Doreen did. How did that work?

Yet it kept Nan happy and content, and, considering Nan's age, Doreen was more than okay with that too. It was just so very strange that everybody else was having all these great things happen in their lives, while Doreen felt as if nothing was happening in hers. And yet that wasn't true, and she knew it. It was just how she felt right now, which wasn't good either.

Morose, she decided that she would do something she absolutely hated doing. If she was already in a pissy mood, she might as well get some unpleasant chores done. With that thought, she got up and grabbed the vacuum, then proceeded to torment the animals by vacuuming the whole house, both floors, even inside the closets, finding every nook and cranny. When she was finally done, she turned off the vacuum and looked around. No animals were anywhere to be seen.

She had just headed back downstairs when a hard knock came on her front door. Mugs tore out from under her desk at the side of the kitchen, barking like crazy. Frowning, she opened the door to see a huge older man standing there, glaring at her. Mugs sniffed his legs through the screen door but then walked back to the kitchen, as if disinterested.

Doreen attempted a smile for the seemingly unhappy man and greeted him. "Hello."

His gaze narrowed and locked on her face. "I'm looking for a woman named Doreen."

"Yes," she replied cautiously, "that's me."

His eyebrows shot up. Then he shook his head, looked around, and asked, "Are you sure? Isn't somebody else here?"

"No, I'm sure nobody else is here," she stated, staring at him. "This is my house, and you came here, so what is it you want?"

He looked down at the note he held in his hand. "It can't be you."

"Why can't it be me?" she asked in exasperation.

"For one thing, you don't look old enough, and, for a second thing, you don't seem as if you could handle this job."

She straightened her messed-up clothing, pushing wisps of hair off her face, then decided to give it up. "That doesn't change who I am. Plus, I still don't know what you're doing here, but you're the one who sought me out. So why don't you just tell me what you want, instead of insulting me."

He flushed and groaned. "Sorry, I didn't mean to do that, but I was looking for a detective."

"You found her," Doreen declared. "Some people call me the *amateur detective*, and I do a lot of that work, but, if you want to be technically correct, you can call me an amateur sleuth."

"I did hear you didn't have any credentials, and that worries me."

She stared at him and asked, "Do you want to explain what's going on?"

"Yeah." Still, he didn't speak for a long moment. Then with a deep breath, he began, the words tumbling out, "My niece is about to be charged with murder, but I know she didn't have anything to do with it."

"And how do you know that?"

"Because it's not who she is. She wouldn't."

"Okay, so presumably she has an alibi or a reason why she's not involved or something."

"No, and that's the problem. She doesn't have an alibi, and she did see her boyfriend before he was killed."

"Ah, and that's the most recent murder we have in town here, I presume?"

"Yes," he confirmed. "It just happened, but I know she didn't kill him."

"Okay, and you came to me why?"

"I want you to prove that she's innocent."

She winced. "I'm not sure how you expect me to do that. I have limited capacity to act with current cases. Cold cases are altogether different."

"I heard that too. You have limitations on what you can deal with."

She studied him. "I'm glad to see that the rumor mill is fairly accurate these days."

"My niece would never kill anyone because she's still

trying to figure out what happened to her mother."

"Her mother was murdered?" Doreen asked, frowning at him.

He nodded. "Yes, but it was quite a few years ago now."

"How many years ago?" she asked, eyeing him carefully.

"At least ten or so, I think." He looked down at his hands, as if mentally counting his fingers. "Yes, it was ten."

"And whereabouts did this happen?"

He shrugged. "Alberta."

"Okay, so when did the family move here?"

"Right afterward, a large portion of the family moved here. One of the family members here had inherited a farm and had employee housing, so there was room for everyone to get settled into a new location. Everybody was pretty fed up with the whole rigamarole that had happened in Alberta, so they came here."

"And now you've been here for ten years."

"Yes, and we've not had a lick of trouble," he pointed out. "Now, all of sudden, the local cops are looking at my niece."

"Looking at your niece is one thing, but charging her with murder is something completely different. Do you think her mother's murder had anything to do with this current murder?"

He frowned at her and shook his head. "I couldn't imagine how. ... That wouldn't make any sense to me."

She nodded. "If you want to give me the details, I can talk to the police, see if I can get an idea of what I can work on. I can work on cold cases and can partially look into the current one, if it somehow connects to a cold case."

"I'm much less worried about something that nobody could solve from ten years ago. I'm trying to confirm my niece doesn't end up being charged for something she didn't do in the here and now."

Doreen invited him inside and noted that Thaddeus remained asleep on his stoop. Even Goliath didn't move from under the kitchen table. So her animals weren't at all worried about this stranger in their home. Doreen led her visitor into her kitchen, where she picked up a notepad and began, "Give me the information about your niece and the case of her murdered boyfriend, and I'll also need your contact information. Plus, I want a full file on the deceased mother." When he glared at her, she tilted her head. "You may not see that it's connected, and maybe it's not, but it could be my ticket to getting access to work on this current case because both murders share a connection to your niece."

"I don't understand what difference it makes."

She smiled up at him. "It makes a big difference because I'm engaged to be married to the detective on the current murder case," she shared.

His eyebrows shot up, and he asked, "Is this some marital thing?"

"No, it's a *law* thing, but it's okay. I still need that information from you," she noted, facing him. "Your contact information and your niece's contact information."

He groaned. "I will give you mine, but I won't share Jillian's. She's got enough going on."

Doreen sighed. "I presume one of you has a decent file on her mother's murder."

"Jillian does. She was investigating it. She shouldn't have been, and I told her to lay off."

"And yet her boyfriend was killed, but she wasn't. I heard they were both there together. Interesting."

"Yes," he muttered, giving her a death glare. "Why

would Jillian have been killed?"

"Let's start with details on the current case, the murdered boyfriend."

"He's a chef. Hang on. … He wasn't a chef yet. He's was … working on becoming a chef," he clarified, with a wave of his hands. "He's a heck of a good cook." He winced. "He *was* a heck of a good cook." Doreen just nodded and waited. He groaned and continued. "And there was some dispute at work. I don't even know what it was all about, but he was killed with a butcher knife."

She stared at him for a long moment. "He wasn't, um, chopping up watermelon or something at the same time, was he?"

He looked at her curiously. "I have no idea," he replied, staring at her. "Why would you ask that?"

"Never mind." She gave an airy wave of her hand. "It just occurred to me."

"Right," he muttered, frowning at her. "It just occurred to you? How does that work?" He gave her a look, as if she were crazy.

She beamed at him and added, "Don't worry about it."

He shook his head. "Look. I'm already worried sick. I need to get somebody who can actually help."

"Of course you do, and you're welcome to get somebody else who will. However," she explained, "I do know an awful lot about murder cases, even though you're already thinking I'm crazy because I want the information on her mother's death."

"Digging into Katie's murder is a different story," he pointed out. "I need somebody who can work on *this* case right now and can get my niece off the hook."

She studied him. "Getting her off the hook isn't the

same thing as her not being guilty."

"She's not guilty," he roared.

Mugs barked at him, suddenly in between the two of them again.

Pinching the bridge of his nose, he sighed. "I'm sorry. *Getting her off the hook* is just a turn of phrase."

"But it's a turn of phrase that's very important," she stated. "You may think she's got nothing to do with it but—"

"I don't even know why she was there so late that day."

"She works with him?" Doreen asked, surprised.

He nodded. "The two of them look like … siblings."

She winced and frowned. "And do we know that they aren't?"

"Why would you even say that?" he asked in horror.

"I've seen an awful lot of cases go south because people had no idea what was really going on," she muttered, writing down as much information as she could. Meanwhile, her mind was going off in a million different directions as she tried to come up with other questions she could ask him.

He continued to glare at her.

She shook her head. "Look. I'm willing to look into this and to see what I can do to help Jillian, but you need to know that, if she's guilty, I won't be working to get her off."

"She's not guilty," he declared, then groaned. "I don't think we should even be having this conversation."

"Maybe not, but that's up to you."

"Will it be a problem if I go to a private investigator?"

"Nope." Then she mentioned the one she'd worked with in the past. "Talk with Corey and tell him that you've spoken to me about it."

"What difference would that make?"

"He'll talk to me if we come up with anything," she

shared cheerfully.

"Oh, so you'll work with him?"

"Sure."

"Fine then," he said, giving her a sideways look. "You haven't talked about money though."

"No, I haven't. What's your name?"

"I am Zev Burgon."

"Okay, Zev, talk to the private detective, if that's what you want. I'll contact you if I come up with anything."

"And what about … a fee?" he asked, staring at her hesitantly.

She raised her eyebrows. "It would be nice to think I got paid for any of the cases I've already solved," she admitted, "but I haven't been so far, and I certainly won't start charging now."

Chapter 3

AS SOON AS Zev left—and it had taken a little bit more pushing to get him to go—Doreen sat down in her living room and just let some of the information flow through her brain. Could there be a connection between the murder of a decade ago and this current one?

Of course.

Was it likely? After all, the murders were ten years apart.

Probably not.

And the fact that the family was in Alberta when the mother had been murdered was an interesting twist. It didn't necessarily have anything to do with the niece, but, if she was on Mack's suspect list, then Doreen wanted to know. Now that didn't mean Mack would tell her, but some things needed to be shared. So she picked up her phone and called him.

Mack answered, but he was a little distracted. "I don't have any information for you," he warned.

"I might have a little bit for you though."

"What do you mean?"

"I just had a very strange visitor at my front door."

"Oh?" he replied, wariness sliding into his tone.

Then she explained about the visit.

"We're looking at his niece," he confirmed in exasperation. "Yet it's not as if we've made any decisions, and we sure haven't arrested anybody. It's so typical. People go off half-cocked, and they jump to the worst conclusion."

"I did tell him that he may want to get a licensed PI, and I directed him to Corey in town," she shared.

"Yes, but you also heard *cold case*, and now you're all over it."

She hesitated. "I heard *cold case*, and obviously we don't have any way to know whether it's connected to this one or not," she clarified, "but the fact that Zev even showed up here …"

"Why are people jumping all over this?"

"Because they're scared," she offered. "It's his family, and they've already been through the grinder with the police over the mother's death some ten years earlier—but it was in Alberta."

"I understand. I get it," he said, with a groan. Then in a calmer tone, he added, "I just wish they wouldn't keep bringing you into it."

"I don't think we can stop that, particularly at this stage. However, I do wonder about the mother's case."

"Of course you do because it's a cold case," he stated, with a note of humor.

"Therefore, I'll ask if you could pull the files."

"Even though it's an Alberta case?" he asked.

"Yes."

When she hesitated, Mack was all over her. "What are you thinking?"

"I don't know, but the family moved here ten years ago, after that murder. Already a lot of their relatives were here, so they joined them after the ugliness of Jillian's mother Katie's murder."

"So, everybody who had some connection or involvement in that ten-year-old case moved here?" he noted. "That's just great. And now they're all in the midst of a second murder."

"That's one of the reasons I thought you needed to know about this. Plus, I'll need you to clarify just what's going on with Katie's murder case and who, if any, were considered suspects back then."

"Oh, gee, let me guess. You want me to find that out too."

"I would think that, in the course of your investigation into this current case, you would want to know about that previous murder, and you would check it out anyway."

"Obviously I would want to know," he muttered. "So, fine. I'll do that much but no guarantees."

"Of course not," she said in a gentle tone.

After a moment of silence, Mack sighed. "Sorry I've been a bit of a bear. And how are you?"

"I'm okay," she muttered. "A little bit out of sorts."

"And you're thinking this case might pull you out of the doldrums?" he asked, humor threading through his tone. "Just a juicy little murder, even if it isn't in your own backyard?"

"I haven't dealt with anything quite so far away," she noted, "and I can see how that could be an issue but maybe not. It is a curiosity."

"It is—a curiosity that could impact what I'm doing as well."

"Exactly, so, in the spirit of cooperation—"

"In the spirit of you getting information you want, you

mean," he pointed out wryly. "Yeah, you told me."

"Yes, but isn't it interesting that Zev came to see me in the first place?"

"That seems to be more of the norm now," Mack muttered. "It would be great if people would just tell the cops what they knew and wanted, so we didn't have to go through all these shenanigans. But it doesn't seem as if criminals have gotten any more honest or ethical in the years that I've been on the force."

She laughed. "No, I don't think so," she conceded. "Not only that, I suspect they may be worse. They've gotten smarter and have a lot more ways to hide their crimes, and they can do everything more quickly."

"I know," he agreed. "And, on that note, I'll get back to you. The captain's calling." And, with that, he ended the call.

Doreen sat back and looked at the names Zev had given her, then quickly settled down in front of her laptop and started an internet search. Just as she was about to go through the pages and pages of results, she had a thought and checked Solomon's files. She had all the shortened digital summaries in her phone but also had hard-copy printouts in a binder. She put on some coffee and then sat down with her phone to see if any of Solomon's unsolved cases dealt with this Burgon family.

Nothing came up on Katie's murder, but the Burgon family was mentioned as potential eyewitnesses on another matter, with some questions for them. This seemed totally unrelated to the Burgon family's two murder cases. Still, she pulled the physical file and reviewed it in full. Not much was here, yet she found a direct link to the family on yet another of Solomon's files.

"Another case? A third case?" she muttered to herself, as she looked down at her summary notes regarding a possible suicide or an actual murder of yet another Burgon family member. "Why would this same family be involved in all these murder cases?" She pulled the Burgon file, which had a few notes of dodgy business practices, but no reference material to back it up. However, a single handwritten note stated *Alberta connection*.

She sat back, stared at it, took a picture of it, then sent it to Mack. She didn't know what was going on here, but there was an Alberta connection between one or two of Solomon's unsolved cold cases and now a current case.

When Mack phoned her a little later, he asked, "What is that from?"

"Solomon's files," she shared.

"Oh boy," he muttered.

"Yeah, I know," she replied, "and I don't really understand what it means. There's not much information, but that note about a connection to an Alberta case caught my eye."

"I phoned Red Deer to get the details on the mother's murder and talked to one of the officers put on the case. He told me how the mother was home alone, the family off bowling for some teenager's birthday party or something that Jillian had been invited to. When they came home, Katie was dead. She'd been killed in her own house."

"Sexual assault?"

"No," he confirmed.

"Thank heavens for that." Then another ugly thought hit Doreen. "Did the daughter find her?"

"I think the uncle may have been there with Jillian, but I don't know for sure. The information in the database is minimal, so I've asked for a hard copy of the file."

"How long will that take? And I bet it's incomplete too."

He gave a bark of laughter. "That's just the facts of life. When we want more, we get less, and, when we want less, we get more. I've got to run."

And, with that, he was gone again.

Chapter 4

FOR THE NEXT little bit Doreen couldn't do a whole lot, outside of making notes and doing some internet research. Her animals seemed to know when she was head-down into her work and pretty much left her alone. As long as she fed them morning and night, opening the rear kitchen door for them to access the backyard, they all seemed happy enough—until they wanted to see Nan or just to walk down the creek. That suited Doreen just fine.

Then she took a break from her laptop and apologized to the animals for leaving them behind and went to the library to see if she could come up with anything there, in terms of the current murder in town. Doreen searched for Katie Burgon, murdered in Alberta a decade ago, grumbling as she went back and forth with the microfiche articles, finding a lack of information.

The librarian came over and asked if she could help. After Doreen explained what she was working on, the librarian nodded. "That's a pretty modern murder in microfiche terms. There's probably a whole lot more information on the internet, especially since it happened in Alberta."

"I did look at that," she shared, "but there isn't a whole

lot there either. It doesn't seem to be widely covered."

"And that happens too. You know it does."

"I understand, but it's frustrating when searching for information, and it seems these journalists pick and choose who they report on."

"It would typically be a one-paragraph article with a by-line, not a whole lot more," she pointed out. "So, if you can find that one short entry, the byline will give you someone to contact for more. Other than that, it'll just be whatever is in the police files."

She nodded. "And Mack is pulling those for me."

"Oh, good," the librarian replied in delight. "I'm really glad you're working so closely with the police."

"Me too. Sometimes it works out very well," she noted, as she stood up, then looked down at the few pages she had printed off. "Just not a whole lot is here."

"No, but you could check some of the archived newspapers and see what's available."

"Yeah, will do," she agreed, and, with a smile, she headed back to her car. In the mood for Chinese, she made a quick stop at Mr. Woo's. When he saw her, his face lit up. "I know I'm showing up midmorning," she noted, "but I just wondered if you could whip me up something to take home for lunch."

"Of course, of course, of course," he stated. "Do you want to pick off the menu, or do you want me to make you something?"

She looked at him in delight and nodded. "If you could just make me something, that would be wonderful."

He disappeared into the kitchen, muttering something to himself, but she didn't have a clue what. When he returned, he had a bag with two containers stacked on top, and he held it out to her.

She handed him her credit card, and he refused it. "No, no, I can pay."

"No, no, no, you no pay," he declared. "You did for me. I do for you."

"No, no, no, no, no, no," she argued. "I can't do that. It's not right."

He glared at her, and she glared right back. He refused to take her money, and she refused to accept the food. Finally she relented. "Fine, but … only this time." He just nodded and didn't say anything. She glared at him. "Otherwise I won't come back."

He frowned, and she nodded happily. "See? You don't like that either, but I won't take advantage."

"No, no good for business if you no come back."

"Maybe it's not good for business if I'm here, and you don't let me pay," she muttered. "Seems as if everybody is struggling these days."

He snorted. "Some places bad."

"Sure, some places," she muttered, "but I am not bad and the places I go aren't bad. That's part and parcel of what I do."

He nodded. "You take it." And he shoved it at her.

She glared at him, but her shoulders slumped. "Fine, thank you." Yet she wasn't happy. In the meantime, Doreen realized there wouldn't be any compromise reached right now, so she snatched her to-go bag, muttering as she walked back out to the parking lot.

She went home, her mind trying to figure out how she could get him to accept payment. Otherwise she wouldn't get her favorite Chinese food anymore, and that would suck. As soon as she got home, Nan called her.

"Any news?" Nan asked.

"No, not yet, … at least not on that case."

"Oh, so you've got something else?" Nan perked up.

"As a matter of fact I do, but I also have another problem."

"What problem?" Nan asked. When Doreen explained about Mr. Woo, her grandmother laughed. "You could just accept the free food."

"But I want to go back and have more Chinese food," she explained. "If he won't let me pay, I'll avoid going there."

"Tell him that what you did was good enough for one payment and for you to pay next time."

"I don't know if he'll accept that."

"But this is the first time he's done it, so maybe all he wanted was to give you free food *once*," she suggested.

"Maybe." Yet Doreen was doubtful. He'd been so determined.

"Besides, you did save both his life and his business, so the least you could do is allow him to pay you back a little bit."

Doreen groaned. "Fine," she muttered, trying to suppress her intense frustration. "I'll think about what my options are."

Nan chuckled. "You do that. In the meantime, did you say you have another case?"

"There's a curiosity."

"I like curiosities," Nan stated. So, Doreen filled her in. "In Alberta and in Kelowna?" Nan asked.

"Alberta is where the mother was murdered, and we don't know that it's connected at all, but Mack is happy enough to have me dig into that one as long as I stay out of his current one."

"Yes, yes, of course," Nan muttered. "And Alberta is far enough away to keep you out of trouble, at least mostly."

"Parts of that province, true, but Calgary is in the southern region, and it's what? … Maybe a four-hour drive from here? So easy enough for someone to make the round trip in one day," she muttered. "Anyway, the next thing is this name, *Burgon*. It's somehow connected to an old murder or just a possible suicide here. Solomon's files had *Alberta connection* handwritten in that file."

"Burgon, Burgon, Burgon. *Dave* Burgon?" Nan cried out.

Doreen frowned at her phone. "You know a Dave Burgon?"

"Sure, used to," Nan stated. "The family at least."

"This is a big multigenerational family, and Zev Burgon approached me, asking for help. Somehow Katie's daughter, Jillian, appears to have gotten herself in trouble over this latest Kelowna murder. Her boyfriend, the cook, was killed at work. Jillian also works at the same place as her boyfriend."

"Oh, so the police think it's a lover's tiff or something?"

"I don't know what they're thinking, and you can bet Mack isn't telling me."

Nan burst out laughing at that. "No, I can see Mack keeping mum on this one. He is as stubborn as you are."

"It would sure make my life easier if he wasn't."

"Of course, but that wouldn't do much toward making his life any easier," Nan quipped, giggling.

Doreen glared down at her phone again. "I don't think it's that funny, Nan."

"Oh, it's absolutely hysterical, and you know it, child,"

she declared, still chuckling. "But don't you worry your head about it. You've got other things to worry about. You need to hunt down the Burgon family."

"What do you recall about the Burgon death case here?"

"Daryl Burgon, Old Man Dave's brother, committed suicide a long time ago—somewhere around the time of that Alberta murder in the family, I think. But Daryl had cancer and wasn't hanging around for an ugly end is what the rumors were all about. I remembered thinking I was right with him on that viewpoint back then. I don't remember much else."

Doreen nodded. "The newspapers didn't have very much on it at all, nor the murder in Alberta. Now Solomon's files did mention an Alberta connection but no explanation as to what he was thinking regarding what kind of connection to that particular file. His files for the most part have been in the province of British Columbia, not the others."

"If there was any squashing of the news, I'm sure Old Man Dave Burgon had something to do with that, but he passed away a few years ago. So, as soon as he was gone, everybody started talking about how the family seemed to slip from one tragedy to another. Besides, I think the coroner ruled Daryl's suicide as an accident, but no one believed it. I certainly didn't. But then I agreed with Daryl's philosophy on skipping an ugly end."

Doreen suggested, "Old Man Burgon may or may not have tried to squash the information on Daryl's death, but I can tell you that the newspapers did not run very much about Katie's death."

"Right, and I don't remember there being any solution to the case, but did you say it was solved?" Nan asked.

Doreen sighed. "That's a good point. I don't have anything saying it was, but Zev told me that Katie's murderer was never found. So, we've got two murders involving the Burgon family now, plus Daryl's suicide." Doreen started jotting down notes.

"That's fascinating. Old Man Burgon will be rolling over in his grave. He hated bad publicity."

"Why would he try to suppress it?" Doreen asked curiously.

"Because they ran a pub and restaurant downtown, so any bad news or negative press would be enough to dry up that kind of business. They established their business here probably ten years ago, and suddenly they were big business—important people, you know? They appeared out of nowhere to become someone."

"Do they still run it?" Doreen asked.

"The family does, last I knew," Nan suggested, slowly searching through her memories. "I can't remember how that one all played out, but I do remember him having a fit over any gossip that could potentially kill his business. They used to have a deli on the side of the pub. However, they got into trouble with the food inspector or something. They were always selling out-of-date stuff, so it was a mess. It became a community joke, and Old Man Burgon was fit to be tied over it. He had a really ugly reputation for a while. Maybe things improved when the restaurant replaced the deli, but I'm not sure I believe that either."

"You really don't like them much, do you?"

"It's not even about liking them or not, but, when you realize that Old Man Burgon ran a sloppy business, it's not a good look."

"Maybe not," Doreen noted, thinking it over. "Yet, if the family is putting their heart and soul into the place, ...

it's hard to see it go downhill over some rumors."

"Maybe so. I can't say anything either way," Nan muttered. "All I can tell you is, at that time, Old Man Burgon was fit to be tied over it all, but he didn't garner any sympathy. He was well known for cheating people."

Doreen nodded. "That'll cause bad feelings everywhere."

"Absolutely, and he was just a difficult person. He always seemed cranky and miserable, generally not someone you would want to do business with."

"Which then begs the question as to how the business managed to survive."

"His booze was cheap, at least in the restaurant, but you had to order food while you were there."

"Which is also normal," she pointed out. "That's how restaurants make money. Sell the food at a bargain price, then make it up on the booze or vice versa."

"Sure, but people didn't want the food, or, if they did, they didn't want to buy that much of it."

Doreen didn't say anything and just let her grandmother vent.

When Nan was done, she muttered, "Okay, now I'm really tired."

"That was a lot of venting, and, from the sounds of it, you've obviously been upset about this for a long time."

"I didn't realize how these little injustices really piss me off," Nan admitted, with a chuckle. "I'm sorry. I must have sounded as if I'd completely lost it."

"Not at all," Doreen lied. "On the other hand, … Old Man Burgon is gone."

"He is," she agreed, "so maybe the family can recover businesswise."

"He's been gone for quite a while, so if they're still in

business, I presume they might have recovered, or at least held their own. They've either changed their systems or their people."

"I have no idea how they're doing," Nan stated. "It was quite the business at one time. Nowadays, I just don't know."

"Good enough," Doreen said. "I'll dig some more and see what I can come up with."

"You do that. You're always so good at the digging part."

"I haven't really found very much this time, at least not yet."

"It's early," Nan declared in a bright, bolstering tone. "You will. I'm sure of it." And, with that, she added, "As for me, I'll go have an afternoon nap."

"Is it already afternoon?"

"It sure is. That's why you got your Chinese food early, remember? So now you can sit down and enjoy it."

That reminder just made Doreen feel bad as she stared down at the free Chinese food. With Nan off the phone, she warmed up a plate, realizing that Mr. Woo had also given her enough for several people. She hadn't even noticed it when she'd stormed out of the restaurant. And she shouldn't be upset at him since he was just trying to say, *Thank you,* but it felt like charity, something she didn't want.

There was a time when she was more than happy to accept it, and that's because she was darn hungry back then. She wasn't as hungry now, and she wanted to pay her way, which Mr. Woo didn't seem to want her to do. Nevertheless, she enjoyed her lunch, finding it delicious as always. Then, with the animals in tow, they all headed down the river just to clear Doreen's head a little bit. It was beautiful outside but too cold to enjoy it for long. By the time she made it back home, Mack was pulling into her driveway.

She walked to the front door and opened it, Mugs racing outside to give Mack the usual joyous welcome.

He laughed, bent down, and cuddled Mugs for a minute.

"I don't know," she began. "I swear, he's happier to see you than me."

"Nope. He just knows that I'm a friend." And, with that, he came inside, packing some groceries.

"Are you cooking tonight?" she asked.

"I went shopping and realized that you probably were out of a few things by now," he shared, "so I picked them up. And, if we're cooking this week, I figured I could pick up a meal or two, and we could learn to cook as we went along."

"That sounds good to me," she said, as she trailed behind him, wondering what the bags contained.

There was a certain amount of joy every time he went shopping, partly because she never really understood what to do with half of the groceries that she saw in the stores. They didn't look the same as the dishes she'd been accustomed to seeing on her plate when she had first moved here. So it always gave her pause to realize she wouldn't have a lot of the dishes she had been used to. Then, all of a sudden, Mack would come by with groceries, and soon there would be a dish that she almost recognized, which would make her smile, exactly as Mack had intended.

As he unpacked the groceries, she watched. "Were you planning on cooking tonight?"

"No, I wasn't planning on anything," he admitted, with a smile, as his gaze landed on the Chinese take-out containers. "Seems to be a good thing, considering you picked up take-out." He looked over at her.

"Now you're just pissing me off too."

He frowned at her. "You want to explain that?"

She raised both hands in a huff and explained the problem.

"Ah, so he wants to say, *Thank you.*"

"That, plus I don't necessarily feel like taking charity anymore. … I am helping people, so it's not as if I'm asking for handouts."

"Right," he said, leaving it at that, while she kept talking.

"But it feels like charity."

He smiled at her and asked, "In what way?"

"I don't know. I just don't want him to feel that he has to do it."

"Did it feel as if he had to?"

"No," she wailed, raising her hands in frustration. "Never mind. Apparently … I'm not making sense."

"You're making perfect sense, but I think sometimes you have to give other people a chance to say, *Thank you,* in whatever way that they know how." She frowned at him, and he nodded. "Just think about it. What is it that he does?" He smiled at her.

Doreen sighed. "He makes Chinese food."

"So, it's his business. It's his restaurant. You helped him. Heck, you saved him, both his business and his life. He just wants to do something for you, and this is what he knows to do. His food is what he is proud of, and he wants to thank you with some."

"I suppose," she grumbled.

He laughed. "You suppose?"

"That makes sense. I just don't want him to feel obligated."

"I think he probably *does* feel obligated to some degree—or at least grateful. And grateful is something you should manage to deal with."

"I can manage just fine," she snapped. "I just don't want him to feel as if he has to do it for me."

"You told him that, and he acknowledged it and has done what he's done anyway," Mack pointed out. "So, you now get to acknowledge him and your feelings and move on."

"But I want to still have Chinese food," she cried out, facing him. "And I'll feel terrible if I go in there and he does it again."

He smiled. "I'll go with you next time, and we'll see what he says, but you have to give people a chance to thank you. It's just being gracious. Of all the things you know, that is something I'm surprised you don't have down already."

"Knowing is one thing, but having it directed your way is a completely different thing," she muttered. "And why would you assume I would know? Just because I know all about being a hostess and being gracious?" she asked, raising her hands in frustration yet again. "Apparently I've forgotten way more than I ever remembered."

He chuckled. "I won't argue against that at all," he noted, "because I happen to like you just as you are."

She glared over at him. Then her shoulders sagged. "Thank you."

"I mean it. I'm not just saying that."

"I know," she murmured, as she walked closer, and he opened his arms. She stepped into him for a hug and added, "He just kind of ... set me off."

"And that's fine. You're entitled to feel what you feel, but you also need to understand how he feels. If he wants to do this, you let him do it."

"*Great*," she muttered, "as long as I'm not sixty-five, and he's still trying to give me free food."

Mack burst out laughing. "Hey, if that's the case, I won't argue the point because I happen to love his Chinese food."

"I know. Me too," she admitted, "which is also why I don't want him to feel as if I was taking advantage of him."

Mack groaned, resting his chin on top of her head. "There's a big difference between his trying to thank you with food and your feeling as if you're trying to take advantage. It's not the same thing."

"There was a point in time that I was hungry enough to do it," she admitted, looking away from his piercing gaze. "And just knowing that I came that close makes me want to pay double sometimes."

His arms tightened around her, and he added, "No, that's not how life works. We all get those thoughts sometimes, and we all have things in our heads that we wish we didn't have, things we would like to feel differently about," he shared. "Yet you can't hold that against him. He is just trying to be him."

"I know. I know," she muttered.

He burst out laughing. "And yet it's still so hard for you."

She shrugged. "It is hard."

"Did you talk to my brother at all today?" he asked, as he stepped back, walked over to the Chinese food, and lifted the lid. When he looked over at her, she motioned at him.

"Eat," she prompted him.

"I didn't have anything for lunch, and I didn't know if you'd eaten already," he explained. "So I figured that, worst-case scenario, we could just make omelets."

"Your omelets aren't the *just make an omelet* kind," she clarified, as she sat down beside him and watched as he served up a big plate of the Chinese food. "Your omelets are a whole meal."

"Are you sure you don't want some of this saved for tomorrow?"

"No, I'm fine," she replied, smiling at him. "It does me good to see you eat."

He nodded, eyeing her. "Now you know how I feel."

She winced and then nodded. "Okay, fine," she muttered, "point taken."

"And, no doubt, that's also how Mr. Woo feels."

She groaned. "Got it."

He burst out laughing and told her, "Not sure you do quite yet, but we have hope."

She sighed, "I'm really not that stubborn."

"*Uh-huh …*"

"I'm not," she declared, glaring at him.

"No, of course not." And he picked up his fork and started to eat.

Chapter 5

WHEN MACK WAS done eating, Doreen got up, made coffee, and the two of them settled into the living room. He looked around as she sat down on the floor.

"You could sit in the other chair," he suggested.

She shrugged. "I'm okay on the floor for a while. I'm trying to figure out what furniture I want."

"It's a good time to figure it out," he replied, "though you seem to be pretty comfortable without furniture."

"I know, but I understand that you need bigger furniture."

He raised his eyebrows at her and shrugged. "I don't know that I need *bigger* furniture, but some furniture would be nice," he clarified, with a laugh. "These matching chairs are great for short-term sitting, but, long-term, I'm not sure they'll be the easiest on my back."

"Right. So, before you move in, we'll have to go furniture shopping." He just nodded and didn't say anything. "Or is that an issue?" she asked, looking at him.

"No, not at all, but, until we're ready for me to move in, you might change your mind a multitude of times between now and then."

She frowned at that. "I might, but I don't know why I would."

His gentle smile blossomed. "Because what we want can change over time," he shared. "There's no rush right now."

Doreen sighed. "Nan was at me again about the wedding too."

"Don't worry about it," he replied comfortably. She looked at him sideways, and he nodded. "I'm fine. You don't have to worry. I won't start pushing and getting angry about it."

She nodded. "Thank you. It's nice of you to not add more pressure," she muttered. "Still, plenty of other people are pushing."

He chuckled. "That's just because your friends include an awful lot of older people, and, looking at the possible years ahead of them, they may be wondering if they'll make it until your actual wedding."

"I get it, but we also have to consider how big we'll make this wedding." She rolled her eyes at him. "Sometimes I think I just want to run away and have a tiny wedding someplace off on a remote island."

"We can do that too," he stated, nodding. "I'm not opposed to it."

"But then what about all those people?"

He grimaced. "I can't imagine telling your grandmother that we did that, without her."

She stared at him and then winced. "Oh my gosh, me neither." She gave him a half laugh. "Although I don't think she would be mad."

"No, but she would be heartbroken."

"And I can't imagine your mother would take it any better."

"*Ugh*, no. Probably worse."

"So, as you can see, I'm still working my way through all the decisions and thought processes."

"Take your time," he told her, patting her hand. "Just take your time. It's not an issue."

She smiled, then hooked her fingers with his, and added, "Thank you for being a nice man."

He looked down at their fingers clasped together and closed his free hand around them. "You do realize a lot of men would take that comment as an insult."

"Yes," she noted bluntly. "However, I also realize that you're not *a lot of men*." When his eyebrows shot up, she smiled. "You're a whole lot better than that. You wouldn't distort words from somebody's mouth and get upset about them," she added, with a shrug.

"No, I sure wouldn't," he agreed, "but I would have to ask what you meant."

"Of course, but whatever. It doesn't matter," she replied, with a smile.

Just then his phone rang. He looked down at it and winced.

"Work?" she asked him worriedly.

He nodded as he stood up and answered it. He listened for a few minutes and then replied, "Okay, I'm coming." He looked down at her and tilted his head. "At least I got dinner, so thank you for that." He walked to the door, looked back at her, and said, "Don't forget to lock up."

"I won't."

When she hesitated, he rejoined her and gave her a kiss. "And thank you for not asking questions." Immediately the words on the tip of her tongue died in her mouth, and she glared at him. He smiled and then burst into an all-out chuckle and headed off.

"Glad I can make you smile," she muttered.

"You always make me smile, but it was definitely something much softer tonight," he noted, with a laugh. And, with that, he was gone.

She stared out the window, wondering what new calamity had hit the town, resulting in Mack being called out at night. She wished she could have asked him something about it. But she didn't want to bug him, and she didn't want to be anything other than—

"Other than what?" she muttered to herself. "Doreen, you're being a fool. You could have just asked. He was expecting it." It was nice that he didn't have to explain anything to her. Yet it did feel weird to think that he was heading off on a case, and she literally knew nothing about it.

Soon afterward Doreen got a phone call from Nan. "So, what happened?"

"What happened?" Doreen repeated.

"Richie couldn't get anything out of Darren," she grumbled. "So I'm calling you for the latest."

"I couldn't get anything out of Mack either," she shared.

Silence came from Nan's end. "Wow," she muttered. "What's going on with this place? All our sources have dried up." And, with that, she ended the call.

Doreen stared down at her phone and wanted to laugh. Yet she also recognized that she was siding with Mack on this one, even when, in the past, she would have told her grandmother how Doreen hadn't even asked Mack for details on this one.

Groaning, she pulled out her phone and sent Mack a quick text. **How about now? Can I ask now?**

He called her, chuckling. "You held out longer than I expected."

"Yeah, well, I was trying to be good. Even Nan called, wondering what had happened. She was grumbling about all our sources drying up, since Richie couldn't get anything out of Darren either."

"That's a good thing," he stated. "These are active cases. Remember that."

"*Active cases. Remember that,*" she mimicked, then groaned. "Fine. Were you able to get me all the files from Alberta?"

"I put in the request," he replied, "and you'll get them when you get them."

"Fine, fine, fine," she muttered. As she went to hang up, she added, "You'll be careful, right?"

"I will," he said, surprised, but his tone was gentle. "You try to get a good night's sleep."

"What will you do?"

"I'll work on a new angle regarding this *something that happened*, and, no, before you ask, I won't tell you what it is."

"If it was dangerous, you would tell me, wouldn't you?" When silence came, she groaned. "Of course you wouldn't because, not only would you not want me to worry but it would be connected to an active case, so you wouldn't say squat."

And, with that, she ended the call on him.

Chapter 6

T HE NEXT MORNING, Doreen woke to her phone ringing right beside her. She picked it up to see it was Nan. "Now what has happened?" she asked her grandmother.

"Did I wake you? I'm sorry, child. I didn't even think about the time."

"What time is it?" Doreen muttered, as she brushed the hair off her face, so she could look at her phone and check the time. "Good God, it's only six."

"I'm sorry," Nan replied. "I didn't think."

"What's got you so excited?" Doreen asked.

"The Burgon family, child. Another one of them just died."

Doreen threw back her bedcovers, then grabbed the notepad beside her. "What news do you have?"

"Just that one of the older generation was found dead."

"Okay, but that could have just been old age, right?"

"No, but she's at least sixty," Nan clarified. "I get it that you think *old age* happens to anybody, anytime."

"It does," Doreen pointed out. "People die unexpectedly all the time. And just because you say, *old age*, that doesn't mean they are your age."

"That's good," Nan replied in a snappish tone, "because she's only sixty-something."

"Okay, do we know anything else?"

"All I heard was *suspicious circumstances.*"

"Okay, I'll see if I can get more." Doreen ended the call, raced to the shower, and, as soon as she was dry and dressed, she headed downstairs. There she put on some coffee and fed the animals, checking their water bowls. "Thanks, guys, for being so patient with me when I am working." Then she opened up the back door so they could get outside all on their own. Afterward she brought up her laptop, hunting through the recent newspaper articles, looking for something, anything that would tell her what was going on.

She found nothing.

Frowning, Doreen then went to the larger Vancouver news site, but nobody was covering last night's happening in Kelowna, outside of a small byline confirming that a body had been found.

Doreen sent Mack a text. **It's one of the Burgon family, isn't it?**

He called her later and said, "I see the grapevine is operating as usual."

"Yes, but it's grossly ineffective," she muttered. "We're all looking for a little bit more than what the newspapers are saying."

"Did they identify the family?" he asked.

"No, Nan did."

Silence followed. "Of course she did," he finally muttered. "Although how she knew that, I don't know."

"I don't know either, but, if you want to know, you better contact her directly."

"No, it's fine," he replied. "And, yes, it is one of the Burgon family—the daughter of Old Man Burgon. She was sixty-something. I think sixty-four."

"How did she die?"

"She was in the kitchen."

Doreen groaned. "Oh no, hang on a minute."

"I know," he interrupted her. "I know where you're going with this."

"Oh, I'm going with this all right," she declared. "The question is, are we on the same track?"

"Unfortunately we probably are," he conceded, "but that doesn't mean you can get into my case."

"And this is the same kitchen where the cook died, right?"

Mack went silent, then finally answered her. "All I'll say is, yes, but don't ask me anymore." And, with that, he ended the call.

Doreen sat back, thinking about it, then called her grandmother to fill her in on what Doreen knew to date. "Same kitchen where the wannabe chef just passed away. Mack still didn't give me a cause of death—a stabbing or whatever—not once I understood that both crimes occurred in the same kitchen."

"Oh, that's fascinating," Nan noted. "Who is killing cooks?"

"I don't know, but the food can't be that bad." Nan's shocked silence followed, and then Nan snorted, which quickly turned into huge guffaws. Doreen smiled.

"Terrible timing for jokes," Nan said, when she could finally talk, "absolutely terrible."

"I know," Doreen said. "On the other hand, it eased up the tension a whole lot."

"Oh my." Nan giggled. "I'll have to tell Richie that one."

"Maybe not right away," Doreen shared. "It is definitely sad that we've got two people dead in the same kitchen in the same week."

"It is absolutely sad," Nan agreed, her tone turning serious. "However, you sure know how to turn something sad into a joke."

"I shouldn't have though. We need to be respectful."

"Sure, we do," Nan conceded, "yet that was a good one." And Nan was gone before Doreen could warn her again about not passing on the joke.

She groaned. "Not exactly good of you, Doreen," she muttered. Sure, it was just a quip, and it was meant to ease up the tension, but she certainly didn't need to make fun of murder. Feeling horribly guilty, she got down to work, trying to make some sense out of this.

But what was there to possibly make sense of murder? Two people had passed away in the same kitchen, just a matter of days apart. Then she remembered that Old Man Burgon had a pub *and* a restaurant. She called Nan back and asked, "What was the name of the pub and restaurant that the Burgon family owned?"

"Something like the Rocking Horse Post. I'm not sure on that but something along that line."

"*Rocking Horse Post*. I read that they do craft beer," she shared, having seen something about that.

"I think so, but I don't really remember."

"Okay, good enough." She ended the call this time and sat down at her laptop and started searching. It didn't take long at all, and she had the business name and started to run a history on the family and their pub and restaurant. The businesses had been involved in quite a few lawsuits, even a couple cases involving food poisoning. That was interesting too. Did somebody lose somebody and was now blaming the people who worked there? That was the only motive she could conjure up here so far.

As she worked her way through other possibilities, she lost track of time. When her phone rang, she assumed it would be Nan again, but instead it was the uncle of the young woman he'd thought would be charged with the one death, the first one involving the wannabe chef. Doreen shook her head at that too.

"Is this Doreen?" he asked in that same bristly tone.

"Yes," she replied.

"The private investigator is really busy right now and can't take on the case. When I told him that you recommended him, he suggested that I should just get you to do it."

"I don't know about *just getting me to do it*," she replied. "The PI has access to resources that I don't have, but I can look into it."

"I heard from my niece this morning, and I don't know how bad things are, but she's pretty worried, and now apparently something else has happened, but she was too upset to tell me about it."

"Yes," Doreen noted. "Another death in the same kitchen. I believe it was a Burgon family member."

A shocked silence came on the other end. "Oh my God."

Doreen continued. "I've already pulled a bunch of files and have a few questions I want to ask Jillian." When he hesitated, Doreen added, "I can also get the information from the police, so that's hardly an issue—or maybe from employees at the Rocking Horse Pub."

"Good God," he muttered. "I always hated that name."

"If they're involved with craft beer, it goes along with it. The names of some of those beers are something else."

"I think that's half the challenge," he muttered. "Anyway ... I'll give you Jillian's contact information, but she may not want to talk to you." He finally gave her the number. As Doreen wrote it down, he added, "Jillian didn't have anything to do with this murder either."

And, with that, he ended the call.

Chapter 7

DOREEN WASTED NO time and phoned the niece. When a woman answered, her voice so tired and exhausted, Doreen suspected that Jillian had been crying all night. Doreen winced, then hesitated for a moment before introducing herself.

"Oh, it's you," Jillian replied. "I've had people tell me how I should contact you and get you to help."

"I did speak with your uncle," Doreen confirmed, "and he did want me to look into the case to see if we could do anything to help you."

"I don't even know if there's any reason to worry any-more," she shared sadly. "My aunt also just died in the restaurant. Thankfully I wasn't there to see that too. I think I'm quitting. I'll head back to Alberta."

"Not if you're involved in a murder investigation. You likely won't be allowed to leave the province. I'm not even sure you can leave town."

"I can't do it right away anyway, but I can't say the move here has been a good one."

"But your family was already here for about ten years, right?"

"Sure, but not for long, not for me," she clarified. "I did my schooling back in Alberta, but I hated it there and wanted to come back here, so I did. That turned out to be the worst decision ever."

"And was the chef who passed away also your partner?"

"Yes, we were engaged, planning for a summer wedding. Now we'll plan a winter funeral instead."

"I'm sorry," Doreen whispered. "That's got to be even harder."

"It's always hard, but this just makes no sense. He was the sweetest guy, through and through."

"Any idea why somebody would want to kill him?"

"No, none at all," she cried out. "You don't understand. He's just not the guy who people kill."

Doreen wasn't sure there was a type for getting killed, but, the more Jillian talked, the better potential Doreen had to get more information about everything.

Jillian continued. "He's one of those guys who brings you flowers and who picks you up after work because you're tired. He's the one who will arrange to have food brought in so you don't have to cook, just because he knows you're tired. He was one of the good guys," she wailed, tears flowing through her tone. "You know that saying about only the good die young? I never really understood it until now."

Doreen sighed. "I'm sorry. It's a hardship to lose somebody you care for."

"I thought I would spend the rest of my life with him," she whispered. "And now? He's … just gone."

"And he was stabbed, is that correct?"

"Yes, stabbed, … multiple times."

Doreen wrote that down on her notepad. "I'm so sorry to ask these questions. I know this is a really tough time to talk to you."

"The police have done nothing but talk to me," she muttered, her voice fading with emotional exhaustion. "So not sure your questions will make it any worse."

"Were you there at the time of your fiancé's death?"

"Yes, but I got hit from behind and the police seem to think, because there was very little bruising, that I might have just done it myself."

"Ah, but instead you were knocked out cold, didn't see what happened, and woke up to find your fiancé dead?"

"Yes," she whispered, sobbing anew. "And that was a sight I'll never get out of my head."

"I'm so sorry," Doreen whispered back. "Was anybody else working at the time?"

"No, it was just the two of us."

"Did you keep the doors locked?"

"No, we didn't worry about it. We had each other, and we did this often. We were doing prep for some event the next day, where they had booked a couple meeting rooms, and we were catering," she explained. "So, it required a little bit of extra prep work, and that was fine. We were happy to come in to do the work."

"Which is nice of you," Doreen noted. "Not everybody is happy to do that."

"No, they aren't," she agreed, "but we were both okay to do it. We were working on getting more skills and experience so we could, you know, move up in life," she shared. "So, it shouldn't have been a big deal for anybody that we were working there."

"When you were hit from behind, did you hear anything?"

"No, I didn't hear a thing," she wailed, "and that's also

something that'll haunt me. I still can't begin to wrap my head around it."

"Maybe he came rushing to your aid."

"That doesn't help me feel any better either," she replied bitterly.

"Right now I don't think anything will help you feel better," Doreen pointed out. "You've lost somebody you cared for, so now it's all about the *what ifs*. *What if I'd woken up earlier? What if I had been standing somewhere else in the kitchen? What if I'd heard something?* There will be a long line of *what ifs*."

"Oh, yeah, you're not kidding," she quipped, with a mirthless laugh. "That seems to be all I'm asking myself right now."

"Was there any other way in and out? Would there have been anyone you would have suspected?"

"No, and no," she replied. "Obviously there was the back door, and that's how we all came and went, particularly in the evening. The restaurant itself had just closed, and the pub section was still open, but we were in the back prep kitchen which isn't open to the public."

"Hang on. … The pub was open?"

"Yeah, the pub part was open, but they were just winding down and like I said that area isn't open to them."

"But there could have been any number of people out there still, right?"

"Sure," she muttered, then stopped. "That's right. Anybody who knew the restaurant or knew the building layout would have known they could have come straight back there," she cried out. "And that just means there are any number of suspects."

"Right," Doreen agreed.

"Interesting how I hadn't thought about that," Jillian noted, her voice gaining in strength.

"Sometimes you need to talk to people just to get a better idea of what could be going on because you don't think of everything right away," Doreen pointed out.

"I didn't think of it at all, and now I have to wonder if I forgot something else … or missed something important."

"Maybe," Doreen said, "but that's not the issue right now. If you do come up with something important, then you need to contact the police."

"Why not you?" she asked, her tone turning belligerent. "I really don't want to talk to them anymore, especially that big guy."

Doreen winced. "Are you talking about Corporal Mack Moreau?"

"I don't know who he is, but … he's big, and he grumbled a lot and growled—totally growled. I was terrified."

"I can understand that being scary and off-putting," Doreen began, "but that corporal in particular is very good at what he does."

"Maybe, but, if he thinks I had anything to do with this, he's barking up the wrong tree. So, the sooner he gets it right, the better off I am," she stated, but then she started to sob again. "I miss Barry so much."

"Of course you do," Doreen muttered. "Nobody wants to go through this."

"He's … he was a good man," she murmured. "A really good man. He didn't deserve any of this."

"How old was he?" Doreen asked.

"Twenty-nine. One of the things we were talking about at work was what we would do for his birthday."

"And when is his birthday?"

"Next Wednesday."

"Did you make plans?"

"No, we were still discussing it, trying to figure out what to do, what would be special," she muttered, sobbing again. "And instead of having a birthday party, I'll be burying him," she muttered.

Doreen couldn't argue about that. "Let's hope that, by then, we have answers, and maybe, if nothing else, you can put him to rest."

Leaving Jillian still sobbing, Doreen ended the call.

Chapter 8

WITH HER THREE animals in tow, Doreen headed down the river for a breath of fresh, albeit cold, air. She needed to think, to get her mind cleared. She should go down to the pub and get an idea of the lay of the land there. Maybe, when she got back from her walk, she would. But right now, just all these threads ran in and out of her mind, yet having no connection that she could see, at least none she knew of yet. That was literally her problem. It wasn't a case of no connection, but Doreen had yet to see any meaningful connections. It would take however long it took before she understood what was going on here.

As she wandered down the river, Mugs was playing near the edge and getting wet. She kept calling him back out again, but he wasn't having it. Goliath didn't seem too interested in coming for a walk, but, now that he was outside, he was avoiding the water like the plague—whereas Mugs seemed to be having nothing but fun with the frigid river. As soon as she got down a little bit farther, Mugs was in the river again. Giving up on reining him in, she smiled at his antics. When it was time to leave, she called him back, but he wasn't having it.

"Mugs, come on," she muttered. "That's enough already."

He turned and barked and ran down the river some more. She raced after him, but that just made it a game in his mind. By the time she finally caught him, got his leash back on, and started to drag him home again, she was soaked and getting colder. As they neared the house, Mugs realized where they were going, then raced forward, this time half dragging her up to the rear kitchen door. As she got inside the house, she was shivering like crazy.

Knowing that she was seriously cold to the point that she needed to do something about it, she unhooked the dog, grabbed some towels, and rubbed him down, which warmed her up slightly. Then she headed upstairs for a hot shower. When she came out, she wrapped up in more towels and burrowed into her bed.

Mugs found her there.

"See what you did?" she asked him.

He immediately burrowed into her and her towels, thinking that was great fun. She groaned but laughed at his antics.

"It's a good thing that I love you, buddy."

He woofed at her several times, then grabbed at one of her towels and tried to pull it away from her.

"I'm coming. I'm coming," she muttered.

She got dressed again, went downstairs, and made a big pot of tea. As she sat here wondering what was coming next in the craziness of her world, Richie phoned her. "Richie, what's the matter?" she greeted him.

"Nothing," he replied, "nothing at all. But somebody has a birthday coming up, and I wanted to know when and where you want to do the party?"

Her jaw snapped shut, and she groaned. "Oh my gosh, I completely forgot about Nan's birthday."

"I understand," he replied, "and that's why I'm calling. I can't let you forget."

"No, Nan would be heartbroken," she murmured.

"She would, indeed. That gal likes her time in the limelight."

Doreen winced. "Which is amazing, considering that I can't stand the limelight."

He chuckled. "So, in that case, why don't we have it down here at Rosemoor?" he suggested. "I was thinking that maybe you could come for dinner too that day."

"Sure, I can come for dinner," she agreed.

They settled up on the night for the party, which coincided with Nan's actual birthday. Richie confirmed that was one of the days available for booking at Rosemoor. As Doreen went to get off the phone, she asked Richie, "Have you got any ideas for birthday gifts?"

He laughed. "I'll give her flowers because that seems to be a safe thing, but for you? I have no clue."

"Right," she responded sourly, "thanks for that."

He burst out laughing. "You're the detective, Doreen. You figure it out."

She winced at that, then nodded, not quite sure what else to say. She ended the call but now had something else to worry about too. She sent Mack a text, reminding him that Nan's birthday was coming up and asking him for a gift idea.

When no answer came right back, she figured he was as stumped as she was and wondered what he gave his mother on her birthdays.

As if reading her thoughts, Nick phoned her soon afterward.

"Are we done with all the paperwork yet?" she asked.

"Almost," he stated. "I'm sending what should be the bulk of the paperwork for right now, and I need you to sign it, digitally of course, and send it back to me."

"Okay, will do," she agreed. "While I have you, I'm trying to figure out a gift idea for my grandmother, as her birthday is coming up. I texted your brother for ideas, but he was no help at all."

"That's not shocking. How old will she be?"

"I have no clue," she admitted, "and believe me that I'm not asking her either."

Nick laughed. "Is she still worried about her age? She's not yet to the point where she's proud of having made it another year?"

"No, not yet. And I thought she was eighty-three, but, if she heard me say that number out loud, I think she would get very angry, very fast."

There was a smile in his tone when he suggested, "In that case, don't say it. It doesn't matter how old she is, and, if it's her birthday, she might even be trying to hide that it's her birthday too."

"Maybe," she muttered, "but she's not allowed to. Besides, she likes all that attention. Luckily I've already gotten a phone call from someone reminding me that I had already forgotten her upcoming birthday," she shared, "and I can't have that happen."

"No, you don't know how many more she's got, so let's at least make the most of them. Make it count while you can."

"Exactly, but I don't know what to get her."

"I have no clue," he replied. "I'm sure you'll figure it out." With that cheerful note, he rang off.

She glared down at her phone. "How come *I* have to figure this out?" she muttered. "How come *I* have to figure everything out?" she asked, raising both hands in frustration. "How come nobody else is figuring out stuff for a change?"

With a sigh, she sat down and started a Google search for gift ideas for old people, then realized that Nan would be offended by that too. Nan was hardly old, given the context in which she lived. Yet she was old in the sense of being compared to mainstream society. She was at least eighty, maybe even eighty-five-*ish*.

Doreen didn't even know. She didn't have any documentation to give her that information either. As she stared down at the animals, she wondered what she could do for a special gift for her special grandmother.

She started thinking about it and realized that photographs and that sort of thing were very popular gifts for seniors. As she continued to scroll the internet, she came across an advertisement that caught her eye and made her smile. *Pet portraits.* That was something Nan would love, but when she saw the name of the local photographer who was doing the portraits, her smile turned to one of deep satisfaction, and she nodded.

Perfect.

Because, sure enough, it was a Burgon, a Danny Burgon. With that, she picked up her phone, and, when she got no answer, she left a message, saying she was interested in getting portraits done of her three pets for her grandmother's birthday. She understood it was a very short time frame but reached out anyway, hoping that maybe they could fit her in.

Then she sat back to wait, and, while she waited, she went back to work. If she could get a picture of the three animals for Nan, that would be an ideal gift as Nan absolutely loved them. Although she would also want a portrait of Doreen, but that was a whole different gift idea altogether. Besides, when people got older, some didn't want gifts or didn't want photographs because that just reminded them how old they were.

Doreen had heard of various people letting go of extra possessions as they aged because they relied on their memories instead. However, in many cases, they then lost their memories too. Still, Doreen had done something constructive, and, if it wasn't possible to get it done by this photographer, then maybe it would be by someone else. The fact of the matter was, Doreen was looking for an excuse to talk to the Burgon family and to sort out more about their history, and this provided an awesome opportunity.

When the call was returned ten minutes later, she spoke directly with Danny Burgon, who arranged for an initial visit the next day.

"So, are you bringing two dogs?" he asked.

"No," she replied, with a laugh. "I am bringing a dog, a cat, and a bird."

When silence came on the other end, she wondered if that had tipped him off to her identify. Maybe he would refuse to see her.

"That'll be a first," he noted. "I'll have to see what they look like and how they interact. I might end up working with photographs instead of them directly."

"That's fine," Doreen replied. "We'll come down, and you can make an assessment for yourself."

"Good enough."

Beaming a fat smile, she got to work making dinner, just in case Mack showed up. When he was as busy as he was, she had absolutely no way to know. But also, when he got this busy, he just needed a hot meal that he didn't have to cook for himself.

Doreen was trying a new recipe that she had tripped over on the internet, while she'd been researching the Burgon family yet again. As she put on the final touches, putting it back in the oven for the cheese to melt, Mack drove up.

Mugs let her know by caterwauling at the front door, as if somebody had died. She walked over just as Mack opened it. He bent down to give the wiggling Mugs a big hello, then smiled at her.

Doreen shook her head. "You would think he knows that it's you."

"Oh, he knows," Mack confirmed, laughing. Mack held up a bag that had dog treats inside.

"Right," she muttered. "So what you're really doing is bribing my dog into liking you."

"No, not at all," he declared, "but, if he wants to think that, I won't dissuade him."

She laughed. "He doesn't need more dog treats, you know? He's not exactly a slim puppy anymore."

"I see that," he agreed, studying Mugs's waistline. "Are you worried about it?"

"No, not really, but, if I were to take him back to his vet, he would be horrified."

"I'm sure it's probably just as bad for the pets to be overweight as it is for their humans," he conceded, patting his own muscled girth.

"Maybe," she replied. "I don't think it's a problem yet with him, and I hope it never gets to be. He's already plenty active, and, if I'm supposed to take him outside and get him even more active, I would probably die running after him."

He burst out laughing. "You do take him for lots of

walks already."

"I do, but less so with the cold weather," she pointed out.

"Of course, and that's to be expected. Again, don't keep putting all this pressure on yourself."

She shrugged. "Easy for you to say."

"I know." He gave her a smile. Then his nose wrinkled, and he sniffed. He looked over at her, one eyebrow raised.

She shrugged. "I don't know if it's edible."

His face cracked into a smile. "I won't say it's *not* edible," he shared. "I'm pretty darn sure that it will be fine."

"That's just because you're hungry," she pointed out.

He grinned. "That's the perfect time to test a recipe, when you're hungry, because you'll either scarf it down, which will mean it's absolutely wonderful, or you'll still scarf it down and say it was good enough, but maybe you don't need to repeat it."

She frowned at him, yet nodded. "That's really smart."

He rolled his eyes at her. "I know this may be a news flash for you, but generally people would consider me smart."

She wrinkled up her nose and grinned. "News flash," she repeated. "Most people wouldn't think I'm very smart at all."

He bopped her on the nose and added, "News flash, … that's old news. The current news is our Doreen is the smartest gal this side of the forty-ninth parallel."

She frowned at him in astonishment.

He laughed. "You just don't see yourself how everybody else sees you," he pointed out, "but we'll work on changing that."

"Do they really think I'm smart?" she asked, as she trailed him into the kitchen.

"Look at all the cases you've closed," he began, turning to look at her in astonishment.

She shrugged. "Sure, but some of those were about you too."

"Sure, some of them were, and some of them I was still trying to figure out what the heck was happening, when you already had it solved," he admitted, then shrugged. "And some of them didn't make any sense to me even after you'd solved them. Yet somehow the pieces all fit together, and you get confessions. So, most of us are just, like, yeah, … *that's a Doreen case.* We don't understand how or what, but you know how it works, so it's a *Doreen case.*"

She faced him, and her smile, though slow in coming, was deep and heartfelt.

He nodded as he put his arms around her. "Smiles like that will get our wedding date moved up."

She gave him a powerful kiss. "Thank you."

He sighed, wrapped her up tightly, and just held her. "Back to that whole self-confidence thing, where you are your own worst enemy."

"I think that's exactly why it's called a self-confidence problem," she noted, "because anybody who has self-confidence issues is their own worst enemy."

"Yeah, but now that Mathew's gone, I was hoping you would park a lot of that."

"I have parked a lot of it," she said, with a laugh, "or buried it anyway. Burying him meant burying a lot of those issues, and I am absolutely ecstatic to come back as strong as I have," she shared. "Yet there will always be times when I get caught by surprise, and it pops back up."

"And that's okay too," Mack told her. "It really doesn't matter. This isn't a test."

"Good," she muttered, "because I can tell you that I would fail."

Just then the oven timer beeped, and she gasped, raced over, and bent down to open up the oven. Seeing her dinner was not burned at all, she gave a crow of delight and pulled out her chicken dish. She looked over at him and said, "Hopefully this will be worthwhile."

"It's already worthwhile," he stated, as he snagged up plates and gave her a smile. "I didn't have to cook. It's been a long day, and I have a hot, fresh meal waiting. Believe me when I say, *That's perfect.*"

And it was. She beamed as he ate everything on his plate and had seconds. He sat back, looking at her and back again at his empty plate. "See? … Like I said, *perfect.*"

Chapter 9

THE NEXT MORNING Doreen woke up, hopped out of bed, and raced through her morning routines. As soon as she opened her email, she found a message from Mack, with a file attached. He also added a happy face emoji and this text: *This is the Alberta file on the mother's murder, and it's coming to you with the captain's blessings.*

She grinned at that. She had helped the captain on a couple cases that were personal, so he had absolutely no problem with her helping on various police cases that she found interesting. There was a lot to be said for that cooperation.

She sent a thank-you message back to Mack and printed off the case file. Not a whole lot was here. Jillian's mother, Katie, had been stabbed while everybody was away from the home. No sign of forced entry. It was a usual killing mode, and yet it couldn't have been a stranger in this case, not unless some guy had popped into her corner of the world, looking for a shower or something, and had decided that her house looked to be a good one to break into, and then things got ugly.

As there was no sexual assault, that just added an odd

tone to Katie's murder, in Doreen's opinion. This could have been someone she knew. Doreen read the file further. No foreign DNA was found. No motive either. So Doreen was stuck trying to find something that made sense. As she had often found, nothing about murder made sense. What could possibly make sense when it came to murdering a woman in her own home?

Yet it happened so often that Doreen started to wonder what the stats were about women being killed in their own place. It seemed pretty high to her, which was just sad. You would think that you were safe in your own residence, but unfortunately that wasn't always the case.

As Doreen went through all of the file, she read that the suspected murder weapon was a kitchen knife procured from the home itself. Which usually meant the killing wasn't planned. Instead a weapon was used in the spur of the moment. At least that's how Doreen figured the experts would look at it. The woman had been stabbed three times, once in the chest, once in the neck, and once high up in the shoulder. The first one appeared to be high up in the shoulder and was more hesitant. The ones through the chest and the neck were definitely more forceful stabs to finish the job. Seemed personal to Doreen.

Something else that Doreen found interesting was that both of those chest and neck wounds would have been fatal, as the artery had been cut in the throat, while the chest wound had gone directly into the heart. So, was that evidence of somebody knowing how and where to put those strikes? Because Doreen couldn't imagine sliding a knife into the heart as being something that everybody would be capable of doing. Would a knife bounce off bone or slide in along a rib? Or was it just a lucky blow? Or did this person have medical knowledge?

Or did this person just have …

She stopped, winced. "Considering," she said out loud, "the number of cooks in this plot, maybe it was literally somebody who had butchering experience."

Not something she particularly wanted to contemplate, but also not something she could ignore.

She quickly glanced over the paperwork once more, highlighted a few issues, wrote a summary, tacked it onto the paper copy, and put it all in a marked file folder for later. This information here she would need at some point in time. But there just wasn't very much to go on right now. She sent a text message, after she was done, asking Mack for any information on the latest murder.

He phoned her. "You can't be happy with what I gave you, *huh*?" he grumbled.

"Not if it's connected," she replied.

"And we don't know if it's connected," he pointed out.

"Sure, but do you realize that's three murders, all related to the Burgons?"

"Two," he corrected, with a sigh. "The young man who was killed wasn't part of the same family."

"Not yet, but he was engaged to Jillian, so soon to be part of the family."

"I know. Anyway I've got to go. I'll talk to the captain about getting you some information."

An odd note filled his tone, and Doreen wondered about that. Instead of asking him, she just said, "Good, thank you."

"I don't suppose you have anything in your head right now that I could take to the captain, do you?" he asked. "It would make it a little easier to get you that additional information."

She laughed. "If I don't have all the information," she muttered, "how the devil am I supposed to come up with any answers or theories? I need the information before I can say anything. Unless somebody thinks too many cooks are in this broth." And, with that, she ended the call on him.

She knew she got the saying wrong, but, as she kept getting other sayings wrong, it was now a joke between them. When he sent her a heart emoji, it just made her stop and sigh. Something was so wholesome about him. That whole good-guy thing was awfully compelling. She knew he wouldn't take it very kindly if she were to use that phrase in any comment or message, but it was true. Something was just very wholesome about Mack, and, for her, that was worth so much.

Her earlier marriage had been filled with verbal and physical abuse and strict rules of Mathew's own making. Now that he was gone, Doreen was still trying to deal with the emotional aftermath, plus all the related estate paperwork too. Which just reminded her how she was due for an odd visit to her former residence. And yet she knew that it needed to happen. Still, in a way, it was probably a healing thing for her to do. She just didn't want to do it alone. She had discussed this unpleasant trip with Mack, but they hadn't exactly set up dates and times for these inspections of Mathew's various Vancouver properties.

Mack would need time off from work in order to spend a few days with her there. And it really was okay with her if it didn't happen right away. However, she also knew her delay would hold up selling all those houses. So the in-person inspections were definitely something she needed to do in order to get those estate things of Mathew's wrapped up. Not to mention Scott from Christie's was going down there too, and he might need Doreen's help to find some of Mathew's hidden rooms full of stuff too. Something else she really didn't want to contemplate.

Scott called her next.

"Hey," he greeted her. "I'm just checking in because you had mentioned going down to assess the antiques and whatnot in your ex's estate." Scott could barely keep his enthusiasm in check. "And something about secret rooms."

"Yes," she confirmed, "but I don't think I can get there for a couple weeks."

"That's fine," he replied. "No way I can get there that fast anyway. I just wanted to know how long we have to be out there and how many days I need to plan this trip for."

"Considering Mathew was as big a hoarder as my grandmother, potentially a couple days."

After a moment of silence, Scott noted, "You're really surrounded by them, aren't you?"

"Apparently," she replied, with a laugh. "Yet that's okay. We'll get it sorted out one day. No need for a fuss."

"Yes, we will," he declared. "And obviously you've been blessed yet again by the money gods."

"Funny you should say that," she quipped, "because I had somebody ask me if they could pay me to solve a case that their family is involved in. I refused it because I just didn't feel I should."

"Also," he pointed out, "you don't need to. If you want to help on these cases, you can do it without having to charge the families, if you so choose. But, then again, if you feel your time is worth something, nothing is wrong with charging them something."

"*Hmm.*" She pondered that. "I guess I hadn't really considered it from that aspect either."

"You might want to consider that some of these people probably would take advantage of you anyway, and you may very well want to have some contract or some payment system set up—not because you need the money. Besides, you could always give it away to charity."

She perked up at that. "Yes, I can."

Scott suggested, "It would be good for you if there were some written agreement between both parties."

"That's also something I hadn't really considered," she admitted.

"Here's something else to think about, and I'm only bringing it up to protect you," Scott explained. "I would hate to see something go south on one of these cold cases of yours and have somebody trying to sue you when they find out that you have money."

"Oh, *great*," she muttered. "Aren't you a ray of sunshine today? You're just filling my day with all kinds of possibilities."

"People will be people," Scott stated. "So, as soon as they find out that maybe you have some money, the world could look different to them. Especially if you planned to help them, but it didn't turn out the way they thought it should. Then they could come back after you, expecting some restitution in the form of a monetary settlement."

"In other words, I should get my soon-to-be-brother-in-law to help me write up a contract."

"If he's a lawyer who handles contracts, then yes. Otherwise get a lawyer who does that," Scott pointed out. "Just to confirm that you're in the clear. The last thing you want is for somebody to come along and to make your life even more difficult, when you were just trying to help them." He sighed. "Even somebody who gets convicted in your cold cases could turn around and try to sue you as well. We live in a very litigious society."

"Oh, that's great to hear too," she muttered. "Now I don't want to do anything to help people."

"Of course not," he noted, with a sigh. "I do know this from personal experience. Some people are looking for more than they often get with us, and they seem to think, just because we have a contract in place to sell an item, that same contract would guarantee them a certain set price, but it just doesn't work that way."

"No, it doesn't," she agreed, "and that would be foolish on their part."

"But people—"

"Will be people," she finished for him.

"Yes, as I'm starting to find out over and over again." Scott laughed. "It's just sound business advice, Doreen."

"And thank you for that. … I'll talk to Mack and see what time frame we're looking at to get down to Vancouver and to start dealing with some of Mathew's stuff."

"And you really think he had some valuables down there?" he asked curiously.

She snorted. "Yes, I know he did. He had a temperature-controlled room for the paintings, but, if you ask me what paintings, I couldn't tell you."

He groaned. "You know that's a tease for a guy like me, don't you?"

"For you probably," she agreed, half snickering. "For me, absolutely not. He would tell me what it was, and then he would say things like, *You don't even know what that is, so no point in telling you more.*"

"So, for you, this is just something to move out of your life," he pointed out. "However, for me, who may have never seen some of these particular artworks in person, it will be a fascinating process."

"Let's hope I can get there sooner, rather than later," she muttered, "but it will be a while still."

"Understood," Scott said cheerfully, and, with that, he ended the call.

She immediately contacted Nick.

"Hey," he greeted her. "Problems?"

"Not so much problems, just a question." Then she explained Scott's concerns about potential litigation.

Nick whistled and replied, "He's quite correct. Just because you want to help doesn't mean everybody will take the help as being a good thing. And, once people find out you have money, then you will more likely have to deal with issues along that line."

"That's not fair though," she cried out. "How are you supposed to help people if everybody just wants to turn around and take something from you?"

"I don't have any set rules as to the rights or wrongs in any of this," he explained, "but, if you do things on behalf of others, they need to sign a waiver that you aren't responsible for the outcome, that they cannot sue you, and that there's no reason for them to come back against you and bad-mouth you or cause you any other harm."

"Oh, wow," she muttered.

"I know, but Scott's right, and … I should have thought of that ahead of time."

"It's not as if I haven't kept you busy," she muttered. "Not to mention you do have other clients."

"I do, and yes, you're right," he confirmed, "but still it is a concern. It's not something that I handle myself very much, but I do have another colleague here who does, so let me talk to him. I'll explain what the issue is, and we'll see what we can come up with."

With that, Doreen had to be satisfied, so she ended the call. Then she checked the time and noted that she was getting close to her portrait appointment. Immediately she packed up the animals, looked up the address, and headed down to see the artist.

As she approached the address, she noted it was a new area of town for her. It was Glenmore, but a little bit farther out than she was used to. As she drove to the address, she saw the landscape turn into an emptier countryside, a spaciousness. When she pulled into the driveway near an couple older-looking houses, she pulled up to the side, where a dirt road with a bit of gravel was around the main part of the house.

She frowned as she got out because, as much as she had liked the portrait work that she had seen online, it didn't look as if any of his sales money went toward fixing up his house. Then she also knew what that was like, and, if he was literally just making ends meet, then it also made sense. She hoped that he was a decent artist because she really wanted to get this portrait done for Nan for her birthday in just a few days. Considering Doreen was quickly running out of time, and everybody likely expected something unique from her, she hoped beyond hope that this would work out.

She walked up to the front door, thinking about all the fancy houses she had been in over her lifetime, but she felt a real sense of timeliness to this one. It wasn't so much not cared for but more about withstanding the passing of time. And something was very appealing about that. When the door opened, the woman in front of her frowned.

Doreen smiled. "Hi, I'm Doreen. I think I'm at the right

place. I'm here for a sitting for pet pictures."

The woman's face cleared immediately, and she nodded. Ushering her inside, she noted, "Go straight down the hallway, then to the left."

With the animals in tow, Doreen moved through the living room, noting that, although clean, it didn't seem as if anybody had put any time or effort into updating the interior in decades. She stepped into the other room as directed to see a man in a wheelchair, fussing over something on a table in front of him.

He looked up and glared.

She raised an eyebrow and noted, "I think I'm on time."

His face cleared, and he groaned. "Sorry," he muttered, giving her a look. "I was busy and lost track of time."

"Yeah, that happens to me too."

He eyed the dog and nodded. Then his gaze landed on the cat, and he frowned again. "I don't know about the cat," he shared. "Generally they don't cooperate."

"Maybe not most cats," she clarified, with a bright smile, "but I think he might surprise you."

"I doubt it. Cats are just generally cranky."

"And some cats like having their pictures taken." He stared at her in disbelief. She gave him a beaming smile and added, "I need all three of them in one portrait."

"Three?" he asked. "I don't see a third one."

At that, Thaddeus poked his head out from under the curtain of her hair and cried out, "Thaddeus is here. Thaddeus is here."

He stared at her in astonishment. "Good Lord."

"Yes," she replied, shifting her neck ever-so-slightly to ease the weight. "Thaddeus is also quite a character."

"Well," he muttered, frowning as he pondered it.

"You do pet portraits, right?"

"Yes, but I do one at a time."

"And yet I told you on the phone that I had three animals," she pointed out, hating the hint of desperation in her tone.

"And I explained that I would have to see them and that you would have to bring them here."

She nodded. At that point, Mugs laid down, and Goliath walked over, stretched out beside him, sprawling up against his belly, tucked in between his legs, his head literally on Mugs's front paws. The artist's eyes lit up, and he immediately grabbed the camera and started taking a ton of photos.

"That is pretty amazing right there," he admitted, as he kept talking excitedly, but he didn't get any closer. She wasn't sure whether it was the wheelchair or if he was choosing not to, just as part of his artistic work.

When he was done, he beamed. "Now that I can do."

"I also need this one included too," she added, pointing at her bird, still on her shoulder.

Danny frowned at that. Meanwhile, Thaddeus flew down to the floor, and Goliath lifted his head to watch him. Then the cat flopped back down with Mugs. Within seconds, Thaddeus had climbed atop of Mugs and settled in, as if showing the world that he was king of the castle. Danny gave a bark of laughter, and just then Thaddeus put one foot on Mugs' head, literally as if the king of the castle.

Snickering, Danny took several more photos. He turned to her and asked, "Is it okay if this portrait is more comedic?"

She nodded. "I'm not sure there's any way to do a serious portrait, not considering this group of animals."

He nodded. "It does seem as if they have quite the relationship."

"Oh, they do," she murmured. "They absolutely do. But they all love each other and go to great lengths to protect each other."

He stared in wonder and added, "I've never seen a collection of pets like this."

She didn't say anything, just smiled.

"I think I can do something with this," he declared, "and I'm really excited about the thought of trying."

"Good," she murmured, "because this would be for my grandmother."

He nodded, not seeming to care who it was for. "When do you want it by?"

She gave him her grandmother's birthday. He frowned, and she just waited. "It would be expensive," he began.

Her eyebrows shot up because she had found no website for him and had seen no prices on his social media pages. Yet she hadn't asked for an estimate either. He didn't bring up that subject when they spoke on the phone either. She was also fighting the priciness of everything right now. Just because she had the money—and there was a difference between being frugal and just plain cheap—she wanted to watch her spending.

"How much?" she asked cautiously, not wanting to appear too interested either way.

He frowned as he thought about it and finally said, "Probably about five hundred."

She considered that and then nodded. "As long as it's a good rendition, then that would be fine."

He glared at her. "Of course, it would be a good rendition."

"I didn't really see very much of your work, just those few photos on your social media pages," she pointed out, "so pardon me. I'm not trying to insult you. I just don't know what your work looks like in person." When he eyed her in astonishment, she shrugged. "Not much was online."

"Ah, well, there are definitely some pages on there that give you an idea. I am sure you can look up the pictures yourself."

"And I did see some," she noted. "I'm just really hoping you can pull this off on time."

"Of course I can," he stated, changing his tone. He looked back at the animals. "I still can't believe that they're just lying like that. It's as if they're posing."

"Partly because I think they can read my mind."

"That's amazing, but, looking at them right now, I would say they can," he conceded. "I've never seen anything like it." He grabbed a pencil and started sketching by hand now.

She watched as he zoned out right in front of her. She smiled, absolutely appreciating an artist who could do that.

A few minutes later, he stared at her and shared, "I just really want to get at it."

She nodded. "Is that my cue to leave?"

He winced. "Would you mind? As much as I want them to stay here so I can create a live portrait, I'm not sure how long they would hold that pose."

"Probably not long," she replied, "so good that you got your photos to go by."

"I've got quite a few photos," he said, as he picked up his camera and started looking at them from the back preview window. He smiled and nodded. "They really are something."

"I know," she confirmed, "and my grandmother absolutely loves them."

"In that case, it's a beautiful gift," he admitted. "Okay. I'll need to shuffle around a few things, but, if you're okay with the price, then I'll get it done on time."

"I'm okay with the price," she murmured, telling herself off for the thoughts going through her head. It was for her grandmother, and, for Nan, it was worth anything. Doreen asked, "Do I get to see it in between?"

He frowned, then shrugged. "I guess that's fair enough."

She laughed. "Or are you one of those artists who doesn't want people to interfere with your work until it's done?"

"Kind of," he noted reluctantly. "Also, if you don't like it, but I'm already in the swing of things, it's really hard for me to change direction. And that's the problem with doing custom work," he muttered.

"Do you only do custom work?"

"No, I do a lot of my own," he stated. "However, I don't have the same social media presence that a lot of artists do. So it's a lot harder to sell that way."

"What about a gallery showing?" she asked him curiously.

He shook his head. "No, I don't have any exposure to that either. It's more or less people like you, who come along and want something, and I just work away at it," he shared.

She smiled and nodded. "Have you been here long?"

"A lot longer than you apparently," he said, adding a chuckle, "if you haven't heard of me before."

She smiled. "I've only been here a little over nine months. So …"

He nodded. "My family has been here for quite a while,

generations even, for some of the family anyway," he muttered, and then he winced. "I don't know if I'll make that deadline after all."

She froze. "What do you mean? You just said you could."

"Yes, but we've just had a death in the family." He frowned as he stared at the doorway. "I'm okay to not go to the funeral and all that mess," he muttered. "I probably wouldn't be allowed to participate in a lot of it anyway."

She winced. "I'm sorry, and of course that's really bad timing on my part then."

"It's not as if you knew," he noted, with a wave of his hand, "and to some degree it wouldn't matter in terms of my work because I have to work in order to pay the bills." He looked around, then frowned. "And I really could use the five hundred bucks."

"I don't know what to say," she replied. "That's something you'll have to figure out, but I do need to know that you can complete it by her birthday. It would be terrible if you had to stop somewhere along the line and not finish on time. I need it by my grandmother's birthday. It will not be okay to show up empty-handed."

"No, I wouldn't do that," he stated, as he waved his hand. "I've got a decent start already, so maybe I'll just continue." He looked at his other cameras that he had here and frowned, then turned to her again.

"Did you have somebody else's project started already?" she asked.

"Not for somebody else. It's just a picture I was doing for myself."

"Oh nice," she said. "I imagine that's a huge problem when you're an artist, where you have to do things for other people for the money, but it would probably be much more rewarding to do the work that you want to do for yourself."

"It is, but I do need the money, so I do the work for other people too."

"Right," she replied, not sure if she should apologize as she felt she was interrupting him. "I guess the question is whether or not you feel as if you can do this timely and want to do this or not," she stated. "If it's a no, then I need to figure out something else for my grandmother."

"I'll do it," he declared, then winced. "I hate to harp on the money aspect, but I do need the money, so that's my answer."

"Good enough," Doreen said. "And do you think you have enough pictures?"

The animals were starting to stir, but he nodded. Then he looked at them again, shook his head, and added, "I've never seen anything like this."

"They've come to understand a lot of what I do. It just takes time, and they have to wait for me," she shared, with a laugh.

"Do you work?"

Doreen sighed. "It's a completely different world for me now. I am single after many years of marriage."

"Right," he muttered, "that's never easy either. Although my wife and I have been together since time began, I think," he stated, with a harsh laugh, "sometimes it still doesn't get any easier."

She looked at him in surprise. "The marriage doesn't?"

"No, the marriage doesn't," he acknowledged, "but then I'm hardly anything to write home about."

She studied him carefully and suggested, "The wheelchair has nothing to do with it. The gift is in being you. The gift is in the artwork you draw for others and for yourself," she shared. "If you can't be you, no point in trying to be somebody else because that doesn't work long-term."

He looked at her and nodded. "I believe you, but, when I don't provide very much in the way of income, it makes other people think that I'm not doing enough. Even though I am in a wheelchair, I never really saw myself as disabled. So, once you hear that label applied to you, and you realize there's something to it, it's hard to shrug it off."

"Of course it is, but then maybe it's just not a good relationship."

"No, it probably isn't," he agreed, "but being alone sucks too."

She smiled and nodded. "I'll give you that. It really does."

"So, you're still recovering from your divorce?"

"Kind of, and maybe not," she replied, with a smile. "I am now engaged to be married again, but my ex-husband was murdered not very long ago," she shared. "That threw things into a big uproar. So, I'm still settling his estate and tying up everything." She shrugged. "It does leave me in an odd position."

"We'll have to do that with my sister's place too," he muttered. "It's just a mess."

"I'm sorry." Doreen frowned, wondering if she should say anything. "I did hear about a woman killed just recently in a kitchen."

"Yeah, that's her," he noted. "Pretty heartbreaking all around."

"I'm sorry. Did she have family outside of you guys, like children?"

"No, no children," he replied, "and, if anything good is

in the whole mess, that's probably it."

"I'm so sorry. That's not easy."

"No, it sure isn't," he muttered. "She's my sister, though we weren't close. She was always telling my wife that she should leave me because I wasn't a whole man."

She stared at him and gasped. "I don't like her already."

He gave a bark of laughter. "Doesn't matter whether you do or not, since somebody obviously hated her a whole lot more."

"And that's not anything anybody wants to deal with," she pointed out. "As I know, murder itself is incredibly invasive, what with the police, the media, just everything." She shook her head as she stared out of the window.

She didn't even need to pretend anything in this instance. Her relationship with Mathew had been quite rough, but having been the prime suspect in his murder had really opened her eyes to the whole process of what people go through in police investigations.

"Yeah, not fun." Danny turned to her and asked, "Did the police look at you for the crime?"

She nodded. "They absolutely did. Thankfully the bad guy was found out to be his long-term assistant," she shared. "And that helped get me out of the limelight."

"That's good because, without that, it's pretty rough."

"You're right," she agreed. "It was terrible." She looked down at her animals and smiled. "These animals really helped get me through it."

"Good for you, and this should be a great gift for your grandmother." He hesitated and then added, "I hate to return to mundane business, but I don't do any commission work without a deposit."

"Ah," she replied, with a nod, "that's understandable."

"I would like 50 percent upfront."

She asked him, "Card?"

"Not if I don't have to," he said, with a sigh. "Too many fees."

She nodded. "I'm not sure what cash I have on me."

"You can go to the bank and come back, if you like," Danny suggested. "As much as I've already started it, I won't allow myself to work on it further, not until I at least get that much."

"In other words, you've been burned before."

"I absolutely have, and it's not anything I want to go through again."

She pulled out her wallet to see what she had. She'd gotten into the habit of carrying cash, and she was planning on going shopping, but this was important too. "I don't have that much on me. I do have $150, so I'll leave that with you, and I'll go to the bank and come back."

"Good, thank you." Danny accepted the money gratefully.

"Give me a few minutes."

He nodded. "It'll take that long just to get to town."

"I know. I wasn't really planning on the extra trip." Then she shook her head. "I should have asked ahead of time."

"And I should have told you ahead of time," he noted, "but I'm not very good on the business side."

"You're doing fine. I'll be right back." She got all the animals ready and left the room. As she headed out the front door, the woman called out to her.

"Did you leave a deposit?"

"I left him part of it," Doreen clarified, "and I'll run to the bank now to get the rest of it."

The other woman stared at her but didn't say anything.

Doreen, an odd feeling in her stomach, headed out and went straight to the bank. It took about twenty minutes to get through the lines, and then she drove back out to the house. Nobody answered when she got there. Frowning, she knocked several times, and then wasn't sure what to do. She picked up the phone and called him, and he did answer. "Hey, I'm at the front door trying to bring you the rest of your money but getting no response."

There was silence at first, and then he spoke. "Are you here for a painting, or are you here snooping?"

"I'm sorry?" she asked.

"My wife recognized you."

"Recognized me how?" she asked. "What do you mean? I want a painting for my grandmother."

More silence came, but he finally replied, "Hang on."

She waited at the front door, wondering what difference it would make if they did recognize her. She really did want the painting for her grandmother. And the fact that the animals had posed so beautifully just added to it.

When he opened the door, he studied her for a long moment. "My wife says that you're that amateur detective."

"I don't know about *amateur detective*," she clarified, "but I am certainly involved in a lot of the cases in town, yes," she stated, looking at him. "What's that got to do with anything?"

He frowned, looked back into the house, and added, "I'm not sure, but she seems to think that you came here for some other reason."

"I came here to get a painting done of my animals for my grandmother," she repeated, "and, if your wife knows anything about me, she knows that these animals are very dear to my heart, and, as I've already said numerous times, the portrait is for my grandmother's birthday. Goliath and Thaddeus were hers when I arrived here, and I took over their care as Nan is in a home."

He nodded. "And you don't have any other reason?"

"Is there anything else that I'm supposed to have a reason for?" she asked in exasperation. "You've already told me that your sister passed away, that it was murder. You brought it up. It's not as if you told me any class secrets or anything. It's not as if I was asking you questions about that either."

"I don't know anything," he muttered. He glanced back in the direction where his wife would be and finally nodded. "Okay, fine, I'll continue with the painting."

"I would hope so," she stated, staring at him, because, at this point, she really did want that painting.

And, yes, she had thought it was a great idea to get it done, regardless of the fact that he was apparently part of the same family. Doreen sighed. "Anytime you want to talk to me about any of this mess, feel free," she offered, "with or without your wife's permission." She gave a nod to the interior of the home. "Especially if you're concerned about something."

As he looked at her, his gaze narrowed, not in anger, more in contemplation. He nodded. "We'll see." And, with that, he accepted the money in her hand, handed her a receipt then shut the door in her face.

She slowly walked back to the car, not even taking the animals out this time. As she sat here in the driver's seat, thinking about what had just transpired, she saw Danny's wife at the front window, staring out.

Doreen started the vehicle and slowly backed out of the driveway. That was a very interesting response from him.

And also a very interesting response from his wife. Doreen didn't always think guilty people did things like that, but it did seem as if guilty people always did those things. And she didn't have a clue what on earth was going on, but it was obvious that something was up.

She lifted a hand and waved at the woman, who frowned back at her, then up came her middle finger.

Doreen laughed, put the vehicle in Drive, and slowly drove away.

Chapter 10

DOREEN THOUGHT LONG and hard for the rest of the afternoon about the artist and his wife and their response to her visit. Obviously the wife hadn't been happy once she realized who Doreen was and had tried to stop her husband from completing the job. The problem was, it was also obvious that they needed the money. Doreen didn't know just what was pissing off his wife, but something was and it seemed to be something that she was quite prepared to make Doreen's life difficult over—as well as her husband's life. If he was any good—something Doreen was still worrying about—then it was obvious that he could make some decent money as an artist.

Although this was a small town, and he would need further exposure to the wider world, it could very well be a godsend for him to get that exposure and to get out there for some name recognition. He could potentially make some decent money. She didn't know if he wanted to enter that rat race, but who knows? Maybe he did. It depended on whether his art was a passion and enough so to do what he loved and to ignore all the rest.

Doreen got home and immediately made a pot of tea

and sat down to wade her way through the research into the Burgon family. The trouble was, she couldn't blame the couple's behavior. Obviously an awful lot of family stuff was going on and was now surfacing to the public at large and involved plenty of family history. So they weren't necessarily to blame for any of that—and certainly not for the recent events.

Doreen could see that Danny and his wife hadn't had an easy time of it. Of course that just made her even more curious as to just what was going on. If she had had any easy answers, she would have done something about it already. Then again, there were never easy answers in this cold case stuff. In fact, so much of the time, it seemed as if there were no good answers at all. With that thought, she sorted out as many of the family lines as she could. When Nan called later, still in a fussy state, Doreen made a sudden decision. "Hey, why don't I come down, and we'll have tea?"

"Good," Nan muttered. "I could use a visit. Is something going on?"

"No, nothing's really going on," Doreen replied. "I'm just a little bit frustrated."

"I'm sorry," she murmured. "Come on down. Let's have tea, and maybe it will shift the mood," she muttered. "Getting old is not for sissies."

Doreen winced because she couldn't argue with that. She could only hope that she made it to old age in as good a physical and mental state as Nan had. Yet Doreen had no guarantees on that either. She packed up the animals, who were a little bit sluggish about going anywhere, until they realized that she was heading down the backyard to the river. And then there was no holding them back. They raced along, dragging her with them.

Doreen gasped, as she finally reached the patio to Nan's place. The animals jumped onto her little patio and then directly through the open sliding door. Doreen followed them, finding her grandmother. "Apparently everybody needed to come see you," Doreen muttered, still gasping.

Nan laughed at that, her mood lightening. "At least *they're* happy to see me."

"What's the problem?" Doreen asked, eyeing her grandmother sharply.

Nan shrugged. "Just every once in a while, you have a fight with some of the people around here, and things don't go so well. Then you find yourself wondering if you're really where you should be or if it would be better to be off doing something else."

That sounded serious enough that Doreen stopped and stared at her.

"Don't worry about it, child," Nan replied, waving her hands. "I get like this every once in a while."

"I'm sorry. It doesn't seem to be a whole lot of fun."

"No, it isn't fun, but that's what happens when you have people in your life. Sometimes you want to do things without people, and sometimes you want to do things with people. Yet then you have to sort out which people, and that's tedious and time-consuming," she shared. "Still, it's not your problem."

Doreen chuckled. "It might not be my problem, but it sure sounds as if it's somebody's problem."

"Yeah, ... mine," she muttered, with an eye roll. "They want me to determine all the entertainment that we should be doing over the next while. But why me?" she asked. "I don't want to do that."

"Did you tell them that you didn't want to do it?"

"Sure, I told them, but they didn't listen."

"And did you get yourself in trouble for having criticized the schedule after somebody else had already done it?"

At that, Nan shot her a look, which revealed so much that Doreen had to hide her smile. "In which case," she added, "I'm sure they figured that you thought you knew better. Therefore, you should make up the schedule and have everybody else argue with you."

Nan harrumphed at her granddaughter and didn't say anything. Doreen waited but knew better than to push it.

"I might have mentioned *something*," Nan conceded, "but really, who could blame me? … The whole dratted schedule was stupid."

Doreen nodded again. "But, if it was stupid," Doreen nudged, "then you should have a better idea of what to do."

"That doesn't mean I want to though," she wailed and then pouted.

"Why not?" Doreen asked. "That sounds perfect for you. You get to have control and to order everybody around at the same time."

Nan frowned at her and then snickered. "I do like ordering people around."

Doreen smiled. "I know you do, so maybe you can reconsider. This might be a good thing for you."

"*Hmm.*"

Nan didn't appear to be thinking about reconsidering at all. But Doreen also knew that, if she let it be a little bit longer, Nan would succumb to the temptation of making everybody else's plans and making everybody else's life happen on Nan's time schedule. And Nan would enjoy it. Yet maybe times have changed for her. Maybe she didn't want to engage with others anymore. Doreen shook her head. It was awfully hard to know from one day to the next.

"So, why don't you tell me what you've got going?" Nan asked.

Knowing that she couldn't even mention the painter, Doreen shrugged. "I don't have a whole lot still. We've got a family from Alberta. We've got two separate murders here—in the same kitchen, no less—and I don't have much in the way of answers yet."

Nan studied her. "Surely you've been doing something."

Doreen winced because she couldn't say anything about *that*. "I have been doing a lot of research, but none of it has been fruitful."

Nan backed off. "I'm sorry, child. I'm not trying to make it sound as if you aren't doing anything."

"You did quite successfully make it sound as if I'm not doing anything," Doreen quipped, followed by a laugh. "But the difference is, I'm still working the case. I'm just ... not necessarily getting anywhere. And that is always a challenge, especially early on," she muttered. "I just feel as if all these people have all these answers, but nobody wants to say anything."

"And we haven't found anybody in this home or the other home who's connected, right?" Nan asked.

"No, none that I can find," she stated ruefully.

"And everybody who seems to be connected appears to be dead?" Nan had stated this with such relish that Doreen frowned at her. Nan shrugged. "Sometimes dead is not a bad place to be."

Doreen winced. "And you could be right. I just really hope that *dead* isn't a place you're planning on going anytime soon."

"Good Lord, no," Nan declared, looking at her. "However, that doesn't mean I don't appreciate it if some other people choose to go."

"Ooh, you really are having a tough day."

"No," she clarified, "I'm just wallowing in being miserable. I brought it on myself, and now I don't really know what to do about it."

"Are we still talking about the schedule?"

"Of course we are," she snapped, looking at her sideways. "What else could we be talking about?"

Doreen studied her grandmother's face for a long moment and asked, "Did you and Richie have a fight?"

Nan glared at her. "Now why would you say that?"

"Because there's very little in life that upsets you more than when you're on the outs with your friends."

Nan's shoulders slumped. "He's the one who told me to take over the job."

"Ah, so it was his job beforehand?"

"Sure, but it was stupid."

"If it's stupid, then you need to take it over and do a better job. Otherwise, maybe you should apologize to him for whatever you said." At that, Nan reared up, but Doreen shook her head. "No, you and I both know that sometimes we just need to suck it up and to not make a big deal out of everything."

At that, Nan stared at her. "When did you get to be so wise?"

"I would say from you, but you would probably just laugh it off and say that it couldn't possibly be."

"True," she admitted, arching her brows, "and you have become very wise. I just didn't realize how much you have managed to make things happen in your world, and here I'm stuck, trying to make things happen in mine and not getting anywhere."

That was such an odd thing for her to say that Doreen faced her and asked, "Is something else going on here that I don't know about?"

"No, no, no." Nan gave another wave of her hand. "I'm just fussing."

"I know, but it's also not normal for you to be fussing—which means something's upsetting you."

"Doesn't matter if it is or not. And it's still just the same old thing."

"Then it seems you need to sit down, make up a schedule, and take it over to Richie, involve him in it, and see if he agrees that some of these suggestions might be better."

"You mean the two of us do it together?" Nan asked.

Doreen smiled. "Sometimes the best way to get people on your side is to involve them in the process," she noted, "particularly if you've put some noses out of joint when you stated your viewpoints."

Nan snorted. "Of course I put noses out of place," she declared, "and I think that's what I do best."

"You certainly know how to do it. But I don't know if you do it the best, or if the best is even what you want to do," Doreen clarified, as she eyed Nan. "You didn't used to be terribly abrasive."

"Yes, I did," she spat. "You just never saw it because you love me."

Doreen smiled. "And I still love you," she said. "However, if you and Richie are on the outs, you know that you won't feel better until you make up."

She snorted. "I don't know about that," she snapped, waving both hands now. "I'm certainly not ready yet."

"Then take your time," Doreen said, holding back her smile. "But remember that there is only so much time, and you don't want him to just not wake up one morning, especially if you haven't had a chance to clear the air."

"I'm not apologizing."

"I didn't say you should. Yet the bigger person, the one who apologizes, does the best."

"I'm still not apologizing."

"Nope, I know. I heard you," Doreen replied, still holding back a smile.

Nan shook her head. "You're making too much out of this."

"Of course I am," Doreen conceded. At that, Nan just glared at her. Doreen smiled. "And maybe you aren't making enough out of it."

"What do you mean by that?"

"Think about it. You're in a good position, in good health, and you're a whole lot younger than he is. So, maybe he's finding things a little taxing these days. If so, your comment may have made him feel a little old and useless," she explained. "You know how that feels."

Nan's shoulders slumped yet again. "That's not fair."

"And why not?" Doreen asked.

"It's just not, and of course he's feeling that way. We … we all feel that way."

"So why would you want to add to how bad he feels by piling on or letting him continue to feel that way?"

Nan sighed. "You can't just fix everything because you want things to go your way."

"And you can't just have everything go your way either," Doreen noted.

Nan stared at her. "I'll think about it."

"You do that. In the meantime, are we having tea or not?" Nan was obviously struggling, so Doreen replied, "I guess that means we aren't having tea. Nan, I was happy to come out for the walk and for a visit, but, if you need some space and time, that's okay too."

"No, I don't," she grumbled. "I really did need to see you."

"In that case, let's make a pot of tea, sit down, and we'll have a conversation about something completely unrelated."

"Good," she muttered. "I was really hoping you had something on the case to keep me busy."

"Did you know any of the family here locally?"

"No, I sure didn't," she replied. "I would have told you if I did. Seems as if I don't know anybody anymore. They've all changed and grown. The town seems different now."

"The town is, indeed, different now," Doreen confirmed. "It's not the way it was so many years ago, and that's what happens. Life goes on, and everyone … moves on."

"I don't like it."

At that, Doreen burst out laughing, and Nan glared at her for a moment, then a reluctant smile tugged at her lips. "It's good to hear you laugh," Nan said.

"It's good to laugh," Doreen agreed. "I didn't have a whole lot of that in my world before."

"I know, and that's one of the reasons I enjoy seeing you around Mack. He makes you smile, and that's incredibly important."

Chapter 11

"MACK ALSO MAKES me feel good about myself," Doreen added, her smile beaming as she gazed at Nan affectionately. "All in all, I think he's been a very special addition to my life. And, no, I'm still not pushing for a wedding yet."

Nan slumped back and glared at her.

"I know. I know. You all want it in *your* time frame," Doreen noted.

"We want it while we're alive, child," Nan muttered. "As you just told me, we don't know when or how any of us will leave."

"And that goes for me too," Doreen noted. "I have no way of knowing if I'll be here in another few days."

Nan's eyes widened, and she paled.

"Relax, Nan. I don't say that to worry you. I'm just saying that I won't get pushed into this wedding."

"You're so stubborn," Nan noted, and then she laughed. "And I heartily approve of it."

"That's good," Doreen agreed, rolling her eyes, "because you still won't get me to jump into it before I'm ready."

"You need to be comfortable doing this on your own,"

she agreed, with a nod. "And, as much as we all may want you to jump right in, it does have to be your choice."

"Thank you," Doreen replied, a smile on her face and in her tone. "Hopefully you'll remember that, even in a few days."

"No, I probably won't—particularly if I won't be around for much longer," she muttered.

"Are you actually having that feeling, or is this more about *I'm feeling rough and don't like my life just now, so I'm hoping I won't be here in a few days?*"

"No, it's never that," Nan admitted. "It's just when I get tired."

"But you also know what the fatigue is from." At that, Nan turned and glared at her. Doreen just held up a hand. "I'm just calling it the way it is."

"Yeah, but what if I don't want to hear the way it is?"

Doreen grinned at her. "But you do want to hear it because you already know what the right thing to do is. You just don't want to do it. Maybe I'll set up a betting pool as to how long the two of you will be on the outs."

Nan gasped in shock.

Doreen shook her head. "Don't look at me like that. That's exactly what you would do," she pointed out. "For all I know, somebody has already set it up."

"They wouldn't dare," Nan snapped, but she frowned, as if going through all the people she knew, and then nodded. "I bet somebody already has."

"I bet somebody already has too," Doreen agreed, with a chuckle.

They sat down with their tea as Nan started going through the list in her head again. "I wouldn't be happy if they did that though," she added.

"But you do it all the time, and you do it with everybody in your life. So you have to expect that, when you're on the outs with somebody, they'll do it to you too." Nan just glared at her, and Doreen nodded. "I know you don't want to hear that, and I get it. Yet you're telling me that it doesn't matter with your bets, so why not with theirs?" she pointed out. "You can't do things like that to other people without their jumping at the chance to do it to you."

"Fine," Nan muttered, then she glared at her. "Who would you bet on?"

Doreen shook her head. "Oh, no way," she said. "You're not asking me that. First off, I don't know anything about the betting that you're doing, and, second, no way I would pit myself against you guys. You're both stubborn enough to confirm nobody won."

At that, a real smile crinkled up on Nan's face, and she had a good laugh. "You do know me, don't you?"

"I absolutely do," she stated, "and I know that Richie is just as stubborn as you are. He's also a good friend. Good friends are hard to find these days, Nan. You've got a lot of people here you are friendly with, but Richie? ... He is somebody who's been here for you all the time. And it'll hit you awfully hard when he goes one day."

Nan slowly nodded. "You're right about that," she muttered. "Just having him as part of all these cases has made life so much more fun."

"True enough, and here we are in the middle of another one. It's surprising to me that you're not hot on the trail to help me out."

"That's because you haven't given us a job," she noted.

"Didn't think I had to," Doreen replied. "Remind me of

a single time when that happened? Did you ever wait? Or listen?"

Nan's gaze widened. "Oh, now that's an interesting point. I hadn't considered that."

"Of course not, but, from my point of view, you're all sitting here, waiting for me to solve it, and I could use a hand," she pointed out. Even if she didn't, she wouldn't tell her grandmother that. It seemed to be the one thing that kept everybody here happy and involved. "I think the day you guys all decide that it's not worth doing is the day you might as well not get out of bed."

"It'll be the day that we *don't* get out of bed," Nan declared, looking at her. "It'll be the day we can't get out of bed."

"Exactly, so pitch in and give me a hand on this one," Doreen said. "I would think we could get it done, but, at the moment, we're still stuck."

"So, what do you want us to do?"

"I need to know who's working at that restaurant, and we need to talk to them in such a way that Mack doesn't think we're interfering."

Nan started to laugh. "Oh my." Nan tried to stifle her laugh and failed badly. "If he finds out …"

"I know, and he won't be happy, which is why I need help."

"Oh, perfect, and it is a restaurant, right?"

"It is a restaurant, yes, though I don't know if they're open after the two deaths. Who'll run the kitchen? How many people does it even take to run a whole restaurant, I wonder."

Nan frowned. "I think Cleavis might help. He's a chef and has been around the restaurant scene a lot, so we should talk to him."

"That's nice, but who is he? Do I know him?" Doreen asked.

"He's relatively new," Nan began.

"When you say *relatively*, what does that mean?"

"I don't know, a couple months, maybe a couple weeks. I don't know."

Doreen heard an odd note in her tone. "Nan, have you been stepping out on Richie with this chef?"

"Richie and I are not an item."

"Is that what this is all about?"

"No," she stated, glaring at her. "I just think Cleavis is a more interesting character."

"Of course, because he's new. However, if you start breaking hearts around here again, you've been fairly …" She stopped.

"Fairly what?" Nan asked, turning that gaze on her.

"Fairly quiet about your little alliances."

"I'm no different now," she stated, "but Richie did seem to think I was stepping out."

"If you weren't, and he doesn't believe you, shame on him. However, if you were, and you're lying to him, then shame on you."

Nan's jaw dropped. "My goodness, you certainly ended up picking a side very quickly."

"I'm not picking a side," Doreen clarified. "There are no sides here. You and I both know that life is far too short for that. Who is this Cleavis, and what does it take to talk with him?"

"Probably not much since he's hanging around me pretty consistently."

"I would say, good for him. You're a mighty fine woman

to hang around with."

Nan looked at her, preened slightly, and added, "He mentioned that too."

"Of course he did, and he sounds like a bit of a ladies' man."

Nan thought about it, then nodded reluctantly. "That's probably a good way to put it."

"In that case you're pushing all the buttons to trigger Richie's insecurities."

"He shouldn't have so many," she snapped. "We're friends."

"Good, I'm glad to hear that."

"And it would be nice if Richie would believe it too." Nan sniffed as she pulled out her phone and left a quick text. "Cleavis is coming down," she announced, setting aside her phone.

"Okay, good." Doreen eyed her grandmother and asked carefully, "What about inviting Richie too?"

"Oh, that'll just set off a fight, and it won't be pretty. You have no idea."

"No, I don't, but it would be nice to think we wouldn't have fights at your age."

"That would imply we're not worth fighting over," she snapped, "and that won't work out so well." Nan gave Doreen a curt nod.

When a heavy knock came on Nan's door, Doreen got up to answer it. She found a large man, similar in size to Richie, leaning heavily on his cane.

He slowly made his way into the room, then took one look at Nan and smiled. "There she is. How's the prettiest woman in the place doing today?"

Doreen looked over at her grandmother, not at all surprised to see her blushing. "Good Lord," Doreen muttered to herself. Just then she heard a shout from the hallway, and she looked out to see Richie. "Hey, Richie," she greeted him. "How are you doing?"

He moved slowly toward her and sighed, then took one look at Cleavis, and his face closed up. Doreen quickly stepped out into the hallway and whispered, "Richie, I asked Nan to call him, so I could pick his brain about the restaurant industry, a chef's life and all. I don't know if you heard, but we had a second death at the same restaurant."

Immediately his face lit up with curiosity. "Really?" he asked, as he glanced back at the room and sniffed.

"You know that we need to find out as much as we can."

He nodded. "That's possible, but still, he's a little too flirty."

"That may be, but you also know, as soon as you make a scene, she'll go in the opposite direction."

He laughed. "She already has. That woman will always drive me nuts."

"Maybe so, yet I hope you guys are willing to get past all this, before the betting gets a little too crazy." He stared at her, and she nodded. "Do you really think people aren't doing that here?"

"I would hope not." He sniffed again.

"Think about it," she suggested, patting his shoulder. "You and I both know how many times you two have had bets on other people around here. So it would make sense that somebody was already putting something together about you two. Unless you guys can, you know, bury your differences and fast, that's just the way it'll be."

"But it's not fair."

"Nothing is fair in life." Doreen smiled at him, wondering why they hadn't considered the possible fallout from their own riff. "You two can settle your differences on your own. Now, if you want to come in and be a part of this conversation, you have to behave yourself."

His big, unruly brows pushed together, and he glared at her.

She nodded. "I won't tolerate any fighting, but I could really use all the help I can get on this case."

Immediately he relented. "That makes sense. … Okay, fine. I'm coming in."

"Leave the attitude outside."

Chapter 12

DOREEN WAS SURPRISED to have Richie nearly brush her aside so he could get into Nan's living room faster. She went in behind him, and Nan stood there, glaring at him. Doreen stepped between the two of them. "Now, let's not forget that we're here because we need answers." She turned, looked at the new arrival with a smile, and greeted him. "Hello, I'm Doreen." Mugs walked over trying to sniff the new arrival. Goliath in typical cat mode ignored him, and surprisingly enough Thaddeus snoozed missing the new arrival completely.

"Hi, Doreen. I'm Cleavis with a *C.*"

"Versus *Cleavis* with what?" she asked, frowning.

He burst out laughing. "That's the thing. As far as I know, *Cleavis* is only ever spelled with a *C.*"

She wasn't even sure how to approach that, so she decided to avoid that topic. "I do thank you for coming, Cleavis with a *C.* I'm hoping you won't mind answering a few questions about the restaurant industry."

"It's a mess. I can tell you that much."

"Pretty sure everybody in this place looks at their own industry as being a mess," she noted, with a smile. "Not exactly sure what part of it is a mess though."

"It's very competitive. I think the statistics in Vancouver—before COVID hit—noted that a restaurant closed every day of the year, and a new restaurant opened every day of the year."

"So, is that a bad thing then?" she asked, frowning at him. "That is the way life often is. Some people make it, and some people don't."

He nodded. "But, if you're one of the ones who don't make it, then it's devastating."

"Of course. I get that. What about locally? What are the stats in Kelowna?"

"With not as many people, it could be even more cut-throat," he suggested. "You've got to think about the reality that somebody out there will always do better than you. Some places take off really quickly, and some places just really struggle."

"And what about the Rocking Horse Pub and the attached restaurant? Do you know anything about them?"

He snorted at that. "Those two businesses have been in and out of trouble for years."

"What about now?"

"I can't say I really know," he admitted, staring at her. "Is there a reason we're talking about it now?"

"We're talking about it because of two murders there. Part of the Burgon family came over from Alberta, and the niece's fiancé was murdered a few days ago here. He was just a young man, and he'd been working in the kitchen when he was stabbed. Now, as of last night, an older woman has also been murdered in the same kitchen. Alice Burgon."

He paled at that.

"Did you know her?"

He frowned. "I know of her, but I hadn't heard about the murders."

"Exactly, and I don't know if Nan has mentioned anything to you, but I do a lot of amateur detective work and sometimes help the police."

"Sometimes?" Richie snorted. "You're in their way all the time."

She glared at him. "That may be, but I prefer to think that I'm offering my assistance to them."

He frowned and nodded. "Darren says that they wouldn't have closed half those cases without you."

"I'm not trying to take any credit either," she clarified. "All I want to do is help close these cold cases—and some related current ones. So, the question I have is"—Doreen turned to face Cleavis—"what can you tell me about the history of that restaurant?"

"It's a mess. Dave Burgon, the original owner of the pub and restaurant, was a right terror, and he used to rent out rooms above the pub. There was even talk about his getting involved in some minor prostitution, all in order to make some money when times were tough."

"He prostituted himself?" she asked.

He blinked and shook his head. "No, God no. He had a couple of prostitutes and rented the rooms up there by the hour."

"Ah, so he operated as a pimp, or was he renting rooms in order to make ends meet?"

He frowned and nodded. "You know, that's a good point. I'm not sure which, whether he got a kickback or just rented rooms."

"Right. So, we have to keep an eye on that issue as well," she muttered.

"Why?" he asked. "That old man was just bad news, and he's dead. It would take a better man than me to miss him."

"He was that difficult?" Doreen asked Cleavis.

"Yeah, he was that difficult. If he didn't like you, he poured your pints on the skinny side. If he thought you were pretty and were likely to give him a run for his money upstairs in bed, your pints got a little bit heftier. For all I know, he may have slipped something into their drinks too."

"But you don't know that though, right?" Doreen asked.

"No, I don't know that," he confirmed, waving his hand. "That's just what the rumors were."

"Right, well, rumors being what they are, we also have to keep an eye on that too." She shook her head.

Nan started to laugh. "If Mack could hear you, he would be so proud of you."

"No, he wouldn't. He would be telling me that I was barking up the wrong tree and wasting everybody's time," she retorted, with a knowing smile for her grandmother.

"But look at you now? You're trying to keep the conversation on track and not let rumors and innuendos dominate the discussion."

She shrugged. But inwardly she couldn't help but smile. And as if he knew Thaddeus stirred in her hair, grumbling slightly as if upset at being disturbed. The others had settled down to wait for her.

Cleavis continued. "I can't really tell you a whole lot about the family, except that, in most cases, they were okay. Old Man Dave Burgon was a bit rough on everybody. Dave just seemed to think that what he said was never to be contested. If you didn't like it, that was your problem, not his. He wasn't an easy person to get along with, but I didn't really have any personal beef with him."

"Okay, that's good to know," Doreen noted. "And what about this woman who was murdered ten years ago in Alberta? Katie Burgon? I understand she was married, but her husband left her and was never seen again. I presume that's why she went by her maiden name."

"As far as I know, she was okay. She was one heck of a cook in her own right, but her world was in Alberta. Some of the family moved to Kelowna after her death and more moved here later."

"Ah, okay."

"I think Alice would have been the current owner of the pub and restaurant."

"Okay." She wrote that down. "What was she like?"

"A chip off the same old block, just like Old Man Burgon," he noted. "Again, I don't have any personal experience, so everything is hearsay."

"Good enough," she muttered. "And when we're talking hearsay, what hearsay have you heard?"

He shook his head. "I'm not really sure I can tell you very much on that score. Just that, when times were tough, the Burgons got a little tougher."

"*Hmm.* Is there any reason to believe that anybody would still be harboring something against Dave for all those tough times?"

"Sometimes memories are short. Sometimes they're long. Old Man Burgon was in the property business at one point in time, whatever that means. I just know that, when he was expanding his restaurant and trying to move to a new location, things got a little ugly. I think he may have managed to squeeze out a couple people so that he could have their places. And, when I say, *squeeze out,* I suspect that he was pulling some strings to make things difficult for the other restaurants, effectively shutting them down and then hoping to buy them out before things got too bad. He did that to the competition a while back too."

"And to you?"

"No, not to me," he replied, with a shrug. "I didn't particularly care for his dealings but I made no bones about it, so it was a little easier for me to stay clear."

"Interesting," she murmured.

"I've done a lot of things in my life that I may not be proud of, but I never actively tried to hurt somebody's business. Yet you can bet that Old Man Burgon did. That I know for sure. At one point, he and I had words. The old man … Well, … he was old, and I guess I was too," he admitted, with a shake of his head. "You forget just how old you are. Looking back at things, we were crazy to even be fighting over these things, but it is what it is," he conceded, with a shrug. "The restaurant business has changed a little bit, but it's maybe even more cutthroat now."

"You think it is?" Doreen asked, frowning.

"Oh, I think an awful lot of people are suffering out there, following the peak COVID years. The delivery services took a big fat knife and cut themselves a hefty profit. People want to stay at home more than going out to the restaurants, and that's having an effect on the industry too."

"So, you stayed involved in the industry back then?"

"No, I stayed *interested* in the industry. I'm well past the point of being involved in anything."

"And does anybody in your family still have a restaurant?"

"Sure, my grandson runs it now. We lost my boy a few years back," he shared, his voice thickening. "Nobody should live to see their son die."

"I agree with you there," Doreen replied, "but who could still be around with potentially any knowledge of how that restaurant business is run today?"

"Do you think it's really about how the business is run?" he asked.

"Considering that a young man's been killed, and now Alice, the older woman, has also been killed, it makes me wonder if it was mistaken identity. If you've got your hair up in a ponytail, and I understand Barry did have his hair up, it could be that he was just in the wrong place at the wrong time. And determined to not let it go, this killer came back and took out the person he really intended to take out the first time." When Nan stared at her, Doreen shrugged. "It's just a working theory."

"It's not a bad one," agreed Cleavis with a *C*. "When you think about it, there has to be a reason for taking out two people. Unless it's just to ruin the business, maybe as payback for when Old Man Dave ruined somebody else's business."

"But as you pointed out, the old man is gone."

"Right, but we don't know if the remaining Burgons were carrying on with the same business practices, in which case that could have stirred up some petty unpleasantness."

"It's possible, I suppose," Nan interjected, but she sounded doubtful.

Doreen smiled at her. "I'm just tossing out ideas to see if we can find anything plausible," she murmured. "We don't have a whole lot of Burgons we can ask any more, but with Alice now gone, … I guess the next question would be, who'll take over in her place? Was somebody pressuring them to sell out or to close the restaurant? And what were they prepared to do in order to get it?"

"Oh," Nan muttered, raising her eyebrows.

Doreen shrugged. "We can surmise all we want, but it doesn't really help us until we can get those answers."

Nan nodded. "I see what you're saying. I always think of a restaurant as being lots of hard work, so I don't know why anybody would try to take it over."

"It's also an expression of art, an expression of love," Doreen noted. "If somebody has a passion for it, and you thought you had a job there, where you could really work at creating dishes, something that really appeals to you. Then say the aunt decided to sell or something. You find out that not only are you losing your job but you won't get a piece of the pie either—since the aunt will need it for her retirement."

"I've certainly seen those things happen," Cleavis confirmed. "I sure don't want to think of people killing each other over it, but it is a valid point."

"You have to look at *all* the reasons people kill each other," Doreen suggested, turning to give him half a smile. "We keep coming up with all kinds of doozies, but, at the core of it all, it's usually jealousy, revenge, or greed. In this case, it could be any of those."

"I don't envy you the job of looking," Cleavis stated, with a grimace. "It seems to me to be a job for the police."

"It absolutely is a job for the police," she agreed. "Yet the police are pretty overworked. That's why I lend a hand every once in a while."

"And a mighty fine hand it is too," Nan stated, with a chuckle.

With that, Cleavis got up to leave. Then he looked back at Doreen and suggested, "You could always contact my grandson, who runs my business now. He might have some more current insights."

Doreen nodded. "Either you can give me his contact information or send him a message that I would be interested in talking to him."

"Will do," he replied, "but remember that he's got nothing to do with anything. Keep him out of trouble. He would just be a source in terms of how the industry is working today."

"That's fine," she said. "It also would help to have an understanding of how somebody could sneak up on these people."

"What do you mean?" he asked.

"When you're alone in the restaurant, as the cook Barry was, all alone as far as I understood, except for his fiancée, Jillian. She got knocked out cold and, when she came to, she found him dead, where they had been working."

He stared at her. "Seriously?"

She nodded. "Yeah, seriously."

"That's not a good way to go."

"And think about the trauma to the young woman who found him dead but didn't see or know what happened. Of course the cops are very interested in her involvement."

"*Of course.*" Cleavis gave an eye roll. Then he added, "You should be looking at her. What if it would be her restaurant now? Was she connected to Alice just because she wanted the restaurant?"

"I don't know," Doreen replied. "*We're all still looking for answers yet.*"

"Good luck with that." Cleavis slowly made his way to the door. "You will definitely need it." He looked back at Nan and said, "I'll talk to you later."

Nan waved and got up. Cleavis walked out the door, and

she closed it behind her. They spoke for a few minutes in the hallway before Nan stepped back inside her apartment again. She looked over at Doreen. "Do you think that helped?"

"I'm not sure," Doreen noted. "However, anything I can learn about the industry, anything I can learn about the people involved, is more than I knew before, so sure. ... It helped. Did it help a whole lot? Maybe not, but we'll take what we can get, particularly when we're grasping at straws."

She looked over at Richie, who was studying Nan's face. As Doreen stood up, the animals hopped up as well. She smiled down at them and praised them. "You guys were so good while we conducted our business, even though this visit was longer than we intended." She looked over at Nan and added, "I'll leave you and Richie to consider this. Maybe by the time I get these animals walked home, some inspiration will have struck me, and I'll have some insights into what's going on. Meanwhile, you two need to talk."

And, with that, she made good her escape.

Chapter 13

T HE NEXT MORNING Doreen woke up fairly early, but her mind was already buzzing away. She sent Mack a text, asking if they'd gotten anywhere. He'd worked late last night, had popped by for a cup of tea, then had left fairly quickly. She worried about him when he was working so hard, but he just laughed and pointed out how *somebody* had sent, in his direction, all these cases to be closed. With the station short-staffed, Mack was helping out with all the details. She wasn't sure if he was really upset or if it was just a reminder that she dealt with only a portion of the police work involved, and everybody else had to deal with the rest.

She got a response about twenty minutes later when he phoned her. "Hey," she greeted him, yawning into the phone.

"Are you okay?" he asked.

"A little tired, that's all."

"To be expected, I suppose," he stated in a matter-of-fact tone.

"Maybe. How're you doing?" she muttered.

"We're just not getting anywhere," he admitted in a frustrated tone. "So, do you have anything to help us along?"

"Not yet," she muttered. "I feel as if I need to know a little more about the Burgon family though—as in, whom hated whom, and who loved who."

"Why?"

"Because it has to be an inside job," she shared. "How many people know who's working at night after hours? And was the young man's murder a case of mistaken identity, or was it to put the family on notice? Then maybe they didn't listen, or maybe something more was going on under the surface."

"So, you're thinking blackmail?" he asked.

"I'm not really thinking anything at the moment. I haven't had my coffee yet to spur on my thinking."

He burst out laughing. "I hear that. I came into the office early because I couldn't sleep."

"*Uh-oh*," she muttered. "Right. That's what happens though. You get all these thoughts running around in your head, and you stay awake, wanting to check on them. Any surprises in the autopsies?"

"Nope, none. Cause of death was stabbing in both cases. The difference was, Barry was stabbed in the back, while Alice was stabbed in the front. Yet the chest and neck were involved in both killings."

"So, very similar stab wounds."

"Yes, and again with a kitchen knife."

"That kitchen will have to replace those knives soon," she muttered. "And that was the manner of death for Katie, Jillian's mother in Alberta. Stabbed with a knife from her kitchen, in her chest too."

Mack went silent for a moment. "I hadn't considered that."

"I would imagine these knives are very special, and people who use them are very attached to them."

"Possibly," he replied. "I think chefs tend to be pretty protective about their knives."

"I think anybody in a shared environment is territorial about their equipment. I don't know any mechanic who would be happy to have somebody come along and use his tools, potentially not treating them as well as he would like."

Mack laughed. "No, we've had more than a few cases of that going bad too."

"So, when you think about it, there definitely could be something along that line."

"Sure, but now we're just grasping at straws, trying to find a motive."

"If you find a motive and some answers, feel free to share."

"Same for you," he replied, "but, as you know, if we don't solve this right away …"

"Don't even go there," she interjected. "There have to be answers."

"Sure, but that doesn't mean we'll find them right off the bat."

"And that just means we're back to people lying and cheating in order to stay hidden."

"Of course. Nobody wants you putting them behind bars when, as far as they're concerned, they got away with murder."

"And it could very well be that this group gets away with murder, but I will do my best to ensure they don't."

"Whoa, whoa, whoa. What do you mean, *this group*?"

She frowned. "I just can't see three murders happening in the same family ever, especially not within one decade."

"But Barry, the young cook, isn't from the same family."

"But remember he was engaged to Jillian Burgon, so, except for the formality of the wedding, he was part of that same family. In fact, if money is part of the motive, we also need to consider the fact that maybe his becoming part of the family was enough to sign his death warrant."

"I don't think the restaurant is worth that kind of money."

"I don't know, but there is also the property value to consider. I just spoke with somebody who knew the business when Dave Burgon ran it and said Dave was known for letting out rooms above the pub or restaurant for prostitutes by the hour."

"To make money?"

"Yes, I think it was to keep the business afloat."

"It would be hard to blame anybody for doing anything they could think of to stay afloat in tough times, but that could be crossing the line," Mack muttered. "I'm sure he's not the only one who has pulled something like that."

"No, I don't think so either," she agreed. "What I need is a motive, and it keeps coming back to the odd man out, the fiancé, Barry. So, either this is related to the Burgon family and related to money or even an inheritance, or Barry was just in the wrong place at the wrong time."

"I did consider that last theory," Mack shared, "and it remains on the board, just because we don't have answers. Still, it's pretty skinny."

She laughed. "Are you telling me all these theories aren't skinny? Because, the way I see it, they're all pretty weak."

He chuckled. "And you could be right, but, until we can get better answers, all of these are options. What are you doing today?"

She realized she needed to contact the painter, Danny

Burgon. "I'm hoping to settle on a gift for Nan for her birthday."

"I don't know what you've chosen to do, since you've been secretive about that," he noted, "but you're running low on time."

"I need to get it resolved. Nan and Richie are having a little trouble because of this new guy at Rosemoor."

"*Uh-oh*," Mack said, laughter in his tone.

"I know, but that's not exactly anything we want going on around Rosemoor."

"And I think Richie is still rattled a bit after that other case," Mack reminded her. "Even though it didn't turn out to be his daughter, it did involve somebody he had a relationship with. He was pretty head over heels in love with the child's mother, and that sort of thing leaves a mark. The whole investigation was an emotional roller coaster for him."

"Right," she agreed. "I never even thought of that with this latest upset between Richie and Nan. I need to remind Nan about that."

"Yeah, it would be nice if somebody would cut Richie a little bit of slack."

"Yeah, I don't think these people are very good at cutting each other slack," she added, with a snort. "Somehow there just seems to be a whole lot more upsets."

"And how is that even possible?" Mack asked, a bit of teasing in his tone. "They spend all day, every day with each other. You would think they would have plenty of time to work things out."

"Maybe that's the problem," Doreen pointed out. "Maybe they spent way too much time together."

"That could be," he muttered. "On the other hand, we've seen some really good things happen down there."

"I agree, and, when I talked to management, they were really happy with how excited people were at all my comings and goings on these cold cases and how involved everybody was. I just feel bad that I don't have a whole lot for them to do this time."

"Maybe that's a good thing. You can't be the entertainment for them every day."

"No, I sure can't. I did ask Cleavis to come talk to me about the restaurant industry, since he had that experience. Also I forgot to mention that we need to figure out when we can go to Vancouver."

"Vancouver?" he asked.

"Yeah, remember? To go check out Mathew's houses?"

"Oh, right," he replied in an odd tone. "And when did you want to go?"

"In a couple weeks, but, of course, the sooner, the better."

"Right."

"I really prefer that you come with me," she added hesitantly. "I know I mentioned it before, but we didn't really resolve it."

"No, that's fine," he replied, with a sigh. "It'll be interesting to see where you lived."

"You mean, my gilded cage?" she asked, with a snort. "For all I know, Robin completely gutted the house and changed everything."

"Would he have let her do that?"

"I don't know," she said, "and I don't care. I have her houses to go through too," she noted, with a groan. "And that won't be easy either."

"Do you have to go through them?"

"I suppose I do. There are a lot of things to consider,

and I probably shouldn't just sign off blindly, not without first seeing things for myself."

"Right, and I'm really proud that you feel that way. So, I'll put in for what? Three days? Four days?"

"Or we could take a long weekend," she suggested. "Regardless, we should get all of it done if we took, … I don't know, four days?" Then she frowned and added, "Maybe a week."

He laughed.

"At least this way, we can make it a bit of a holiday."

"A holiday sounds perfect. I'll talk to the captain." And, with that, he rang off.

Chapter 14

DOREEN WOKE THE next morning, bounced out of bed, and reached for the phone to call Nan. "Hey, do you want to go to a restaurant for lunch today? Anything except for the one in question of course?"

Nan came back with an immediate yes. "And we should talk to Cleavis's grandson."

"I was thinking about that," Doreen murmured. "Some discussion is warranted, but I want to go to the restaurant itself first. If it's closed, we'll pick whatever one is closest and maybe talk to some of the local businesses too. The thing is, I was hoping to take the animals."

"So bring the animals," Nan stated. "We could always do takeout—or sit outside, if that's an option."

"It's pretty cold out there," she murmured. There was a pause while Nan appeared to consider that. Doreen repeated, "I don't really want to go without the animals."

"Let's take them, and we can just do our talking and see how people feel about it. If need be, we can pick up food and bring it home."

"Good," Doreen agreed. "I like that idea too."

It didn't take very long to get through her morning routine, and then she found herself just waiting and waiting, frustrated.

An hour later, the phone rang, and it was Nan. "If we don't plan to sit inside a restaurant, why don't we just go now?" she suggested. "I've been sitting here, waiting, trying to fill my time."

"Yeah, me too," Doreen admitted, laughing. "I'll come pick you up." And that's what she did.

When she pulled up to the front of Rosemoor ten minutes later, Nan was already bundled up in a nice wintery coat, standing outside, waiting for her.

She dashed to the parking lot, stepped up over the curb, and got into the car. "Thank heavens you finally got here. I was freezing."

"It's only been ten minutes," Doreen protested.

"It felt like at least an hour."

"But it wasn't," Doreen stated. As she drove off, she looked at Nan and asked, "Do you know where Cleavis's grandson's restaurant is?"

"I do," she said, with a smile. "It's down off Bernard."

She frowned at her and asked, "Bernard is close to the Rocking Horse Pub, Dave Burgon's place?"

"Oh, now that's an interesting point," Nan noted. "I hadn't considered that Dave's pub was near Bernard, which is the touristy area of downtown."

"In that location, you would think they had a good thing going in terms of lots of business."

"Maybe, but I don't really know the ins and outs of it over all these years."

"No, me either," she muttered.

They headed downtown, parked, and, with the animals in tow, they walked around. When they came up to the restaurant in question, the Rocking Horse Pub, a big sign was posted. *Temporarily closed.*

"Ah," Doreen muttered, "so they did have to close it."

A couple stood outside, talking, holding steaming cups of coffee in their hands. Doreen looked over at them, not necessarily wanting to interrupt their conversation but hoping to get a bit more in the way of answers. She hesitantly called out and asked if they knew anything about when the restaurant would open again, pretending complete ignorance of what had gone on.

The woman replied, "I don't know if it'll ever reopen, to tell you the truth. A double murder happened in there over the last few days."

Nan gasped and did a lot better job of acting surprised than Doreen.

"Oh my, really?" Doreen turned and looked back at the storefront. "We heard it was a good place to eat and were hoping to come check it out. We're early, but we were just in the neighborhood."

The older man with this woman added, "I don't know about it being good. It was okay, but nothing compared to when the old man had it."

"And how long ago would that have been?" Doreen asked curiously.

"Oh, quite a while ago." He laughed. "I've been here a long time, so things for me in terms of years tend to look a little differently than they do for everybody else."

Doreen smiled and nodded.

Nan, of course, laughed and replied, "Oh, I hear you there."

"I guess you don't know any details on the murders, *huh?*" Doreen asked.

"No, I sure don't," he replied, with a snort. "But, if it was some insurance scam, now that I would have believed."

"Meaning that they really were suffering for business?"

"Yes," he confirmed, "at least as far as I know."

The woman beside him hushed him. "Now that's just rumors," she said. "You shouldn't be passing on that stuff."

He shrugged. "I tell ya, it might have been rumors, but it was money on the line because that place was empty a lot of times."

"I understood that they were also into catering," Doreen shared, with a wave. "We were wondering about getting them to cater for a party."

"The catering option was fairly new, I believe," clarified the older man, as he frowned and looked at the restaurant. "It's a shame about the kid though."

"What kid?" she asked.

"The first one murdered was a young man, fresh out of culinary school and really excited about it."

"Oh, did you know him?" she asked. "I am so sorry if you did. That's got to be hard."

"I met him here the odd time or two, as I work just next door."

And right next door was … an unmarked building, so that didn't say much.

"I work up on the second floor," he added.

Doreen's gaze drifted upward, and she realized an office suite was up there.

"I'm part of an insurance assessment and evaluation company."

"Ah, so then you must come down here to get your coffee and whatnot on a regular basis."

"I don't know about coffee. I've got a coffeemaker up

there," he shared. "However, I do come down for a lot of the socials sometimes, and I would pop in the restaurant every once in a while. One day I saw the kid trying to unlock the door, and he couldn't get the keys to work. The mechanism was just stiff from the cold, so I helped him out."

The older man shrugged. "He seemed nice enough. He was pretty excited. He and his girlfriend had finally moved over from Alberta, and this was a family business or something, and he was hoping to make a mark of his own."

Doreen's heart broke for Barry. "And that has got to be terrible to hear about that and to know that he was cut down in his prime."

"Exactly," he declared, his tone turning brisk. "I just wish the whole building would go. There's a really ugly history to it."

"What now?" she asked. "I haven't heard any of this stuff."

With a glare in the older man's direction, the woman with him interjected, "My father's a bit of a local historian. So, take everything with a grain of salt."

"It's not gossip," he declared. "I get it that you don't want me talking about this stuff. Yet, maybe, if we talked about what some of these places are doing wrong, we wouldn't have these recurring situations."

Nan stepped forward, smiling up at him prettily, and nodded. "I think that's a really good way to go forward. Unfortunately so many of the young people today are all about staying out of everything and not getting involved."

He nodded, smiling back at Nan.

Nan asked, "What can you tell us about the history of this business?"

He shrugged. "It's not even so much about the restaurant but just the history of the place," he clarified. "I didn't know the young man or his fiancée at all."

"What about the second murder?" Doreen asked curiously, wondering just how much information this guy had.

"All I heard was what was on the news," he replied. "And I believe Alice was the last living daughter of the old man. He had two sons as well. … One is a retired contractor, and one is an artist. God, that son's a bit of a character and lives somewhere out in Glenmore, I think."

"Oh, interesting, so then that's got to be a shock to everybody." Not wanting to really bring too much attention to themselves, Doreen glanced around and asked, "So, is there a good place to grab a coffee at this hour?"

"Not with the animals," the woman said, glancing down at Mugs, who was currently lying down on the ground. "They wouldn't have let you into the restaurant anyway, especially with a cat. That would cause chaos around here with the health inspector and customers."

She looked down at Goliath, who swished his tail with big, wide jerks. "Even if we just pick up a coffee?"

The woman snorted. "No, the restaurants are fairly anti-animal."

"The Burgons weren't the most social of people anyway," her father noted. "And I'm not sure they had to be either." He glanced at his daughter. "Some people just aren't … social."

She laughed. "My father is very social, in case you haven't noticed."

Doreen smiled at him. "It's nice when we get a chance to talk to people. It's often cold and dark this time of year, and everybody is bustling on their way to get to the next point of their day."

The older man nodded. "And I came here to meet my daughter and to just have a cup of coffee with her before she heads back to work again." He smiled at her. "It's always so much fun to see her during the week."

The daughter smiled and gently patted her father's cheek. "If you hadn't chosen to work down here, we could do it more often. As it is, I only get to see him when I'm in this corner of the world," she explained. "Otherwise it's a little bit far for us to travel during our workdays."

Doreen nodded. "Still, it's really lovely for you," she said warmly. "It's nice to even think that such a thing can happen." She hugged Nan and explained, "I've just brought my grandmother downtown to spend a few hours together. We thought we would do coffee, maybe walk around for a bit, and then find a restaurant to try for lunch."

"Oh, there's a good restaurant just around the corner here," he pointed out. "It was a restaurant that'll probably do much better now. These Burgons seem to take a lot of the downtown business, and everybody understood that," he said, with a headshake. "Yet this other restaurant is a family-run business as well." He gave them directions to get there. He frowned as he looked at the animals. "I don't think anybody will allow the animals in."

Doreen sighed. "I can understand that, with the food regulations and such. Maybe Nan can look after them while I run in and grab coffee, at least."

"Now that you could do," he replied, chuckling. They spoke for another few minutes, and then the father and daughter quickly headed off.

Nan turned to her. "You really do have to come to the location of the crimes, don't you?"

"I really do," Doreen confirmed. "And, if I wasn't off my

step on this one, I would have been down here earlier."

"I don't know that it would have been the right time," Nan stated. "I think timing has to come into play as well."

"Maybe," Doreen acknowledged, with a smile, as they headed off in the direction of the other family restaurant. As soon as they got there, she nodded. "This looks much friendlier, doesn't it?"

She opened the door and stepped in and asked, "I'm just here to grab some coffee right now, and we'll think about coming back later to pick up something for lunch, but can I bring in the animals while we order coffee?"

The woman looked at her and her animals and smiled. "As long as you do it fast, and we don't have anybody from the board here, then we certainly allow some animals in," she explained. "So, if it's just for coffee, come on in."

And, with that said, and a beaming smile in her direction, Doreen and the rest of them trooped indoors. Mugs set his tail to wagging, as if certain that would score him a treat. And, indeed, the woman came around and bent down to say hi to him.

"Oh, he's lovely," she crooned. When she saw Goliath on a leash, she gasped and laughed. "Oh my, doesn't he look dapper in that?"

"Dapper maybe, but he's not a big fan. As long as we're on the move, he's good, but, if we stay stationary for too long, he's not impressed to be wearing it."

The waitress chuckled. As she straightened, her eyes widened, and Doreen realized that Thaddeus was poking his head out of her hair. "And who is this?" the waitress crooned, reaching up a gentle finger.

Thaddeus cried out, "Thaddeus is here. Thaddeus is here."

She gasped, looked at her, and exclaimed, "Oh my, you're that sleuth person in town, aren't you?"

"I'm not sure about that exactly," Doreen noted, laughing, "but, yes, some people see me that way."

Nan stepped forward. "She's my granddaughter," she stated proudly. "And she solves so many cases here."

"Good, I hope you can step up and solve the one across the street." She pointed to the Rocking Horse Pub. "That's got us all in a tizzy."

"You're talking about the murders at the restaurant?" Doreen asked.

"Yes," the waitress cried out. "That's been awful."

"Did you know them?" Doreen turned to look back at the closed restaurant.

"I don't think anybody *knew* them," she clarified. "They just weren't the kind of people you can ever really get to know."

"Standoffish?"

"Standoffish, competitive, grouchy. All of that and more. If I just wanted to say hi, they would look at me as if I were there to steal restaurant secrets or something," she muttered, with a headshake. "The new young guy who worked there and his fiancée, they were quite decent, but the older lady? The one who was just killed? She was crabby and cranky."

"I'm sorry to hear that," Doreen replied. "That can make a bad impression on restaurants everywhere."

"That was the thing," the waitress explained. "We're all in the industry, and there's no reason to be nasty about any of it, but she just didn't see it that way."

"So, you couldn't really talk, have coffee, or discuss anything in the industry with her?"

"Oh, no, no, no. That was definitely not something she would ever be strong on."

"How was her health?" Doreen asked.

"I don't really know. She often looked worn out, but she was one of those steely kinds of people, you know? Instead of blood running through their veins, it's as if they have steel in their system. She never really looked anything other than tired, but she never slowed down either."

Doreen nodded. "I've certainly met a few people like that myself."

"That's the thing. Once you've seen the type, you recognize it," she noted, with a bright smile. The waitress turned to Nan and asked, "What can I get you, dear?"

Nan ordered tea.

"If you want to take a table and keep the animals tucked up close," the waitress suggested, "I'm happy to have you here. That way you can stay long enough to warm up."

"Sure, that would be lovely," Doreen replied, with a bright smile. She led Nan to a table and tucked Mugs and Goliath up underneath. Goliath just glared at her, but she nodded. "I know, Goliath. You want to get moving."

"I can't believe you have the temerity to put a cat on a leash," the waitress cried out, laughing.

"Yeah, he can't believe it either," she quipped, smiling at the helpful waitress. "The thing is, most of the time he's really happy with it."

"I've heard some crazy things about some of the cases you've been on. I'm sure they aren't true, but they've made for great reading fun."

"Oh, they probably *are* true," Nan corrected, with a chuckle, looking over at Doreen. "She's gotten into all kinds of trouble."

"The police must not be impressed with some of your antics."

"Lots of times I would say that's true, but yet they've been quite happy in the end to have me involved," Doreen noted.

"Of course it doesn't hurt that she's gotten herself engaged to a detective either," Nan added, smiling.

The waitress seemed astonished and then burst into delighted chuckles. "Oh my, now that's how you make a friend out of your enemy."

Doreen grinned. "Except, in this case, he's been a very good friend, long before we ever became anything more."

"That's a good way to do it," the waitress murmured, then quickly disappeared and came back out with pots of tea. "I've got two different kinds here for you, so let's see if we can get you warmed up."

"You're not open yet, are you?" Doreen asked, noting all the empty tables.

"No, not yet," the waitress confirmed, checking her watch. "For once, I'm ready in decent time too. So I can spend a minute or two just visiting. I'm Marla, by the way." She looked at Doreen. "About that restaurant …"

"Yes?" Doreen leaned forward slightly.

"You know that older lady, she had some pretty-ugly business practices, and I wouldn't be at all surprised if she was killed because of that."

"What do you mean?" Doreen asked.

"Apparently the young man and his fiancée were working on some catering jobs, and that's why they were there that night."

Doreen acted surprised. "I hadn't heard anything about them working so late on a catering job." At the moment she couldn't remember the details Jillian had shared with her.

Marla glanced around the restaurant and shared, "I can't imagine taking on more work on top of what I'm already doing."

"But the fiancé was also fairly new, so maybe he was pushing for it?"

"Maybe." Marla frowned. "Hard to say."

"How is your business?" Doreen asked.

"Rough," she stated. "After COVID, with everybody stuck at home for so long, then came this spurt of people who just couldn't wait to get back out again. So we had a fair bit of business at that time. However, as the costs went up on our supplies, we had to raise our prices. People didn't appreciate that, of course," she noted, with a sigh.

"The other thing during COVID was that everybody has gotten used to having deliveries, and that continues to cut into our profits pretty heavily as well," she shared, a sad smile playing on her lips. "And now with the high inflation rates and the cost of gas and everything? It seems a lot of people have decided to stay with delivery and not come in person. The business crowd is pretty decent though, and that's coming back again. Plus, if we host events on the weekends, I stay open for that. Still, it's just not been the same," she admitted.

"There have definitely been times when I wondered if I could stay afloat, but ours is a family-run business, and I just don't have a whole lot of work experience, outside of running this business," she shared. "So it's more about keeping it because, otherwise, what will I do?"

"Ah, so it helps you to stay busy more than you need the business?"

"Oh, I do need the business," she clarified. "I don't want

you to get the impression that we're rolling in it because we certainly aren't. Yet it is not quite the same thing. I've been here a long time, bought our house many years ago, and thank the Lord it's paid for. So it's not quite the same stress as if I were just starting out. I don't know how the young people will do it today."

"Do you have a family?" Doreen asked.

"Yes, but they've all moved down to Vancouver," she said, with a careless shrug. "They couldn't wait to get out of town and to find something a whole lot more *exciting*," she shared sadly. "My husband and I, we both run the restaurant, and we're doing okay."

But Doreen noted it was obvious from her tone that it wasn't great. "Would you consider shutting it down and maybe retiring at some point?"

"Oh, someday we'll definitely have to figure that out," she replied. "I don't know when, but the goal had always been that the kids would retire up here with us. Yet I think they're more settled down there with jobs that they can handle better and get paid better for. So it may end up being the other way around, and we retire down there," she explained.

"But I don't know that our old house would fetch enough money to enable us to have the same lifestyle that we could have here," she added. "So it's one of those many decisions that come your way as you get older."

"Grandkids yet?" Nan asked.

"Two," she stated, with a bright smile. "Two little girls, and, of course, we would love to be closer just for that reason alone."

The conversation continued around family for a bit as Doreen tried to navigate through the restaurant questions that she needed answers for. "Do you have any idea what could have happened at that restaurant?" she asked suddenly. She smiled at Marla. "Sorry, it just seems so hard to contemplate that something like that could happen here."

"I know," she exclaimed, with a delicate shudder. "I've been struggling to get my head wrapped around it all this time."

"And, of course, as a bit of an amateur sleuth myself," Doreen began, "the questions are endless. Like, is anybody even left in that family? Like, who is there to inherit the business?"

"There's definitely two brothers still nearby. One is retired, I think. The other brother is an artist, though I don't think he ever makes any money."

Doreen just nodded, once again wincing at the thought that this guy may not be any good. It had been a spur-of-the-moment decision to choose him to do Nan's birthday gift, but now Doreen wondered if it was the best choice she could have made. "So, maybe he doesn't want anything to do with the restaurant then?"

"I think his wife does. She helped out a little, but the sister-in-law and Alice? … For being so alike, they didn't get along all that well."

Doreen nodded. "Ouch. That's hard. Although maybe her husband will inherit it, and maybe he'll put his wife in charge to manage it how she wants."

"Maybe. I don't know how that works, but it is possible. It's been in the Burgon family a long time."

"And there's the niece too, the one who lost her fiancé."

"Yeah, I think she would probably go back to Alberta. Her uncle was talking about it. He was in here not that long ago."

Doreen frowned, having just realized that she'd more or less put Uncle Zev out of her mind. Yet he was the one who had brought Doreen into this in the first place. How could she have forgotten him? What part did he have to play in all this?

Chapter 15

SITTING HERE, DOREEN realized that she was really off her game. She was running around clueless on this one, and she needed to get her head in the game. Doreen muttered, "Right, I guess the other brother could possibly inherit too then."

"I don't think he's restaurant material. He's a little rough around the edges and all. I don't think he particularly cares for dealing with the public."

Doreen laughed. "No, a lot of people don't care for dealing with the public, but it's a necessary evil, especially when you're in the hospitality industry."

"And people just don't get that," Marla noted, with surprise. "I don't understand it."

Doreen nodded. "Most of the time I think it just takes the right personality to make a service business a success."

"I've been the right personality all these years," Marla stated. "So, for me, it's an easy thing to do, but it would be nice to walk away at some point and to know that we would be okay."

"Do you think that the Burgon family had business issues?"

"Oh, I know they did," Marla confirmed. "We all have business issues, and lots of times absolutely nothing could be done, and their restaurant would be just as empty as ours."

"Ah, that's got to be hard too." Doreen was trying to get a better sense of this business. "Is there something like insurance for you, to cover times like that?"

"Oh, you mean, in case of loss of business? We must have some. I think it's only after … an accident or a fire or flood or something along that line that it comes into play."

"Or death?" Doreen asked.

Marla stared at her. "You know, that's possible." She frowned as she looked around. "I hadn't really considered that."

"I'm not saying it's a motive or anything. I'm just wondering if that exists."

"There is insurance, but a lot of us don't have it because it's expensive. … Yet it's definitely a possibility."

"Of course," she murmured.

Finally, when they had stayed as long as they could and had gotten what information there was to get, Doreen got up and thanked Marla for letting them warm up inside.

Marla sighed happily. "It was so nice to see the animals and to meet you both."

Just then another person walked in, looked around, and asked, "Are you open?"

"I am," Marla said, and she jumped up and walked over to the front counter.

Mugs came out from under the table, took one look at the newcomer, and started growling and snapping. Surprised, Doreen almost lost control of the leash as Mugs lunged toward the man. She gasped in embarrassment and apologized quickly to both the owner of the restaurant and the new arrival. "Sorry," she said, looking from the man to the woman behind the counter. "He never does this."

The man glanced down at the dog and glared. "You shouldn't have animals in here anyway," he muttered. "That's definitely not how a restaurant should be run."

Doreen apologized again and dragged Mugs away. "It's not Marla's fault. It's our fault," she stated, as she tugged Mugs along. Yet he still refused to cooperate.

For whatever reason, Mugs did not in any way like the man who had just arrived. Even outside, he was still barking, turning back to face the man at the counter, talking with Marla.

Doreen looked over at Nan. "That's so not like Mugs."

"No, it isn't," Nan stated, glancing down at Mugs, who was not interested in calming down much. "But he also must have a reason."

Doreen looked at her grandmother and back at the man in question. "Let me put you guys in the car, and maybe I'll come back and see who he is."

"You'll have to be fast, as he looks like the kind of person to get in and get out without wasting time," Nan suggested. "Let me just sit here on the bench with the animals."

Doreen hesitated, but Nan shook her head. "Stop fussing, child. Just go on back in and do whatever it is you think you can do—although I have no idea what you think you can do. He's not a very friendly character."

Doreen handed her grandmother the leashes, sat them down at the corner on a bench, and rushed back inside. As she came back in, Marla turned to her. "I just wanted to apologize again. I am so sorry, Marla."

The man glared at her and snapped, "You shouldn't

keep a dog like that. He's a hazard to the community."

Doreen apologized again, trying to take stock of the man. "I'm so sorry. He normally loves people."

"I don't love animals," he declared, "and most animals know that."

"And that could be the issue," Doreen noted.

"Anyway," he replied, with a dismissive hand, "just make sure he's not outside when I leave."

"He is actually, but he's allowed to be outside," she pointed out.

Marla worked swiftly behind the counter, trying not to get involved. Doreen didn't want to make life harder for her, so she just held out her hand to the man. "I'm Doreen, by the way."

The man frowned down at her hand. "And?"

She flushed. "I was just trying to be friendly."

"Don't bother," he snapped. "And, if that dog touches me, I'll sue you, no matter what." And, with that threat made, he accepted the coffee cup from Marla, then turned and strode out of the building. Doreen winced at the owner and whispered, "I really am sorry."

Marla just waved her off and shook her head. "Don't worry about it."

Doreen raced outside and headed right for Nan. As soon as Mugs saw the same man again, Mugs started barking like crazy. Doreen managed to grab him just before Nan lost her grip. Doreen then immediately calmed him down. "That's enough out of you, Mugs," she stated in a stern tone. He grumbled at her but slowly attempted to stop making waves.

Some other people had looked over at them, and she just smiled. "He didn't get his pup cup."

Several laughed, but the man just continued to glare at

her and stalked away. She watched where he went, and, sure enough, he headed down to the closed restaurant. She looked over at Nan, who nodded. "Now that is interesting," Doreen whispered. "Who could he be?" she asked, staring at the man.

"Child, did the dead woman have a husband?"

"I don't know." She turned to look back at him, but there was no sign of the guy. "Interesting," she murmured.

"Interesting, but also fascinating that Mugs, who has a great respect for most people, did not like him."

"Mugs has very strong likes and dislikes," she noted.

"And always with people who don't like animals or people who are trying to hurt you," Nan pointed out.

"I can't imagine the guy was trying to hurt me," Doreen countered, looking at Nan. "We were just there having coffee."

"I know, but it's obvious Mugs didn't like him."

There was no getting past that point. Yet she couldn't accuse people of being involved in crimes just because Mugs didn't like them. The fact that she trusted his judgment said an awful lot, but, because she had no idea who this man was, it didn't matter. "Now if only I'd gotten a picture of him."

"You don't need to. That was Randol Biscott."

Doreen turned to see Marla, as she stepped outside and looked down at Mugs. "Your dog's a better judge of character than most people. That Randol man is bad news."

"Is that the murdered woman's husband?"

She nodded. "Yeah, that's him."

"He looks very … *non-restauranty*."

"Exactly," Marla agreed, "and that's what I meant. Definitely not the right person for the hospitality industry."

"On the other hand, maybe there's enough insurance

money that he can shut down the place and go off and have a new life," Doreen suggested, frowning.

"As long as he didn't do anything to create this scenario," Nan interjected.

Marla winced. "I'm really glad I don't have to deal with anything in *that* world. It's hard enough to look at my customers and to wonder how to get them to spend a little more and to come back one more time, versus thinking about them being involved in crimes."

Doreen smiled at her. "We don't come downtown very often, but we'll definitely come back. And I promise that I'll leave the animals at home."

"You don't have to leave them home on my account. Once we get the outer patio set up, you can absolutely have the animals here," she offered. "We obviously prefer to have them outside, unless it's a therapy dog, just because of incidents like this one."

Doreen shook her head. "Yeah, Mugs is great, but he's far too opinionated to pass muster as a therapy dog," she shared, with a chuckle. "He has very strong feelings, one way or the other."

Waving goodbye, the group of them headed back to Doreen's car. They hadn't gotten very far when Mugs started up again. She looked down at him and asked, "What is your problem?" But when she turned, sure enough the same man was walking toward them. She stepped off to the side and kept Mugs close.

He snorted as he walked past. "Yeah, you better keep him away from me. Dogs like that need to be shot."

"No, they don't," she bellowed. "It's very obvious that you're not an animal lover, and he knows that."

"Of course he knows it. I would shoot him myself if I

had a gun right now," he muttered.

"That's awfully violent talk for somebody who just lost his wife," she snapped.

He froze midstep, then turned to her. "What did you just say?"

"You heard me," she snapped. "Your wife was just murdered, wasn't she?"

He put his free hand on his hips, still holding a coffee cup in the other, and he glared at her. "What's that got to do with anything?"

"You're talking about shooting things with a gun, right after your wife was murdered. You better watch your language before people start thinking you might have had something to do with your wife's death."

Beside her, Nan gasped in shock. "My granddaughter doesn't mean any harm," she interjected in a high-octane tone. "She's just upset that you were threatening the animals."

"I'll do more than threaten them if I find out you're spreading those kinds of rumors," he spat, staring Doreen down. "Absolutely no way I'll allow such talk."

She shrugged. "Then don't be so quick to tell people that you're ready to shoot their animals."

He took a step toward her, and Mugs started to growl. Only this time it was different. It was farther back in his throat, like he meant serious business. The man looked down at the dog and glared. Then Goliath stepped forward as well.

His expression turned into astonishment. "Good God, what are you? The epitome of an old cat lady? You've got an attack dog on a leash, and now you've got a cat on a leash too?"

At that, Thaddeus poked his head out from under her

hair and cried out, "And me. And me. And me."

Doreen stared at Thaddeus. "That's a new phrase for you, buddy."

The man started to laugh, but only bitterness filled his tone. "That's just *great*," he muttered. "To cap off my day of all days, I end up with a crackpot. It figures, since this whole place has gone to pot."

"At least now you can sell the restaurant and move on."

He once again glared at her. "Don't pretend to know anything about me and my business."

"Maybe I don't know," she conceded, "but maybe I know a whole lot more than you're expecting."

He stiffened, and such iciness filled his gaze, not with anger, just this cold, relentless stare that never seemed to quit.

Nan stepped closer to Doreen.

Doreen continued to stare down Randol, knowing full well that, when it came to this kind of attitude, no way you could back down because, if you showed fear, these bullies were all over you.

He nodded. "I know what you are," he stated, with a cold smile. "You're just a busybody with no life. An old maid nobody cares about, so all you do is sit around and ruin other people's lives with your gossip. Don't try it, or I'll have you charged in a heartbeat."

She nodded. "I hear you, but you might find it more difficult than you think to make good on those threats."

He stared at her, then narrowed his gaze. "Good God," he muttered, surprise dawning in his gaze. "You're that amateur sleuth in town, aren't you?" He shook his head. "You better not have anything to do with my wife's case," he warned in a dark tone, full of anger and promise. "Because I will have something to say about that."

"Me? If you didn't have anything to do with your wife's death, I would think you would want all the investigative help you could get."

"That's the job for the police," he snarled, "and, if you're smart, you'll leave it to them."

With one last sound of complete disgust, he glared at the animals, then marched away at a clip that wasn't quite running but wasn't far off.

Nan let out her breath. "I keep forgetting how much danger you tend to get yourself into."

"Come on, Nan. Not you too. It's not even that I put myself in danger," she clarified, "but I do know that you can't back down with bullies."

Nan stared at her and frowned. "But, honey, you were instigating some of that."

"I was," she admitted, with a nod. "We don't have very much to go on in this case, and I need an avenue to explore. Just knowing the kind of person *Randol* is, he makes me want him to be guilty."

"But wanting him to be guilty doesn't make it true."

"I know, so, therefore, I have to confirm that he isn't guilty because somebody like that is perfectly capable of setting off on a vendetta to get rid of his wife," she suggested. "And, if that's the case, I really can't let him get away with it."

"But you don't know that he did."

"*Yet.* We don't know … yet."

Chapter 16

DOREEN MADE HERSELF a sandwich for dinner and was just sitting here, staring out into the backyard, when Mugs started to bark with joy. She smiled at him and nodded. "At least it's the right kind of barking this time."

Sure enough, she opened her front door and saw Mack, just getting out of his truck, looking tired and worn out. "Hey," she greeted him. "It seems you're having a run of tough days."

"It's been a hard month," he admitted. "Lots of cases, lots of trials, lots of headaches."

She nodded. "And that just means that you really need the holiday, whenever we can get away."

"Yes, I absolutely do," he agreed, "but we've got cases to work on right now."

"I know, and I kind of got into trouble over one of them today."

He stopped in place, then looked at her and asked, "Is it the kind of trouble that I'm likely to hear about?"

She nodded. "Maybe. Nan was more than a little upset, but I don't know whether she was upset for my sake or just worried about Mugs."

As Mack came inside and realized she was just having a sandwich to eat, he headed to the fridge and pulled out the makings and made himself a couple big ones.

"I wasn't sure if you were coming tonight."

"That's all right," he said, with a shrug. "It's food, and, right now, I'm too tired to care."

He listened as she explained what had happened. "Why do you think Mugs reacted the way he did?"

She really appreciated that because, out of everything she had told him, that was the one thing that concerned her the most. "I've been thinking about it. As a matter of fact, I've spent a fair bit of time searching online for info on that character, wondering what about him would have set off Mugs so instantly."

"Is it literally just because Mugs didn't like him?"

"It's absolutely possible. Although Mugs has this tendency to get along with everybody, until somebody hurts me."

"That's why I was asking. I'm just wondering if something was there that we hadn't picked up on."

"Have you interviewed him?"

"Of course. He was home alone while his wife was at work."

"So, he has no alibi," she stated.

"Nope, no alibi. As far as he's concerned, that has nothing to do with it. At least he claims to have nothing to do with it."

"How come nobody ever has an alibi when they need it?" she pointed out. "Seems if someone needed an alibi, they would have made sure they had one. Pretty arrogant not to. It almost makes him look guiltier."

He looked at her in surprise and then chuckled. "I don't know about guilty or guiltier, but he's certainly not off the hook as far as we're concerned."

"Yet would he have killed both of them?"

"That's the rest of the challenge," he noted, with a nod.

"What did the fiancée have to say?"

"Not much, she's still pretty shocked and traumatized."

Doreen didn't say anything to that. "What about Uncle Zev?"

"He's been cooperative."

"Alibi for the murder?"

"He was with his niece."

"Ah." Then she winced.

"You don't like that," Mack noted, as he took another bite, checking out her expression intently. His gaze held an amusing note.

"It just means that they alibi each other."

He nodded. "Don't worry. We've thought of that."

"Of course you have," she muttered, chuckling. "So, it's a matter of forensics then. Have you gotten anything helpful?"

"We don't have the full lab report yet, but there weren't any fingerprints found on the knife that killed Alice."

"Which means the killer wore gloves."

"Yes, but it's a kitchen setting, and they have plenty of plastic gloves available."

"Of course," she muttered. "Not exactly what I was thinking, but, yeah, you're right."

"That's because you're thinking of the horror movies, where they come into the restaurant with black gloves on, and all you ever hear is the music before the knife raises and comes down, taking somebody out."

She smiled at his description. "A little more graphic than that most of the time—something that I'll have to remember—but, yeah, ... the same idea."

He smiled, but it was obvious he was preoccupied.

"Are you worried that there might be another murder?"

He turned to her and nodded. "That is definitely a concern."

"Which is why you haven't had any rest in the last little while."

"When you've got a case, you've got a case."

She sighed. "I haven't gotten very far. I went downtown and checked out the restaurants."

"So, what did you learn?"

"Everybody's having financial difficulty. COVID was very hard on them, and the aftereffects are still being felt. You do have the option for insurance to a certain extent on some of these places," she shared, "but I don't know that it would be enough to kill over. Everybody says the young man who died was really nice, and potentially he could have just been in the wrong place at the wrong time."

"Meaning?"

"I guess I'm wondering if his death was a case of mistaken identity. Both Barry and Alice had long hair, which was pulled back in a ponytail."

He eyed her as he continued to munch, then nodded. "That's possible. Barry was tall, but so was Alice. Although you would think the killer would confirm it was the right person first, before killing them."

"Depends on whether it was a crime of passion or not," she pointed out.

Together, they wrangled over the details, looking for any answers, and he finally said, "This isn't looking very promising."

"No cameras, no street cameras, no security alarm?" she asked.

"No cameras inside that were on, not in the kitchen area anyway. There are some in the restaurant."

"What about where the fiancée was hit in the hallway?"

He frowned at her. "She was attacked somewhere around the ladies' bathroom. She was just outside the prep room."

"And, of course, no cameras are there," she grumbled.

"Exactly," he said, as he nodded.

"That almost seems as if somebody knew exactly what they were doing and could place where everybody was."

"Yeah, it's sure a good possibility," he admitted. "We have taken into consideration how no cameras were in the kitchen. So we don't have any way to know exactly what happened and how." He sighed. "That's always one of the challenges in a case like this."

"You know that it won't be a stranger murderer though."

"And your reasoning is what?" he asked, as he continued to eat.

Realizing this was as much about Mack testing out her theories and seeing what she was thinking, she replied, "In order for it to be in a restaurant, with an exit and an entrance, and, because they likely used a weapon on hand, I can't see it being somebody who didn't know their target would be there."

She leaned forward, just warming up. "Now, it could have been a robbery that went wrong because they weren't expecting anybody to be there in the kitchen. However, if that were the case, they would have killed them both, regardless of where they were. Even if they didn't hear her music playing in the bathroom, if she had returned to the kitchen and had been surprised by the attacker, she would remember that before being conked on the head—or just killed right then. *Or* somebody had to be there, seeing her go to the bathroom, and chose that moment to make his move," she suggested, thinking about it slowly. "This was *not* a spur-of-the-moment killing. This was someone who planned to kill someone that night. Otherwise it leaves too much to chance to think that scenario happened. Barry had no defensive wounds, did he?"

"I don't have the full autopsy report yet," he noted. "When most people confront a killer with a weapon, they're willing to fight pretty hard to save their own life. He was young, and he was pretty healthy."

"And, if he had no defensive wounds," she pointed out, "it's because he was surprised, since he was attacked from behind."

He smiled and nodded. "You got that right. Still, we don't know that he doesn't have defensive wounds yet."

"Also, you have to look a whole lot closer. Particularly at the jerk I was talking to today, and then potentially at any other family members who may have been at the restaurant that we don't even know about. Because somebody got close enough to take out Barry, and, chances are, Barry knew his killer and likely knew him well."

"Like who?" he asked.

"I don't know, but they had other employees."

"We've talked to them all. No one seemed to know that the prep kitchen was open and staffed at that time. They really are separate areas. It was just these two, who were working on the catering job for the next day."

She nodded. "But somebody knew they were there, and that meant Jillian's Aunt Alice must have known they were there because she was their boss."

He stared at her and asked, "You're not thinking that Alice killed Barry, are you?"

"Even if she did, somebody came along and took her out soon afterward—so maybe not," she muttered. "I don't know. Nothing much makes any sense right now. In cases like this, you start to wonder if you're automatically jumping ahead and thinking you know what's happening because you've seen it so many times before."

He smiled, reached out his hand, and covered hers, then nodded. "Now you're starting to sound like a real cop." She looked at him in delight, and he chuckled. "And, no, that's not an invitation to work on my current cases."

"You do know that I already am."

"I know you are," he confirmed. "We were just discussing it, but you seem to have forgotten that the murders of Barry and Alice are both current cases."

She stared at him and sagged. "*Uh-oh*, I got completely lured into thinking you weren't trying to trick me."

"I wasn't trying to trick you," he stated. "I did want to see what your thoughts were in this case. Yet, while we have an agreement between us, I can also see that you didn't adhere to it."

She winced and then nodded glumly. "Nope, I didn't."

"And yet you have absolutely nothing on your cold case from Alberta."

"It's pretty hard to have anything when it was literally someone who was at home alone, until someone walked in through the door and stabbed her. Plus, no forensic evidence was found to identify her killer. No cameras. According to the Red River Precinct police file, everyone loved her, and she had no known enemies. Her phone and emails offered no information either."

"By what you just mentioned, it's also very likely to have been somebody she knew too."

"That's the thing," she said, eyeing him. "In a way, it's some of the same suspects all over again. We have Katie, the Alberta victim from ten years ago, and Katie's daughter, Jillian, the fiancée in your current case of the death of Barry, and the niece to Zev and the niece to your second murder victim, Alice." Doreen shook her head. "It's definitely not as clear-cut as it could be. Uncle Zev says that Jillian was with him, and I believe him." She frowned, got up, and picked up the case files she had printed off. "So, apparently Jillian's uncle had taken Jillian to an event, while her mother, Katie, remained home and was murdered."

"Where was Jillian's father back then?" Mack asked.

"I don't know." Doreen frowned. "And where's Jillian's father now?"

Mack frowned, shaking his head. "I think Uncle Zev took Jillian to the event ten years ago because I think Jillian's father has been gone for longer than that."

"Yes, but is he dead or is he just lying low and taking out family members?" she suggested. At that, he burst out laughing. She glared at him. "I'm not kidding."

He stilled, caught the seriousness of her tone, and asked, "Seriously?"

"Missing people are missing people. But, if the missing people aren't actually missing, they have one heck of an alibi to take out other people."

"Ooh, ouch," Mack replied. "You definitely need a holiday."

She glanced over at him and muttered, "You too."

He groaned. "I know, but we have to solve this case first."

"I'm all for it," she stated, rolling her eyes. "I just don't know what we're supposed to do."

"Don't tell me that you're giving up?" he asked in astonishment.

"No, of course not," she stated, "but the one that I'm supposed to be working on is a little bit harder."

"No, it's not," he argued. "I will admit that there probably isn't as much evidence, and maybe there isn't as much actual forensic evidence, and you probably don't have much in the way of eyewitness accounts either."

She rolled her eyes again and sighed. "So I have nothing."

He grinned. "And that's how we often feel, but the truth of the matter is, there was a weapon—also a kitchen knife—and Katie was stabbed, and there was apparently no motive."

"All of which," she stated, "applies to your two current cases too."

He slowly nodded. "You're right," he acknowledged, staring at her. "It really is likely that the killer in each of these three murders is from the same cast of suspicious characters, isn't it?"

"I would think so, yes," she agreed. "But the fact that we have two recent murders is what I don't get."

He raised an eyebrow, waiting for her to continue.

"Why not take them both out at the same time? After all, they both work for the same restaurant."

"Because they both weren't in the kitchen that first night," he replied.

"Right, and why weren't they both in the kitchen?" she asked. "Maybe our killer expected them both to be there?"

Mack shrugged. "Or was it because our killer couldn't take out two at a time. Think about it. It would take too much effort, and maybe they couldn't think of a way to get it done without getting into trouble themselves or getting hurt themselves."

Doreen nodded. "Which also would imply that they either thought they were inferior in strength and speed or were taking too big of a risk."

"But to go in again and kill a second time is taking a much bigger risk," Mack stated.

She sighed. "I know." She gave him a smile. "The motivation is still all wrapped up around the restaurant somehow."

"Which wasn't doing well," he pointed out.

"So, who wants it if it's not doing well?" she asked.

"If the business is going under, it's hardly something to kill over."

"I agree, unless they own the building, in which case maybe the real estate value is enough. Or is it more of a revenge thing?"

"Yet why take revenge on Barry, the young cook?"

"Unless it really was a case of mistaken identity."

He frowned as he thought about it and noted, "You keep coming back to that."

"I do keep coming back to that." She shrugged. "I really want to talk to Jillian again, but ..."

"*Mmm*, ... good luck with that," he said, with a chuckle. "We've talked to her several times, but she's not doing well."

"Right, and I can certainly understand that," she stated. "But questions need to be asked so answers can be revealed."

"I'll go by and talk to her tomorrow," he offered.

"I wish I could come with you."

"No, not allowed."

"I know. I know. I know." She raised her hands in frustration. "I get it."

He smiled. "I'm not sure you do get it," he replied, staring at her. "But as somebody who just spent an awful lot of time in court, making sure this last case was locked up tight so we didn't have people running amok all over it, I have to make sure that we end up with convictions that work in court at the end of the day."

"Got it," she muttered. "I still think Mugs had a point though."

"Mugs always has a point, but it's usually at the end of his teeth."

She looked at him and then started to laugh. He grinned, and she shook her head. "You really do know how to lighten the mood, don't you?"

"As long as Mugs is not biting me. I'm much better with the idea of his biting somebody else because he knows that I won't hurt you." Mack covered his mouth as a yawn escaped.

"But he doesn't know that about this Biscott guy," she pointed out, "and it's rare for Mugs to have that kind of attitude from the first second of seeing someone."

"What about the other animals?"

She stared up at where Thaddeus was snoozing on his roost nearby in the living room. "Thaddeus has been keeping himself very hidden lately. It's almost as if he's got this thing about being the element of surprise."

"He certainly is an element of surprise," Mack noted pointedly. "Just think about how many times he stayed hidden in your hair, then peeks out to surprise people."

"I know, and I was thinking about that because he's always got this really odd way of popping out just at the last minute, crying out that he's here."

At that, Mack chuckled. "The animals are definitely full-on all the time," he said, "and the fact that you can handle them as well as you do always amazes me."

"I don't know that I handled Mugs at all today. He really did not like that Randol Biscott man at all," she noted.

"Then you better stay away from him. The last thing we need is him complaining to the city about it."

"Right, I know, but hopefully they would understand that something off is going on."

"It wouldn't matter whether they understood or not. If a dog is perceived as dangerous, you know as well as I do that he will get labeled as aggressive, and it could get really bad after that."

"Mugs can be aggressive," she stated pointedly, "but in a good way. He's saved my butt several times."

"But the very fact that he saved you is exactly what saved him. You can't just have dogs going off half-cocked."

"It's never just him though," she clarified.

"I know. Your animals are a comedy act that never gets old."

"Unless you're a criminal," she pointed out, beaming. "And then, of course, none of my animals are very happy to have any of them around."

"The bottom line is," Mack stated, staring her down, "keep the animals calm around Randol. He's threatened to shoot Mugs, and next time Randol may have a gun on him. Meanwhile, we'll go through all the case stuff tomorrow, or I will," he clarified, looking at her pointedly, "and hopefully we'll come up with some new answers."

"Right," she muttered, but something had caught her attention, and she couldn't let go of it. She gave him a bright smile that only narrowed his gaze as he stared at her.

"Okay, I don't like the look of that smile."

She shook her head. "It's nothing for you to worry about. Just an idea I might have to try out."

"A good idea or a bad idea?"

"Oh, it could be a totally good idea," she declared. "It depends on whether or not the niece will talk to me."

"Jillian won't. I can tell you that right now."

"Okay. In that case, it's no idea at all."

"Good."

When he yawned again, she leaned over, gave him a kiss, and said, "Go home and get some sleep."

"I would love to," he muttered, then stopped to study her.

She replied too quickly, "I promise I won't get into trouble overnight."

He gave her a droll look and pointed out, "I like how you clarified *overnight*."

"I'm trying not to lie to you, remember?" she replied pointedly. "And overnight means overnight. I could very easily get into trouble tomorrow."

"I know," he muttered, as he stood up, then bent down to say goodbye to Mugs and Goliath, both still on the floor beside him. "It's almost as if the two of them are joined at the hip lately."

"I know, and I wasn't sure what that meant either," she admitted, watching them both closely. "Usually Goliath stalks him. But now it's almost like …" She winced and looked at them again. "It's almost like he's being protective."

Mack's expression turned somber. "You stay safe, and keep the animals safe," he said. "I can't imagine how you would handle losing them."

"I wouldn't handle it well at all," she stated. "Anybody who comes for Mugs, comes for me too."

Chapter 17

WHEN DOREEN WOKE the next morning and got her morning routine completed, she phoned Uncle Zev, who had contacted her in the first place.

"What?" he snapped.

She waited for a moment and then replied, "That's an interesting greeting. I wasn't expecting the hostility."

"Nothing good is happening in my world right now," he declared, "so, if you're looking for a good and happy reception, you missed the mark."

"I understand that life has gotten pretty rough for you," she began. "I was hoping that maybe you and your niece would be willing to talk to me."

"Talk about what?" he asked. "Since we moved here, it's been nothing but a disaster."

She winced and added, "I did hear that, and I'm so very sorry."

"You might be sorry, but it doesn't change anything," he snapped, as his voice roughened. "Jillian's really suffering right now."

"I'm sure she is, but maybe, if she would talk to me, I could possibly get a different take on all this."

"She's already talked to the cops. I mentioned you, but she doesn't want to talk to you again, at least she didn't before."

Just then a voice came through the phone, angry, yet obviously in pain, as Jillian said, "Let me talk to her."

Immediately the phone switched hands, and a young woman spoke up. "I'll meet you for lunch, although I won't be eating anything."

"Then why don't I come to wherever you are?" Doreen offered. "You won't have to go anywhere."

After a moment of hesitation, she agreed. "Fine." She provided the address.

Doreen asked, "When do you want me there?"

"Better sooner than later, before I change my mind. I won't be talking very long."

When the phone was handed back to her uncle, Zev said, "I'm amazed she wants to talk to you at all. She's really hurting. I will not take it kindly if you hurt her too."

"I'm not here to hurt her," Doreen stated, trying to keep her tone calm. "All I want to do is get answers for her."

"We definitely need those," he muttered. "So, come on over, I guess."

With that she ended the call, looked down at the animals, and said, "I guess we're heading out pretty quick then."

She got up and bustled around, getting everybody into leashes and harnesses, gathering her things, then headed out to the vehicle. She wasn't at all sure what she expected, but when she drove up to a middle-class home in Glenmore, with the Crown land rising up behind them and a big hill, she was quite surprised at how nice it was. And yet there wasn't any reason to be surprised. There were a lot of these houses around, and they were all quite nice. Yet somehow

Doreen had expected them to be poor, considering the lack-of-customers complaint that Doreen kept hearing.

As she got out of her car with her animals, she walked up to the front door. Thaddeus poked his head out so he would be the first for anybody to see.

Doreen groaned. "Jillian didn't say I could bring the animals." When he just squawked at her, she shrugged. "I know. She didn't say I couldn't bring the animals either. It just feels as if we're pushing the line."

As it was, when the door opened, Zev saw the animals and stared at her, his eyebrows rising, and then he shrugged. "Who knows? Your pets might make Jillian feel better."

"They are very comforting," Doreen murmured. She stepped inside and saw a young woman, early- or maybe mid-twenties, her face swollen and blotchy, as if she had spent the last week crying, which she most likely had. Doreen smiled, introduced herself and then her animals. Jillian bent down to give Mugs and Goliath cuddles, and both appreciated it.

"If you don't mind," Doreen added, when she stood up with a half laugh, "please say hello to Thaddeus, as well."

At that, Thaddeus poked his head out from behind the fall of her hair and said, "I'm Thaddeus."

She gasped and laughed. "Oh my, they are a sight for sore eyes. I used to have a dog, but we lost him about a year ago," she murmured. "It was one of the reasons I felt as if nothing was holding me there in Alberta, so there was no reason to stay any longer, and Barry was willing, so we just picked up and finally made the move. We'd both lived in Kelowna and Alberta, but we needed to settle on one location," she murmured. "Now, it's one of those times when you have to look at life and the choices you made and wonder why all this would have happened."

Doreen smiled and nodded. "I'm sorry. Nothing like trying to come up with answers when there aren't any to be had."

"But this really doesn't make any sense," she whispered. She led the way into a sitting-room-style living area, but it was very sparsely furnished. "I'm staying here with my uncle. After my fiancé was killed, I just couldn't stay in our small apartment without Barry. Yet it is just around the corner from the restaurant, so it was close enough that we could walk back and forth to work, but not so close that we would be on top of each other."

"I doubt that being on top of each other would have been all that much of an upset either," Doreen suggested. "It's nice to have family around." Jillian's eyes welled up, and Doreen nodded. "Can you tell me what happened that night?"

"The same thing that I've told you and the detectives over and over again," she wailed, "and nobody seems to believe me."

"Can you go through it one more time and tell me?"

Shrugging, Jillian began, "Barry and I were there at the Rocking Horse, working on catering stuff, both tired and really worn out. We'd been working very long days, both of us. Sometimes we wondered whether the move to BC was a good idea or not. We talked about whether we should have just chucked it all and gone back home to Alberta again, even though we had jobs and were working and living and whatnot here in Kelowna. It's just that my Aunt Alice wasn't the easiest person to work with," she admitted, sliding a glance over at her uncle.

He nodded and agreed. "No, she wasn't."

"So, Barry and I wondered if we were in the right place," Jillian murmured. "We had all kinds of plans for the restaurant. We could have done some really great things here," she said, "but it just didn't seem to matter what we suggested. … My aunt hated everything."

"And was it that she hated the suggestions, or did she just hate change?" Doreen asked.

Uncle Zev interrupted, "My sister Alice has always hated change, so even having Barry and Jillian there to help her would already have been something she struggled with."

"But she's the one who invited us," his niece protested. "She needed us as she was barely keeping her head above water."

He nodded. "I know that, and I'm so sorry she struggled so much with it because I know how good you guys are."

"Were," she corrected. "I don't think I ever want to work in a kitchen again."

With that, the uncle winced, then looked back at Doreen and added, "This is obviously very difficult for her. Are you sure you need to be here?"

"Need to? Maybe not," Doreen conceded, "but any information I can gather is a help."

"I just can't believe that anybody would think they could do something when the police haven't been able to," Jillian pointed out, looking at her.

"I work with the police as well," Doreen said, "and we have solved an awful lot of cases recently, but it does take people talking and opening up in order to find out who's hiding the truth."

"I'm not hiding anything," she declared, sitting up straighter.

"I'm not saying you are," she murmured. "And I know

this will be a difficult question, but do you have any idea who would want your fiancé dead?"

Immediately Jillian's eyes filled with tears, and she shook her head. "I wouldn't have thought for a moment that anybody would be against him. He's just a big teddy bear."

Doreen glanced over at the uncle, who was nodding. "Barry was a really nice young man."

"Okay, so here's another question. Is there any chance it was a case of mistaken identity?"

Jillian eyed her in surprise. "What do you mean?"

"I just mean that, if Barry had his hair up, maybe from the back he looked like somebody else."

Her eyes widened. "You mean, like Aunt Alice?"

"It is something to consider, isn't it? Alice was murdered right afterward, and maybe it was a case of the killer coming back to finish the job because he messed up the first time."

Jillian sagged back and stared at Doreen. "I hadn't considered that," she whispered. "God, to think that Barry might have been killed by accident makes it even worse."

"There's no good way to die," Doreen noted, "not like this. But it is something we have to consider. So, then you went to the bathroom."

"Yes, Barry and I were working. It was late. I was tired, and I had to go to the bathroom. Barry and I had had a bit of an argument, and I was just fed up. I wanted to go home and to go to bed, but Aunt Alice had insisted we work late, get everything ready for the catering job set for lunch the very next day. To be honest, the catering was our thing. I told her how we could have done it all in the morning, but she didn't want us to leave it to the very end."

Doreen didn't say anything for a long moment. "And what was the catering job?"

"A lunch for thirty at the restaurant the next day in one of the back rooms," she explained. "It was an arrangement the restaurant had on an irregular basis with some of the local companies. They would bring in their employees, and everybody would have a business meeting over lunch," she murmured. "It was good money for my aunt, and it helped keep the restaurant going when times were tight, I guess," she murmured. "We didn't have much choice, so we agreed."

Doreen nodded but didn't say anything, hoping Jillian would say more.

"Let's get real. I didn't want to stay, but it was necessary. What wasn't necessary were Aunt Alice's constant negative comments."

Doreen kept that little nugget in the back of her head. "Okay, so you were tired."

"Yeah, we were both really tired, and I just wanted to go home. Aunt Alice said we had to finish, but I wanted to leave it for morning. I was pissed off at my aunt, which just seems so petty now," she admitted.

"And after that?"

"After that, I needed a minute, so I just had to regroup in the bathroom," she explained. "When I came out of the bathroom, I headed down the hall to see Barry, anxious to apologize and to help, so we could go home, and that's when I got hit. When I woke up, I was on the floor in the hallway outside the bathroom. I didn't know what had happened and was pissed off and upset, thinking I must have tripped or something. It didn't occur to me that I had been attacked until I went around the corner to the kitchen, yelling for Barry and wondering what had happened to him."

"And then you saw him?"

"Yeah, he was on the floor." Her tears welled up once

again. "So, it's not as if anybody else was there. I could tell because the place was empty. It was just us."

"And you called the police?"

"Yes, I called the police immediately." Then she shook her head. "No, wait, not immediately. I went to him to see if I could help him—give him CPR or something. But then I saw the blood pooling around him on the floor. ... Oh God," she muttered. "And I looked around the kitchen. I had been cutting up watermelon, had left the knife on the counter beside it. But when I returned, the bloody knife had been stabbed into the watermelon. It was the knife I had been using just minutes before."

"Ah," Doreen murmured.

"I didn't kill him," she cried out, the tears streaming down her face.

"I didn't say you did, though I'm sure it was one of the things the cops would have picked up on pretty quickly. And when you say that you couldn't do anything for him, what did you do then?"

"Sat there in shock, bawling. I called the cops somewhere along the line, but, before you ask, I don't remember when or how, and that was it," she said. "They came, and I gave a statement. I was let go, and then they brought me back in the next day for questioning. Then the next day and the next day, and now I don't even know where I'm at," she wailed, her voice starting to fade with fatigue.

"Okay, so now that you've had a chance to think it over and to look back on it, does anything stand out to you?"

She stared at her and shook her head. "No, I've gone over it time and time again."

"So, when you were in the bathroom, you didn't hear anything."

She winced. "No, but I had my phone with me. I had put on some music and was scrolling through social media, just trying to get my head back together. I was pissed off and needed to get back on track, so I could get out there and help Barry."

"How much time do you think you spent in there?"

"Ten minutes or more, but, when I came back out, I went down, and I don't know how long I was out. And somewhere along the line, somebody killed Barry," she whispered, her eyes welling up once more.

Doreen considered asking a few more questions, but that was about all that came to mind.

Jillian muttered, "Now you're probably just like the police and think I did it."

"Not at all. We also have to look at your aunt's murder, which came right afterward."

"I know, and that's another reason everybody was so pissed off. As if it wasn't bad enough that one of us was killed, either that killer or another killer came back to finish the job of killing Aunt Alice."

"I can't imagine there being two killers," Doreen shared. "Still, stranger things have certainly happened, but I really can't see it. My guess is a single killer."

"But that makes no sense," Jillian cried out. "My aunt may have had some enemies around here, but they wouldn't have any reason to kill Barry."

"Maybe not," Doreen acknowledged, "but the fact is, somebody did, and, until we can get to the bottom of this, we don't have any answers."

"I don't expect you'll find any answers either," she declared bitterly, "and I don't think the cops are looking any further than me."

"I think they are, but they certainly won't tell you that."

"You think so?" she asked, looking at Doreen hopefully.

"Yes, I do. They will look at everybody, and, when they finally get some evidence to point in one direction or another, then they'll move forward with charges. Until then, we need to do what we can to get to the bottom of this ourselves."

Chapter 18

J UST AS DOREEN was ready to leave, she added, "Listen. I
know this is also a difficult topic, but the fact that your
mother was murdered adds another aspect to these crimes."

Jillian groaned. She turned back from walking Doreen to
the door to sit back down again. "The fact that my mother
was also murdered just makes it all so much worse for me,"
she admitted, crying out in pain. "That was an unbelievable
time, and I just …" She groaned. "I can't imagine again
going through all that I've gone through already," she wailed,
with tears in her eyes. "That was one of the most godawful
times in my life."

"And your father is not in the picture?"

"No, he hasn't been in the picture since forever," she
noted. "I don't even know if he's alive."

"It would be nice to know more about that," Doreen
said, turning to look at the uncle.

Zev nodded. "It would be nice, but nobody has found
out anything about him. I certainly haven't heard or seen
anything of him in a very long time."

Doreen continued. "And I know it's a difficult topic, but
the fact that now three murders have happened in the same

family is quite remarkable. I'm counting your fiancé as family, of course," Doreen explained. "That experience is a trigger for you, whether they're connected or not."

"They can't be connected," Jillian argued. "My mother was killed a long time ago."

"I get that," Doreen said, "and I'm so sorry. It's also got to be hard on your uncle." She turned to Zev.

"That's both of his sisters gone now," Jillian whispered.

His face pale and drawn, he looked over at Doreen. "It's been just brutal losing Katie ten years ago, and now Alice," he murmured. "You think you can finally start to heal from the one loss, but then a second one happens. You just wonder if you've got a target on your back," he muttered. "That's a horrible way to look at life. It was such a long time before Jillian would even live alone."

"And then," Jillian shared, "I didn't even really live alone for very long because I went … I hate to say it, but I went from relationship to relationship, trying to figure out who and what I was and where I was safe. So, it may not have been the ideal methodology for growing up, but, after my mom's murder, I was never really comfortable being alone."

"Like never?" Doreen asked.

"No, I lived with Uncle Zev for quite a while, and then I felt as if I needed to get out and to be an adult again," she explained, tears in her eyes. "It's just not that easy after a murder like that. And now? … I don't know what I'll do."

Doreen nodded. "As you look back on your mother's murder, is there anything that comes to mind?"

She shook her head. "No, nothing. Believe me that I spent a decade trying to sort through it, and I just had no idea. It was really traumatizing growing up that way," she murmured. "If it weren't for Uncle Zev, I don't know what I would have done."

Doreen nodded. "I'm so sorry. That's got to be tough. Were there any suspects at the time?"

"Why are you looking at that murder?" Zev asked in frustration. "It has no bearing on this one now."

"Are you sure about that?" she asked, turning to face him. "Just the fact that this many murders happened in the same family means that chances are good there is some connection. And the MO in all cases was also similar."

"You can make up as many connections as you want," Zev snapped, "but that doesn't mean that they exist."

Doreen didn't say anything at first, just studied him for a long moment. "I understand it's a touchy topic."

"Of course it is," he snarled. "Why wouldn't it be? We're sitting here drowning in a sea, completely overtaken by … evil."

"Yes, of course," she murmured. She turned to Jillian again. "Did your mother have a boyfriend back then?"

"Sure," Jillian said, "but it's not as if she flaunted them. I wasn't a part of that aspect of her life."

"Okay, so you have no idea who might have done it?"

"No, I have no idea," she declared, with a wave of her hand.

Zev interrupted, "And if you try to drag that murder into this one …"

"The police have already got the information on Katie's murder," Doreen told Zev. "And that isn't something you can hide. So, the sooner we can clear up one connection as not being connected at all," she pointed out for Zev's benefit, "the easier it will be on everyone."

Zev just glared at her.

Jillian groaned. "I don't have a clue why anybody would

even begin to think it was connected."

"Because that's the reality of life. Most families don't lose anyone to murder. So, as soon as anything is suspect, our natural tendency is to dig deeper and deeper into it."

"Are you sure you're not doing the same thing but out of curiosity?" Uncle Zev snarled, staring daggers at her.

She turned to him. "No, that's not what I do, but I can see that, for the moment at least, you've had enough of my questions." She got up and clucked at the back of her throat for the animals. They all stood up, and together they walked to the door. "I'm sorry for the need to ask these questions," she said, "but I felt it was important that we clear the air on the matter."

"I don't know what we could possibly have cleared," Jillian replied, staring at her. "We didn't get any answers."

"No, and there are definitely a few more questions I could really use the answers to, just so I can write it off."

"Like what?" Jillian cried out.

Doreen turned to the uncle, still at the doorway. "Did you live near your sister Katie in Alberta?"

"Yes, we all lived close by."

"You didn't hear anything?"

"No, I didn't hear anything. I was out with Jillian."

Doreen nodded and looked over at Jillian. "Were other people around you?"

"Yes," she snapped, glaring from Doreen to Zev. "It was a birthday party, and we had all gone together."

"And where was the party held?"

"I don't know, maybe ten minutes away at a bowling alley," she murmured. "And, when we came home, the lights were off, which was unusual since my mother should have been there."

Doreen turned her attention back to Zev. "I guess one of the questions I have is why you took her to the birthday party and not her mother."

There was a moment of silence, and Zev looked over at his niece. "I took her to a lot of things."

"So it wasn't Jillian's birthday then."

"No, no, it was her friend's birthday. They needed more adults, so I volunteered. And, even back then, I was heavily involved in her life."

Doreen just smiled and nodded. As she got to the front door, she asked, "Are you involved with the family restaurant too?"

Zev shook his head. "I helped when I was younger, but no. I chose a different career path."

Doreen noted his tone remained clipped. Was it because she had overstayed her visit or was there some animosity regarding the family restaurant? "And what kind of work do you do?"

He sighed. "I'm a contractor by trade, but now I serve as a consultant and do a lot of my work from home. For the last several years, I've devoted my life to helping my niece, so I haven't worked full-time."

"That's very nice, but are you able to, … well, are you okay on money that way?"

"No, not particularly. No. … I inherited some money from my sister Katie, if that's what you're asking."

"That wasn't what I was asking, but I guess it is one of the questions that needs to be answered."

"Why?" he asked, frowning.

Doreen turned to Jillian. "Did you also get money from your mother? And, if so, what happened to that?"

Jillian nodded. "I sold the house, and I invested the

money, and I haven't really done anything with it."

"But you told me that you were struggling."

"I did say *struggling*. I don't know that it was financial as much as just plain struggling emotionally, but I did the right thing. I didn't want to touch that money until I was ready to settle down, and that would go toward buying a house. Neither Uncle Zev nor I got a lot of money, and I wanted to use my inheritance in a meaningful way, honoring my mother."

"And now," Doreen said, as she turned to face the uncle, "with this other sister's death, do you know who gets Alice's money?"

"She has a husband, so I guess it would all go to him, … though maybe not. The Rocking Horse was her restaurant, not his. The Burgon family hands down our restaurants through the generations. So the business probably can't go to him, but maybe to my brother or even me."

She stopped, thought about that, and asked, "Your brother's the artist, right?"

"Yes." Then Zev gave half a laugh. "At least he calls himself an artist, though he doesn't make any money. I know our sister Alice was forever helping him with handouts, and they also got a lot of their food from the restaurant just because they didn't always have the money they needed."

"Ah, so he's really struggling too."

"Yes, and I get it. I really do. He's in a wheelchair, and his life hasn't been the easiest."

"What about his wife? Does she work?"

"No, she doesn't work. She plays at helping out at the restaurant but she only irritated Alice, so that soon stopped. My sister-in-law is one of those people who's after money all the time—of the handout variety."

"But there is such a thing as a job."

The niece laughed at that. "Now that's the mess of our family for you. She thought Danny would inherit the restaurant when his father died, and there would be big money waiting for her."

"They've been married for a long time, haven't they?"

Jillian thought about it and nodded. "Yes, so she must have thought something was in it for her way back when. She's not exactly the nicest of people."

Doreen smiled. "Some people don't seem to know how to be nice."

Zev snorted. "And then some people just don't want to, and that would be her. We have very little to do with her because she's not anybody we want to spend time with."

Doreen asked, "So, in your mind, would she have had anything to do with Alice's death?"

Zev frowned at her. "Good God, I didn't even consider that."

"With your sister Alice gone and even *some* of the money coming to Danny, would that be enough to make Danny's wife happy? Would it be just the money that she's after? Would it be … What I'm asking is, will she gain from that and then divorce her husband or something?"

Zev frowned, shaking his head. "Danny gets a disability check each month, and they own their property, so—at least if she stays with him—they both have a house, but I don't know their finances beyond that," he shared, as he turned to look at Jillian, frowning. "But none of that explains why Jillian's Barry died."

"No, it doesn't," Doreen agreed. "And that is something we'll have to sort out soon."

"Good luck with that," he muttered, "because you'll never get a chance to talk to that woman. You might get to talk to Danny, but it won't be easy to talk to his wife."

"Ideally people make wills and plans for who gets what, like a restaurant, before those people die," Doreen noted. "I wouldn't imagine that everyone would want the responsibility of running a restaurant. So proper planning for a family legacy to continue makes these things a whole lot less painful."

"I don't know," he muttered. "It just seems so awful that we're even in this place."

"But, as we well know, when people die, property frequently has to be sold so the proceeds can be divided," Doreen noted. "One of the big things in any investigation involves following the money. So, who benefits from the deaths of Katie, Barry, and Alice?"

"Not me," Jillian exclaimed, with a hysterical laugh. "At least not from my fiancé's death. He didn't have anything and was worth far more to me alive."

"I'm sure he knew that and, in his final moments, was probably only concerned about keeping you safe."

Jillian looked at her and then nodded. "He would have done that. It would have been so like him too. He was a gentle soul."

"Maybe he was looking out for you at the end of the day." Doreen turned to the uncle. "I know this sounds completely off topic, but considering it is now just you and your brother …"

Zev nodded.

"Considering the attacks on your siblings, you might want to take extra care of yourself."

"Why?" he asked, giving her a stare.

"Because your family is dwindling rather quickly."

And, with that, Doreen opened the front door and walked out.

Chapter 19

WITH THE ANIMALS riding along with her, Doreen didn't want to stop and pick up groceries, so she headed on home. Just as she was getting inside her front door, the animals barely waited for her to push the door open and bolted inside. She herself was looking forward to a cup of tea in the kitchen that she'd been thinking about the whole way home, her phone rang.

She answered it absentmindedly and found it was Richie. "Hey, Richie. How are you guys doing?"

"Better," he replied in a jovial tone. "Your grandmother and I have talked."

"That's good," she said. "I hate to see you guys on the outs."

"Ha, me too. Anyway, Cleavis with a *C*'s grandson Denton has time for a phone call, if that's of any help."

"Sure." She grabbed the phone number from him and said, "I'll give him a call right now."

"That's good. He's got to get ready for his day, but he said he would try to fit in a short call."

So, putting on the kettle, Doreen dialed the number. When a man answered, she quickly introduced herself and thanked him for taking the time for the call, and he sighed.

"Ah, yeah, Grandpa was pretty insistent."

"Sorry, I'm just wondering about the state of the restaurant world and how that would work currently. If you were in the kitchen doing prep work, could somebody come up from behind you and stab you without you knowing or hearing anything?"

A shocked gasp came first. "Good God, you don't mince words, do you?"

"My understanding is that you were short on time, so I thought I would get to the point right away."

"That was definitely a point. Okay, keep in mind that I'm a big guy, but, if I were in the kitchen at my prep counter, and I'm chopping away, if I had on a headset, and I was listening to music or lost in my own world, I guess it's possible somebody could sneak up behind me. Yes, that's possible," he said, "but, God help me, now I'll think about that every time I'm in my kitchen."

"I can imagine the image would have a chilling effect."

"Is that what happened to Alice?"

"It's what happened to Barry," she clarified. "From the looks of it, he didn't even turn around and didn't know anyone was there."

"Oh man," he muttered.

"Do you have a security system in your restaurant, including your kitchen?"

"We do have a security system, and I'll go check on that," he muttered to himself, as if making notes, "so thank you for this lovely phone call."

She chuckled. "Hey, maybe it'll keep you safe."

"That would be nice."

"I would never hear the end of it from your grandfather

Cleavis if something happened to you after this," Doreen shared, "so keep yourself safe."

At that, he burst out with a bellow.

Doreen continued. "And if somebody were to come in, how hard would it be for them to get into your back door, say, if you forgot to set the security system?"

"If I forgot to set the security, it wouldn't be hard at all. The way my kitchen layout is, somebody could come around the corner fairly quickly, and I wouldn't really see them. And, if somebody was familiar with the layout, it wouldn't take any time at all. You really think that somebody came upon Barry unsuspecting?"

"Sure. If you're stabbed in the back, that's most likely what happened."

"Right, but, even if he knew who his killer was, potentially expecting a visit, it wouldn't take a whole lot for somebody to turn around and stab you in the back. If you were expecting them anyway, you would say hello and would talk to them for a bit, then carry on with your work. You don't know that somebody will kill you until that knife hits your back."

"Exactly," she agreed. "And, for your restaurant, does anybody log in or log out?"

"No. And I wouldn't sign in anyway. No owner wants to pay the overtime."

"Interesting," she murmured. "Okay, that helps."

"God only knows how it can help at this point," he muttered. "It sounds very much as if nobody has the slightest idea what happened over there."

"We're working on it. However, it won't be a stranger killing if they went into the kitchen of a restaurant where someone was working late at night for a one-off event and at a time when nobody would typically be there."

"And that's another thing," Denton noted in a curious tone. "Do you know why they were working?"

"They were prepping for a catering job for a business lunch the next day."

"That's interesting because generally those are things you would just come in early in the morning and do."

"The boss was the aunt who apparently wanted them to stay late that night to confirm it got done."

"*Hmm.*"

"And you're thinking that sounds off?"

"I don't know about *off*, but it could be that she didn't trust them and didn't want to take any chances on something going wrong on that particular job. Or it was big enough to need some special handling both the night before and the rest in the morning."

"Good point," she replied. "I was just told that Alice was very insistent that they stay late and finish."

"So, *she* knew they were there."

"Right," Doreen confirmed.

He hesitated. "Has anybody considered the idea that maybe she killed him first, then someone else came back and took her out?"

"Oh, it's been tossed about, but, of course, we don't have anything proving it either way."

"Or, if you do, you're not talking," he quipped, with a note of laughter.

"Exactly."

She asked him a few more questions about the industry but didn't find anything else of interest. So, she thanked him for his time and quickly ended the call. Then she reached for the teakettle to make tea, but she didn't even get that far when her phone rang again. She groaned and answered it and found her grandmother on the other end. "Hey, I'm trying rather desperately to get a cup of tea, and I still haven't managed. Can I call you back in a bit?"

"Don't bother now," Nan stated briskly. "Come on down here."

"I've just come in from talking with the family of the two murdered people," she explained. "I really just need a chance to have a cup of tea and to settle for a bit."

"Yeah, well, you can have your cup of tea and settle down here. I'm putting on the teakettle. It sounds as if you need the walk, child. You're getting crabby." And, with that, Nan ended the call.

Doreen stared down at her phone, closed her eyes, counted to ten, then counted to ten again. She really had no reason to be upset, except that she was really, really, *really* looking forward to that cup of tea in her own space, in her own living room, where she could kick back and relax, which was not the same thing as having a cup of tea at Nan's. But it wouldn't make a darn bit of difference now.

She walked back to the kitchen door, grabbed the harnesses, and the animals came running. Thaddeus, who had barely hopped off onto the kitchen table while she was trying to get to the tea in the first place, came squawking, "Thaddeus is here. Thaddeus is here."

She bent down, scooped him up, tucked him up onto her shoulder, and announced, "We'll go to Nan's for some tea."

She looked outside and realized that the walk would probably do them all good, even if she wasn't necessarily enthralled with the idea. Still, she bundled up and headed outside with them. The animals were ecstatic to be going anywhere but even happier to be heading down the river.

She sighed as she walked with them.

"I'm not sure what's going on with this case," she muttered. She tried talking through some of the salient points. Her animals had always been great sounding boards, mostly because they didn't give her any cheek, and, as she was coming to find out, that was nice too.

She chuckled to herself, and, by the time she made it down to Nan's, not only was her stomach rumbling but she was in a much better mood.

Nan smiled at her as she came in. "See? It was a good idea, wasn't it?"

Doreen rolled her eyes. "Maybe," she snorted, "but I still need that cup of tea."

"Hopefully you're also hungry because Richie is here with some treats for you that he got from the kitchen."

Doreen laughed. "I'm so glad that you have a great relationship with the kitchen staff," she murmured, as she stepped into Nan's little patio, where she proceeded to unclip the animals, and they all bolted inside so they could climb all over the people there.

As Doreen went to sit down, a knock came on Nan's front door. She went over and answered it, letting in Cleavis with a *C*. Richie appeared to be completely okay with that too, and right behind Cleavis came Maisie. As they all settled in, they turned their attention to the basket that Richie had brought.

He smacked the first hand to touch it. "Doreen gets first dibs," he muttered. When Doreen frowned at him, he smiled and said, "The kitchen staff told me it was okay to take these as long as it was for you."

"Ah," she said, with a smile. "I'm really happy to hear

that, since I always feel terribly guilty."

"And that would be foolish," he declared, with a snort. "We pay good money to be here."

She chuckled. "Yes, you pay good money to be here, but I don't."

Then she obliged him by snagging up the first thing that came to her fingers in the basket of warm goodies, a big chocolate croissant. She moaned. "You guys will make me fat."

"There's a long way to go for that to happen," Richie quipped, with a snicker, as he passed around the basket.

Everyone grabbed something of their choice, but Cleavis took his time, finally settling on a chocolate croissant.

As Doreen sat there, sipping her tea, she smiled over at Nan. "You're right. This was a good idea."

"Of course it was, child," she stated, with a chuckle. "I've been out of sorts for the last few days, so I figured this was a good way to make everybody feel loved."

"It's always a good way to make us feel loved, but you really don't have to do anything because we already know that we're loved."

Nan just smiled.

"How are things going with you and Mack?" Maisie asked.

"Fine," Doreen replied, her heart sinking as she realized this could have all been a ruse to get her here in order to talk about the wedding. "But, before you jump down my throat, I still haven't set a wedding date."

"That's fine," Maisie noted, with a shrug. "When the time is right, you'll get there."

Doreen looked at her and raised one eyebrow. "Thank you. I appreciate that."

Maisie just nodded as she took another bite of the cookie, the look of absolute bliss that came over her face making Doreen realize that the cookie was probably a better choice. The croissant was very good, but if Maisie's expression was anything to go by, the cookie was way better.

Doreen sat here quite comfortably, with everybody enjoying their tea and treats, until, out of the blue, Nan ordered, "Now, let's get down to business."

Doreen felt herself straighten up, as if she were in a classroom. "And what business is that?"

"You'll update us so we have a good idea of what's going on so far with the investigation," Nan explained, "and then we'll share some news on our side."

"Oh, good," Doreen said in delight. "I'm always happy to hear you have news."

"We have some news, but I'm not so sure it's any news that you necessarily want to hear, but, hey, let's start with yours and get everyone on the same page."

Doreen frowned at that but then agreed. "Not that I have a whole lot, so don't go expecting miracles." She shared her unfortunate encounter with Alice's husband, her phone call to Cleavis's grandson, and her meeting and interview with Jillian.

"Interesting." They all sat back and stared at her.

Doreen nodded. "So, we still have as suspects potentially anybody who was in the restaurant industry and would know what the kitchen layout was. The killer also needed to know when Barry and Alice were working at the Rocking Horse. That's the trick, and, so far, I don't have very many people on that list," she admitted, "and that can stop the investigation cold."

"Even if somebody did know, did they tell anybody

else?" Nan asked.

Doreen sighed. "We can't just assume that somebody was told, say, Uncle Zev, for example. He may or may not have known Jillian was working late that night." Doreen shook her head. "I'll ask her about that, and I'll keep that door open and see if we can get some more questions answered. She was willing to talk, even though she was crying. She's pretty wrecked over the loss of her fiancé, not to mention the fact that she's afraid she's looking good for this murder to the local police, even though, according to her and Uncle Zev, Jillian had nothing to do with it."

"I like how you say, *according to her*," Cleavis noted, eyeing her shrewdly. "Do you not believe that she's innocent?"

"Initially, I don't believe anybody is innocent," Doreen stated. "Not yet at least. I haven't got a good feel for this, and I certainly don't have a good understanding of what's going on," she acknowledged, shaking her head. "Still, I feel as if some tomfoolery is happening."

"Tomfoolery?" Nan's eyebrows shot up, a very happy smirk on her face and a twinkle in her eye.

"Not in that way," Doreen clarified, with a laugh. "I always find myself thinking people are trying to pull the wool over our eyes and getting away with murder."

"Which they haven't successfully done yet," Nan pointed out.

"It's even more than that," Doreen shared, looking at them. "Poor Jillian just lost her fiancé and her Aunt Alice this week. Yet the murder of Jillian's mother from ten years ago has never been solved. That was back in Alberta." They all frowned at her, and she nodded. "So, take that into consideration. According to Uncle Zev and his niece Jillian, her mother's murder has nothing to do with these two recent ones. But Katie—Jillian's mom—was alone in her home and stabbed with her own kitchen knife, just like both of these current murders. However, her mother was stabbed three times from the front, so she faced her killer, like Alice, whereas Barry was stabbed in the back."

"But you don't believe Zev and Jillian on this point, right?" Nan stared at her granddaughter.

"Do you really think three murders in the same family are unrelated?" Doreen asked Nan, looking around at the others too.

"That seems to be a bit of a stretch, doesn't it?" Richie noted. He shrugged, sharing a look at her and Nan. "It is a really terrible scenario for the family, yet not so hard to believe that the killer isn't one of the family."

"Which makes it worse, yet it's not impossible," Nan agreed, "especially given the way these murders were all so similar." Nan sighed. "We've certainly known people who seemed to be cursed with terrible luck in life. One family member dying of cancer, and the next one dying of this, and the next one dying of that. You do have to wonder."

They all nodded.

"That's the thing, when you get to be our age," Maisie added, "it's pretty hard to surprise us."

"Exactly," Doreen agreed. "Even with the number of cases I've worked on, I'm continuously surprised, yet not surprised, at the things people will do to get something they want—in this case, potentially a restaurant. And, from everybody I've spoken to, the restaurant business itself wasn't thriving, so it didn't have a whole lot of value, except for maybe the actual buildings, the pub and the restaurant itself, plus the real estate involved. Yet I don't know to what level that it's financed. If they own it outright, then it could be a fair chunk of money, as the real estate prices in Kelowna have gone sky-high."

A few people nodded.

"That is very true," Nan stated. "So, the real estate value alone, if they were to sell the property, not so much the existing business, could potentially be in the millions."

Doreen nodded. "That's a very recent angle that I was considering. I need to find out more about that particular location and its market value now. I didn't bring it up with Zev and Jillian, as I seemed to have worn out my welcome with her uncle Zev. Maybe it was just because Jillian was in tears again. Yet we did discuss the other Burgon brother, Danny. Apparently nobody gets along with his wife. She doesn't work, even though she doesn't feel they have enough money, yet she is not terribly supportive of her husband's artwork either."

"I don't know what kind of art he does, but it's bound to be a hard living," Nan noted, shaking her head. "Particularly in this town. It's not as if we have high-end art galleries in Kelowna."

"We do though," Cleavis countered, nodding at her. "To you they may not be high-end because art hasn't necessarily been your thing."

"They *were* my thing," she declared, a bit cross, "but more so in the Vancouver scene."

"Ah." Cleavis nodded. "Well, art has come a long way in this town. I'll admit that there's room to grow, but an awful lot of really lovely artists have come out of this region. I don't think I know this particular man though," he added, turning to look at Doreen.

She nodded and moved the conversation along. "There's no doubt that owning a restaurant, if it were profitable and if they could hire a manager to run it, would help provide Danny with some much-needed income," she shared. "He's in a wheelchair, so I don't think he's capable of killing anyone himself, but that doesn't mean he couldn't have arranged it. The police always look to a spouse first as a potential suspect," she noted, frowning. "I need to talk to Danny, but I'm not sure that would be so easy to do."

At that, Richie nodded. "As you told us, Alice was married. So she had a husband. I wonder why he wasn't mentioned as a potential suspect. Have you spoken to him, Doreen?"

Before Doreen could answer him, Maisie interjected, "You're a pretty young thing. He might be quite happy to talk to you."

Doreen grimaced. "I suspect Randol Biscott would refuse to speak to me, especially after meeting Mugs the other day. Mugs did not like him, and, when I say, *he didn't like him*, I mean he hated him at first sight. And Randol threatened to shoot Mugs for acting that way."

Nan gasped. "He was so angry. I hope you told Mack about that man."

Doreen nodded. "I did."

Nan continued. "On the other hand, maybe Randol's our killer, and we can only hope that he's in jail somewhere soon."

Doreen had to smile at that thought. "Randol won't talk to me, not after the way he behaved in response to Mugs barking at him. I can't take Mugs with me, even if I did try to talk to him," she noted, "because he immediately disliked Mugs."

"And he was going into the Rocking Horse restaurant?"

"He had a key and was going into the now-closed restaurant," she confirmed. "So I'm pretty sure that's Alice's husband."

"Or her ex-husband," muttered Nan. "Maybe they were separated."

Doreen pulled out her phone and contacted Zev. When he answered the phone with the usual irritation in his tone, she began with an apology. "I'm so sorry. I'm trying not to be a bother, so I didn't phone your niece, but I have a couple of questions. Was Alice still married to Randol, were they separated or maybe involved in a divorce proceeding?"

Zev groaned. "That marriage was on the rocks from the very beginning. However, I don't know the legal status of it."

Doreen asked, "So, if your sister Alice was still legally married to Randol, you still thought that your brother Danny would inherit from Alice, right?"

"The restaurant has to stay in the family," Zev explained, "so Alice's husband can't have it. ... Jesus, I wonder if he did it."

"If who did what?" Doreen asked.

Silence came from the other end. Zev muttered something under his breath that she couldn't quite hear. Then Zev continued. "What if Randol killed Alice? All I'm saying is, ... what if Alice and Randol had split up, and maybe they've been separated for quite a while. If Alice was going to divorce him, I don't know whether he would be happy about it or not. I don't know if they went to a lawyer to do the paperwork needed for a legal action."

Doreen pondered that. "Would Randol already know that he can't get the family restaurant?"

Zev sighed. "I don't know. Alice kept the family business very close to her chest, but, as a motive for Randol killing her, it's not a bad one. Randol definitely has a temper."

"That's not a bad motive at all," Doreen agreed. "I'll see if I can talk to him."

"Good luck with that. He's not very social."

"Right, and I may have accidentally met him downtown," she murmured. "If he's the same man I'm thinking of, he wasn't very nice at all."

"That would be a pleasant way to describe him," Zev said. "By the way, he hates animals, so don't take them with you. He'll make sure they have an *accident*."

"I already don't like this man."

"If just for that reason alone," Zev replied, "I would be more than happy to see him as the guilty party. Yet, … after what I said about him, I just can't see it."

"Why not?" Doreen asked.

"Because … I'm pretty sure my sister was paying him money to keep him away from her."

"Sorry?" she asked. "As in, he was blackmailing her?"

"Something like that, but I don't know why, and the more I think about it, … maybe he was just done with her and their marriage. Maybe he figured, if he got the restaurant, it would be better than waiting for the money from her every month. Maybe he figured he could just, you know, have it all."

"But wouldn't he know that he wasn't entitled to the family restaurant?"

"He may not," Zev pointed out. "You would expect Alice to make that clear, but she wasn't the nicest person either. Plus, she didn't discuss the business with me or Danny, so why would she talk to Randol about it? He has no restaurant experience."

"Good God," she muttered. "What about you and Danny? Do either of you talk with Randol at all?"

"I don't know that Danny has ever spoken to Randol. Between Randol and Danny's wife, those are two hateful people who are not someone anyone wants to interact with. As for my speaking to Randol, yes, I have occasionally, but I certainly wouldn't brace him over this. When I say he's not a nice man, I mean it."

"Got it," Doreen replied. "Do you have any contact information for him?"

"Sure," he said. "I'll give it to you, but, if you die in the process, you can't hold it against me."

"Oh, if I'm dead," she noted, with a laugh, "I can't hold anything against anyone."

"That's true." He quickly gave her the number.

She waved at Nan, who gave her a pen and paper, and she wrote it down. "Do you have his full name for me?"

"Just Randol Biscott—some silly last name, like the cookie."

"Okay." She stared down at the name. "Do you know if he works? Any idea where he might be?"

"No, I don't think he works. He's just been sucking Alice dry, letting her support him."

"So, part of any divorce settlement may have been alimony that she had to pay to him."

"Maybe. … That would suck, but I guess that makes sense. Although if that were the case," he added, "he wouldn't have killed her because that would have cooked his proverbial goose."

"True," Doreen confirmed, "but that might be worth asking him about."

"I'm just warning you."

"I hear you," she said, "and thank you very much for the warning."

When he rang off, she stared at the people in Nan's living room. "Anybody know this guy?"

They all shook their heads.

She looked over at Nan. "We need a picture of him." She quickly went through her phone to try and find something. "When I get home, I'll contact Mack. Surely the police have already contacted Alice's husband. The death notification is just part of the natural order of things within law enforcement. And, in this case, when someone dies, the spouse is often the first suspect."

Nan nodded. "Don't talk to that man again, Doreen. Let Mack handle it. You know that's what he will tell you anyway, right?"

Doreen grimaced. "I guess so."

Nan continued. "Which is why the police went to Barry's fiancée about her young man."

"Exactly." Doreen pondered that. "It's so sad about Jillian losing Barry—and her aunt too, all on top of losing her mom a decade ago." She looked around the room. "Okay, what else have we got?" But nobody seemed to have anything else to add. "I thought you had something to tell me," she told Nan.

"Not as exciting as what you're finding out," Maisie replied. "You make us feel like slugger bugs."

Doreen laughed. "No, not at all. However, if you want to dredge up any information you can on this Burgon family, then please do so. And, if you know anybody from Red Deer in Alberta, I would love all the information and gossip on Katie Burgon, the woman who was killed there ten years ago." Doreen frowned. "I don't know that Katie used her married name much. Her husband went missing so long ago. Thank goodness that Jillian had Uncle Zev to fill in as her father figure."

"It is rather odd to have three murders in that family, and then for Jillian to have her father leave them too? So sad," Nan muttered.

"It's beyond odd, and Mack can't find a trail on Jillian's father, so we don't know whether he's dead or still hiding out." Doreen shook her head. "Something is off about that too."

"Ooh, another mystery. I like the sound of that." Nan smiled at Doreen. "You're always so good for our entertainment."

"Maybe," Doreen muttered, "but, in this instance, I feel I'm missing something."

"You'll find it," Nan declared comfortably. "You always do."

"No pressure though, right?" Doreen had to laugh.

Nan chuckled. "No pressure ever, honey. But, having said that …"

"Right." Doreen groaned, knowing what Nan was about to say. "*Time is ticking.* I get it."

When tea was done, Doreen got up. After all her animals managed to complete their goodbyes—which seemed to be quite the process these days—Doreen took them all outside and headed back down to the creek, wondering what to do next.

Randol Biscott was not somebody she wanted to talk to on her own. She just barely made it back home when Mack called her. She chuckled. "You know it's been one of those days when I just go from meeting to meeting to meeting," she began, "but you were on my mind, so I'm glad you called."

"That's good," he replied, with a chuckle, "but why is it

a good thing I called? What are you up to now?"

"Did you talk to the husband of the murdered restaurant owner?"

"No, I haven't. One of the uniforms did the notification," he shared, "and it is on my list to do. However, it's not a high priority because he doesn't live here."

"He does live here," she corrected, "at least as far as I know. And Alice was paying him money every month, but I don't know whether that was a court-ordered alimony or blackmail was going on. Yet we met him downtown, and he went to the Rocking Horse and entered with his own key. Plus, he's the one who scared me and Nan when he threatened Mugs."

"That's interesting," Mack replied in a pensive tone. "So you say he has a key to the Rocking Horse?"

"Yes. He let himself into the restaurant, last I saw. And it was closed to the public."

"*Hmm.* I'll need to move up his interview a little bit on the priority list."

"Yeah, you do that, but I need to talk to him too. Not so sure I want to talk to him alone."

"I don't want you talking to him at all, remember?"

"I know, and I know that you'll say it's a current case, but Randol also seems to be quite interesting in terms of all three of the Burgon-related murder cases."

"Do not talk to him," Mack snapped, his tone sharp, "not when Mugs already doesn't like him."

"Oh, well, there's not liking, then there's really hating," she clarified. "You don't understand how Mugs reacted. It was pretty bad and well past *not liking.*"

"*Don't* talk to him, Doreen. I'll reach out to him this afternoon and see if I can connect right away. I may end up going down to the restaurant, if he's there. I was hoping to do another walk-through anyway."

She immediately asked, "Any chance I could come?"

"What good would that do you?" he asked in exasperation.

She snorted. "Why is it *you* want to go?"

"I want to get … Fine, I'll ask the captain for clearance," he muttered, "but no promises."

"No, of course not," she said in delight. "I would absolutely love to go to the crime scene."

"You know something is wrong with you, right?" he asked her in a half-joking manner.

"I know some people would think so," she conceded, "but I also know that you love me. So, if anything is wrong with me, you're okay with that too."

"Absolutely," he declared, his tone super gentle, and then he ended the call.

Chapter 20

LATER THAT AFTERNOON Doreen had worked up her notes and was now struggling against the temptation to contact the man she really did not want to talk to. Yet she also knew Randol Biscott could be a viable source of information. Plus, part of her just wanted him to be the guilty party. As she sat here, arguing with herself, going back and forth on the common sense of going against Mack's warning, Mack phoned her.

"I'm going down to the restaurant right now, and, yes, you can come along if you want."

"*Woo-hoo!*" she exclaimed, jumping for joy.

"I'll take that as a yes," he quipped, laughing into the phone.

"Absolutely," she replied, with a happy tone.

"Okay, I'll be there in ten minutes."

"Okay, I'm getting ready." She quickly grabbed her coat and bundled up the animals. When Mack pulled into her driveway, she stepped outside with everybody in tow.

He looked at her and groaned. "Obviously I didn't make myself clear."

"No, you didn't," she stated, "so I took advantage and

assumed that, when we go sleuthing, we *all* go sleuthing."

"I don't know how the captain will feel about that."

She laughed. "The captain would expect exactly this."

He tilted his head and then chuckled softly. "He probably would."

"And it's not as if it's a working restaurant right now anyway. It's a crime scene that forensics has already processed too," she pointed out. "So nobody can get upset about the animals being there."

"Maybe not," he conceded, "but you do know how to push it."

"That's true. I do," she admitted.

With everybody piled into the cab of his truck, Mack barreled down toward the Rocking Horse Pub.

She suggested, "We could always pick up something for dinner too." When he glanced at her, she shrugged. "We're almost never in downtown Kelowna, and I don't really know why."

"Most of the time we're eating at home, and lately I just haven't had time to go anywhere."

"I understand, and that's another reason I keep bringing up Vancouver. We can actually take time off for a holiday of sorts."

"I'm not against it," he replied. "I'm looking forward to it. We haven't traveled together outside of Kelowna, have we?"

"Vernon," she murmured.

"I would consider that local though," he noted, with a laugh.

She grinned and nodded. "It just seems as if it's a different world."

"Sure, but it's the same for West Kelowna, and you

don't go over there much either."

"I know. It's weird, almost like a different planet."

"Hardly," he said in exasperation, looking at her.

"Okay, maybe not a different planet but a different city."

He just sighed. When they got up to the restaurant area, he pulled down a side street and then into an alleyway, as he parked in the back.

"Oh, even better," she muttered. "I wanted to check out the loading bay area." When they got out, she looked around and asked, "So, is the parking here for the restaurant?"

"I don't know. Why?"

"Just wondering how somebody would get down here," she replied. "Did they drive up? Did anybody see anything illegal? Are there any cameras or anything like that?"

"No cameras along the alleyway," he said. "At one point there were but not any longer. When this whole street was revitalized, with food joints all over the place, some of that went by the wayside."

"Which doesn't seem to be an improvement, if you think about it."

"Some of it was an improvement because the security went inside. These were outdated outdoor security cameras that were mostly broken," he explained. "So it went to more modern technology, and that is controlled from inside the building."

"I don't know if this restaurant had anything like that."

"I don't know, but I did speak to a couple restaurant owners in this area. Most of them would love to have something like that again but haven't been able to afford it."

She nodded. "COVID really did a number on the restaurants, and they're still having a tough time. … We already know a lot of them had to close their doors."

He nodded. "I did hear about that, but I didn't realize it was quite so bad."

"I really think we're supposed to help support the local community," she noted, "which means we should probably do something on a more local level and maybe pick up dinner on the way home."

He looked at her and asked, "Did you eat today?"

She frowned at him. "Of course I did."

He shook his head. "There's no *of course* about it. Did you actually eat today?"

"Yes, I ate today," she stated. Then in a small voice confessed, "I had some chocolate croissants down at Nan's." His eyes widened. "And, no, I didn't bring any home for you either."

He just shook his head. "Did you eat any *real* food today?"

"That is real food," she cried out.

"Only if you had an omelet, or bacon and eggs, or at least eggs on toast beforehand."

"I didn't get a chance," she wailed. "Everybody's had me on the run all day."

They all got out of Mack's truck, and Doreen kept a tight grip on the leashes on Mugs and Goliath. This alleyway was filled with broken glass and dumpsters full of rotting food. Doreen wondered if this had been a good idea to bring her animals here.

Mack had keys to the place and unlocked the back door. She frowned at that and asked, "Did they lock the restaurant when they were inside? Or did they not lock it as Jillian said and anybody could have walked in?"

"I don't know, but it still doesn't explain who would know they were there at that hour, other than Alice. Still, when working after closing time, the doors definitely should have been locked."

As they walked into the restaurant, Doreen lifted her nose and sniffed. "We really should pick up some food on the way home."

"That's the third time you've mentioned food in the last five minutes. So we'll definitely be picking up dinner," he muttered, glancing at her.

"What if it was a burglary gone wrong?"

"Then why kill somebody?" He frowned, looked down at his notes, and stated, "Jillian couldn't remember for sure but didn't think they had locked the back door."

Doreen sighed. "And, maybe in their minds, since she was with him, they had no need to lock the doors at all."

"That's often a misconception people tend to make."

"I was also wondering if he wore a headset, listening to music or something," she added. "He almost had to, right? If not, why wouldn't he have heard somebody coming in? Or was it somebody he knew, and, when he turned his back to them, they killed him?"

He turned to face her. "Seems you already have a theory," he noted cautiously.

"I do," she conceded, "but I have to solve all three murders and untangle the mess before I can get answers for you."

He stared at her. Then his expression cleared, and he asked, "All three?"

"Yes," she declared, nodding at him. "They have to be connected."

He just gave her a small headshake and proceeded to turn on all the big overhead lights. As she walked into what should have been a gleaming commercial kitchen, she noted food still sitting on the counter, along with dirty dishes and a mess everywhere, including that left behind by the forensics unit.

Plus, a big cut-up watermelon was on one counter but now looked wilted and sad. Jillian really had been cutting up the watermelon …

Doreen sighed. "This really won't be an easy clean-up for Jillian, even to hire it out." She had to keep a tight rein on Mugs and Goliath even inside the restaurant. She feared they would eat some spoiled food here—or worse.

"Yet this is minor in comparison to some crime scenes. However, you're right. It does need to be done before it becomes a food hazard."

"Has anybody cleared it so the family can come in?"

"No, I don't think so," he muttered. "And not really an issue right now either."

She turned around and asked, "Where's the bathroom?"

"You need to use it?"

"No, but that's where Jillian was struck."

"Of course. Let's go. We can review this location as to the first murder. Then we'll have a look at it as to Alice's murder." He led the way around the corner, which was out of sight of the kitchen area.

Doreen nodded, thankful the animals followed her with no fuss. "So, when Jillian exited the bathroom, the attacker had to be standing behind this door right here," she pointed out. "So he wouldn't be seen, and he could come right up behind Jillian and knock her out," she muttered. "That lends credence to her story."

"Yes, … but, if she were the killer, she just preplanned that it would fit her story, which just means that she's good at coming up with an explanation that we can't argue with."

She smiled at him. "I hear you, and I'm not saying she's

innocent."

"Good because, until we have proof either way, nobody is innocent in my book."

She held up her hand. "I know the drill."

He snorted. "You may know the drill, but that doesn't mean you listen to it or abide by it."

She rolled her eyes, then headed back to the kitchen and continued their conversation. "The bigger issue is the fact that, if somebody came in through the rear kitchen door, and tried to attack Barry, he should have seen him."

Mack turned, looked at the back door, then at the prep area. "Depends on which counter he was working on."

"According to what we see here, in terms of the knives and the work in progress, it would be this one," she stated, stepping up to it and looking around, the animals right beside her.

Mack stated, "But that also means that anybody coming in would have been seen."

"So, either he knew the person or ..."

"Or what?"

"Or he had no warning. Say, Barry was talking with the guy or whatever, then turned his back on him, unconcerned, then was stabbed from behind."

"I don't think he would have stepped back so quickly to his prep work, not that fast."

"Or," she began, then stopped and frowned.

"*Or* what now?" he asked her.

"Or the attacker was already in the restaurant. The pub was still open, remember? Just because they worked the pub, that doesn't mean they didn't know about the prep kitchen or how to gain access to it."

He considered her, then looked around the kitchen and

nodded. "That's possible and would likely lend credence to the theory of Barry knowing his attacker."

"Exactly," she declared, then pulled out her phone and called Jillian.

Barry's fiancée answered, stating, "I can't help you."

"We're in the restaurant, taking a look right now," Doreen began. "So we do have a couple of questions."

"*Agh*. What is it now?"

"One, what counter would Barry have been working on?"

Following Jillian's description, Doreen stepped back up to the one she had assumed was it. "Okay, good. Now was there any chance that somebody could have stayed inside the restaurant after it was closed? Or is there a way to come from the pub, which was still open, and gain access to the restaurant's kitchen, which was already closed for the evening?"

"The pub and the restaurant share a wall, and a door connects the two, but it's marked For Employees Only. So, anybody still in the pub or the restaurant could have been there the whole time we were," she protested, "but we were there for hours."

"So, they would have to stay quiet, so you two didn't notice."

"Yes, that's what I'm saying. We didn't know anybody else was there, and, if I'd stayed with Barry—instead of going to the restroom to get over my pout," she snapped, "then maybe he would still be alive." And, with that, she burst into tears again.

After Doreen ended the call, she looked over at Mack and shared, "It really does seem as if whoever came in was somebody Barry knew."

"Then how many people could that likely be?"

She sighed. "I know this is not a popular opinion, but I'm leaning toward the idea that Jillian's Aunt Alice killed him."

Mack slowly grimaced. "Do you have some working hypothesis as to why?"

"I'm not sure on the why, but I am a little concerned that maybe the killer got the wrong person."

"That makes no sense to me. Alice, as the boss, knew Barry and Jillian were working late right here that night. So, if Barry was the wrong person, then Alice intended to kill her own niece? If so, Alice would have heard that Jillian was in the bathroom—especially if Jillian was playing music on her phone in there, as she told you. So, when Jillian stepped out of the bathroom, Alice could have killed her, if Jillian was, indeed, Alice's intended target."

"I know, so why didn't she? What would have been her motive for that? What stopped her?"

"I don't know," he grumbled. "I think you're barking up the wrong tree."

"At least I have a tree to bark up." At that, Mugs gave a *woof.*

Mack burst into laughter at that and gave Mugs a quick scratch behind the ears. "Just remember …"

"I know. I know. I know." Doreen groaned. "We're back to that *having real proof* thing."

"Yeah, you're not kidding," he muttered, then went about doing what he was doing.

She watched curiously as he took pictures for his own records. "What is it you came here to look at?"

"A couple things," he replied. "One, I wanted to confirm that nobody was in the walk-in freezer."

She stared at him in surprise. "But how do they get out of it?"

Mack smiled. "There is a safety latch for just those times."

Doreen shook her head. "But how could anyone have stayed in there for hours though?"

"Hard to say," Mack conceded, shaking his head. "Yet I do have to entertain the possibility that somebody was here from the beginning. The walk-in cooler would have been a good place to hide. And, if the killer had come prepared, with winter coats and gloves, it's plausible."

"Would they have been able to stay there for hours though?"

"As I mentioned, with enough preparation, you can do anything."

"Ha, I never even thought of that."

"Oh, wow," he said, looking over at her. "I came up with something you didn't?"

She rolled her eyes. "No need to gloat," she said. Then she stepped into the cooler, gasped, and raced back out. "It must be a great winter coat to withstand hours of that," she exclaimed. "No way anybody can stay in that freezer for a long time."

"Maybe," he replied, as he studied it. "It's set at a fridge temperature, not like the walk-in freezer, but I want to check that out too." When she stared at him, shaking her head in disbelief, he added, "What if the walk-in freezer's not working? What if it hasn't worked in a while? You have to continuously look at all options."

"Then we get to knock them all off the list for being silly," she declared, with a nod. "This was a restaurant, and they would need their freezer."

He shook his head and smiled. "Hey, ... have a little faith."

"*Hey*," she responded, "I'm happy for you to do all these checks because it makes it easier on me as I get to knock them up and down against my hypotheses. And hopefully, at the end of the day, we'll have something that fits this crime—or all three of them."

He gave her a one-arm shrug as he took several photos from inside the fridge.

She frowned. "They would have to hold an awful lot of veggies to make this purchase worthwhile."

"They would," he agreed. "I was thinking about that because there's an awful lot of room in here for a body to be stored."

She gasped. "Meaning?"

He turned to face her. "What if Barry had been killed a lot earlier?"

"Oh no," she muttered, staring at him.

He shrugged. "Again, I just need to know that it wasn't possible."

"But how can you make that *not* possible, when one look at the size of the walk-in cooler tells us that it is definitely possible. But then why would somebody kill him earlier and then put him back in position in the kitchen? Wouldn't he be cold to the touch?" she asked. "Plus, no blood is in here, so, even if they did kill Barry earlier, there would be signs, right?"

"Absolutely," he agreed, "there would be signs. Even if they attempted to clean up Barry's blood pooling in the walk-in, our forensics team would have still found traces."

She frowned at him and sighed. "So you're just joshing me, aren't you?"

He chuckled. "Mentally, I'm just running through all options, and if that were the case—"

"He would have been drugged first," she interrupted him, her mind racing. "Then positioned in the kitchen and killed there, leaving his blood in the kitchen."

He nodded. "That's very true."

She visibly shook. "I'm not so sure this was good idea to have my animals walking around here."

Mack suggested, "We'll give their feet a good scrub when we get back home."

"Or they were both drugged earlier," she suggested, her eyes widening. "Oh, I hadn't considered that." Then she stopped and shook her head. "But it would be so hard to move them. There's that extra weight somehow when the person is not conscious. So that's an awful lot of physical exertion, especially for an older woman like Alice."

"But it's not very far to move them," he pointed out.

"But if they weren't in the fridge for very long, what would be the point?"

"Delaying timelines," he replied.

Her shoulders slumped as she thought about it. "Good God," she muttered. "Of course Alice's husband is big enough—and angry enough."

Mack laughed. "Just because you don't like him doesn't mean he's guilty."

"Are you sure?" she asked. "Because I'm really liking the idea of him being guilty."

Mack just smiled and didn't say anything.

She kept running things through her brain, trying to figure out what the logistics would look like to drug two people, then move them into a cooler, changing the timeline enough that Barry could be put out on the kitchen floor and then stabbed. Jillian would then be placed in the hallway outside the bathroom. "That's a little disturbing," she shared.

"What is?"

"In order to stab him in the back, the killer would have to prop him up against this counter, then stab him, and drop him." She visibly shook, her mind working over the logistics of moving them and whatnot.

"Maybe the killer used drugs that pass through the system very quickly," he suggested. "They might not show up on a tox report that way. That might make them easier to move, if they were somewhat coming to as well."

"On the other hand, I almost prefer this drugged theory," she admitted, "because it's a much kinder way for Barry to die." When Mack looked at her, she shrugged. "He wouldn't have known that he was being stabbed, and he just would have gone from a drug-induced sleep to … a permanent sleep," she offered. Mugs gave another *woof*, as if agreeing. She gave him a snuggle.

"I'm not seriously considering this theory though," Mack told her. "I don't think that's what happened."

"But it could have happened," she noted. "That's the thing about coming here. Now we're seeing other possibilities."

He winced. "But not great ones."

"Maybe not," she admitted, "but it is something that I have to ponder."

He shrugged. "You ponder away. I have a lot of other work to do." And he kept walking back and forth, all around the kitchen.

She watched him until she got frustrated and asked, "Will you explain what you're doing?"

"I'm going through the kitchen again, this time with Alice's murder in mind. This is what I often do because I need to satisfy my own mind that something is possible or not."

"All you did was open up the reality that there are far more possibilities than I had really expected."

He tilted his head. "That's what this is all about," he stated. "It's about figuring out what's possible and then making sure we prove it didn't happen that way because the defense will say most of the evidence we are presenting is circumstantial."

"That would be foolish on their part," she stated. "But, then again, you know lawyers, so who knows what they'll say."

"Exactly," he said, with a smile. "And they aren't dumb bunnies, no matter how much you like to knock the profession."

"I'm not trying to knock them all," she clarified. "I just have an innate bias against lawyers."

"Except my brother."

"Right," she agreed, with a chuckle. "Except Nick."

"Glad to hear that," Mack noted.

She wandered around with her animals now too, contemplating the walk-in fridge concept for a long moment. Unfortunately, it was possible in her mind, but she wondered what it would do in terms of delaying the timeline. And, with that thought in her mind, she phoned Jillian again.

"Seriously?" Jillian snapped at Doreen. "I do have other things I'm trying to deal with, without having this constant reminder."

"I understand that," Doreen acknowledged, "and I'm sorry to keep bothering you, but, if I can't get answers this way, it's much harder for us."

"Fine, what is it?"

"Did you wake up with a headache?"

"Of course I woke up with a headache. What kind of a question is that? I got knocked out."

"And did you have a bruise or swelling?"

"I presume so. … I wasn't too worried about my head. I was more concerned about the fact that Barry was on the floor, … dead," she muttered. "I know they checked me over on the scene and told me that I was fine to go home. They just told me to keep an eye out for my head."

"And did you have a dry mouth or anything?"

"You mean, outside of a dry mouth from all the screaming?" she cried out. "You do realize that I came to and found him dead on the floor, right? And that's not exactly a normal scenario for anybody. I was just completely overwhelmed by everything."

"And I get that," Doreen replied. "That night, did anybody come to the restaurant after closing?"

"Sure, Aunt Alice did, but it was her place."

"Of course. Anybody else?"

"Yeah, a couple men she was supposed to be doing business with, though they were not impressed that we were there. We told her that we could leave, but she told us to go sit in the other room and wait, have some tea, while she did her business with the men. She even brought out the tea and told us to stay there. She mentioned that these men weren't very happy about anybody coming into the restaurant."

"So, after the tea, what did you do?"

"She told us it was all clear, and we could get back to work, and we were to stay here until everything was done."

"And when was that?"

"I don't know, a couple hours. It wasn't very late at that point, but we still had a lot of prep work to do. Honestly, we had an awful lot of work to do, and we just weren't feeling good."

"But you and Barry had a nap, didn't you?"

"Yeah, we did," she muttered. "How did you know?"

Doreen had no idea what to tell her. She herself had no idea what to make of it. The mess just got worse. Even with Doreen poking at her, Jillian hadn't shared everything. "What happened next?"

"We woke up, still not feeling very well at all, but Barry was very conscientious. That was why I wanted to go home because I was feeling sick. I had texted Aunt Alice how we weren't feeling well and that we needed to leave, and she told us that we had to stay and finish."

"Even though you were sick?"

"Yeah, even though we were sick. Which is … that was when the argument between us happened," she muttered.

"Any chance you were drugged?"

A shocked gasp came on the other end. "What?"

"Think about it carefully," Doreen added in a cautious tone. "Is there any chance you and Barry were drugged?"

"But when? How?"

"I'm wondering about the tea that Alice served you."

There was a long sigh at the other end. "I know that Aunt Alice had some issues, and she really didn't like us being here in the first place, but I can't imagine she would ever do anything to hurt us."

"No, but if these two men she was meeting with were people she didn't want you to have any knowledge of, would she have done it?"

"No, I don't think so," Jillian repeated. "I think you're completely out in left field on that. We still did all the work, which we wouldn't have been able to do if we were drugged."

"That makes no sense too, when you could have easily

done all this the morning before the luncheon," she stated, shaking her head. "Okay, I was just working on a theory."

"You'll have to find another theory," Jillian declared, "because that one doesn't fly. We were talking and quite normal. Maybe irritated but normally irritated," she explained.

"Okay, that was just a possibility. Any idea who was there that Alice wanted to talk to so badly, yet didn't want you around them?"

"Don't know who the second guy was, but one was her husband, I think. I really don't like him and want nothing to do with him, so we were happy to stay away from him. He is just plain mean."

"Why was he there?"

"He came in for money, but I don't know the whole story. If you're looking for somebody who may have killed Aunt Alice, I already told the cops about Randol."

"Good enough," Doreen replied, and, with that, she ended the call.

Chapter 21

DOREEN WENT BACK to Mack, and he asked her, "Any luck?"

"No, none at all."

He smiled. "But you went down a pathway, came to a dead end, and that's okay too. Cross off one theory on your list."

"Jillian told me that Alice's husband had come in with somebody else that night. Yet Alice told Jillian and Barry to go stay in another room, while she dealt with them. And she brought them tea and again told them to sit there and to do nothing until she came to give them the all clear."

"Seriously?"

Doreen nodded. "Which is why I was thinking maybe the aunt drugged the tea and all, but Jillian says that they weren't drugged, that they were perfectly capable of getting up and working—after they took a nap because they were really tired, which seems odd to me. But she did say that she told you guys about the visit of Alice's husband and that he was one scary dude."

He smiled. "Yeah, we have heard that about Alice's husband," he confirmed, "but just because he's big and scary and angry doesn't mean he killed anybody."

"Maybe not," Doreen acknowledged, "but I still can't quite see that many killers are here."

"I don't know about how many you've already decided are or are not here," he quipped, "but two deaths could easily be two killers."

"Could be," she agreed, "but it doesn't feel right." He looked over at her and waited patiently. She finally raised both hands. "I don't know. It just doesn't make sense."

"Maybe not, but, as we get more answers, … it will."

"That's the trouble. … I'm not getting answers."

"Yes, you are," he declared, with a nod. "Remember how you go down a pathway, and you go as far as you can, and, if it doesn't pan out, you discard that one. Then you keep working the other angles until you find more information."

She smiled at him. "You really do have a lot of patience, don't you?"

"Sometimes I need it," he shared, looking over at her with a grin on his face. "And sometimes—please don't take this the wrong way—but it's nice to see you flail around a little bit, instead of making us all look like we're completely crazy and half incompetent, the way you usually do as you miraculously solve one case after another."

She snorted. "You just had to say that, didn't you?"

He walked over, leaned down, gave her a kiss on the cheek, and whispered, "Believe me when I say, that mind of yours is absolutely brilliant."

"I don't know about that," she muttered, "as I am feeling totally stumped."

"No, you're not," he argued, looking her in the eye. "You just don't know what direction to go next."

"Isn't that the same as feeling stumped?" she asked, with

laughter.

"It absolutely is not," he pointed out. "It's just a chance to regroup in your head."

"Oh, and I thought that meant *stumped*."

He shook his head. "I get it. For you, it's all semantics, but really it's just a chance for you to sort things out and to ask yourself, *If it wasn't that way, then what way could it be?*"

"I would say, if we're walking away from the whole cooler theory and the drugging theory, which is very convoluted, … but, if it looks like a duck, quacks like a duck, it's probably a duck."

"It is very convoluted."

She glared at him. "Thanks for that."

"Hey, it was an option."

"So, what's your other option?"

"The other option is that they knew the person who came into the kitchen."

"Have you interviewed all the other people who work here?" she asked.

"There are two waitresses, both of whom have been here for many years, and they both finished their shifts that night. They were picked up by their partners, and both had alibis for the rest of the night."

Doreen's shoulders slumped, and she nodded. "Okay, so we're back to her."

"Who's her?"

"The owner, Alice."

He stared at her. "That means we have two killers then. But what possible reason or motive could there be for Alice to murder Barry?"

"That's the real problem I have right now," she conceded, shaking her head. "I'm stuck at that point."

"If you can come up with something about that, then you may get some answers. But Barry was killed, not Jillian, which screws up any motives relating to inheritance and that sort of thing."

"Right," she muttered. "That is a whole different story."

"It is, and, if it was a case of mistaken identity, an angle you seem to like very much," he noted, "you also have to remember that the killer could easily have taken out Jillian while she was in the hallway, instead of just knocking her out. So, instead of mistaken identity, he would have just killed an extra person he didn't intend on killing."

She frowned and nodded. "I guess that's also possible, isn't it?"

"Yes, it is," Mack declared, "and quite likely. If that's what happened, … why would they have left Jillian alive?"

"Only if something interrupted the killer, but then he could have just come back to kill her. We don't know how long Jillian was unconscious in that hallway."

Mack frowned, shaking his head. "So, you're talking about the inheritance angle, right? But that means the entire Burgon family needs to die. So, *again*, why wouldn't the killer come back and take out Jillian?"

"I don't know," she admitted. "That's my sticking point."

"And there is always a sticking point," he muttered. "So, you just keep chipping away at it until something comes loose."

She smiled. "Thank you. Is that Detective 101?"

He laughed, put an arm around her shoulders, and added, "Kind of. I'm done here. Do you need more time?"

"Nope," she muttered, as she looked around. "It's pretty self-explanatory."

"I'm glad you think so," Mack quipped. "It doesn't feel very self-explanatory to me." He gazed around the room one last time. "Let's get going. I think your animals have been on their best behavior for long enough."

She nodded, smiling down at them. "Where to?"

"I thought you wanted to go get some food."

"I do," she said. "A bunch of restaurants are around here, so, as long as nobody else gets killed in these other restaurants, we can assume it's a problem localized to just this one, right?"

He frowned at her. "We hadn't considered that anybody else's restaurant might be involved, but—"

"I know." She groaned. "It's always about the *but*s with you."

He grinned. "For this case, at this moment, it could be a competing business. It could be somebody who had absolutely nothing to do with the restaurant industry, or it could be somebody who literally just … didn't like her."

"Didn't like who? Jillian or Alice?"

"Either—or both for that matter."

"But then why kill Barry?"

"I'm not sure," he replied. "We're still working on that."

She frowned, then nodded. "Okay, I get it. … Did the uncle ever work in this restaurant?"

"I have no idea, but which uncle are you talking about?" he asked.

"Zev," she replied, as she pulled out her phone.

"At this rate, they'll stop answering your calls," Mack said, with a chuckle.

She winced but nodded. "They probably will, but I still have to ask them questions as they arise."

When she called back, the uncle snapped, "Haven't you

bothered us enough?"

"Maybe so, and I am sorry, but, if I don't get answers as the questions come up, it's hard to work our way through all the potential theories to get to the bottom of this."

"Whatever," he grumbled. "What possible question could you ask now?"

"I was wondering if you ever worked at the restaurant."

"Every once in a while, yes, when I was younger. I did that back home for a while."

"Back home?" she asked, in a sharp tone.

"Yes, in Alberta."

"Hang on a minute, are you saying your sister, Jillian's mother, or your sister Alice had a restaurant in Alberta?"

"Yes, we've been in the restaurant business for a very long time. Why is that a surprise?"

"I don't recall anybody mentioning that."

"What difference does it make? Every family has something that they gravitate toward," he stated, "and ours was the restaurant."

"So, a little mom-and-pop diner or what?"

"Alice's was definitely bigger than that," he replied. "She was fairly successful at it, but, then again, she also had more money to get there."

"More money? How did she manage that?"

"Our parents invested money in four restaurants and gave each of us one to run. Depending on how everybody handled their own place, depending on whether they came out doing okay or not, we each had a try at running a restaurant. So Alice did better and ended up with more money than most of us."

"So, your sister Alice, when still in Alberta ..."

"Yes?" he snapped. "Waiting for a question here."

"She was doing okay then?"

"It was before COVID, so she didn't have the same challenges in Alberta that she had here. Regardless, both of my sisters were more adept at running a restaurant, while the brothers, both Danny and I, weren't so interested in that, and it showed," he explained. "But I don't know what the restaurant part has to do with anything."

"Maybe nothing, but was anybody not getting any money they thought they should have gotten from the original wills, when the others were getting restaurants?"

"It's not an inheritance. It's not as if we each got a restaurant when our parents died. It was our life, our family business to have now, while our parents were still alive and well. The four of us kids getting those restaurants didn't all happen on the same day or anything," he added in exasperation. "This was over a period of many years—usually when each of us reached the age of twenty."

"Right," she noted. "So, did anybody think they should have gotten money doled out to them—or a restaurant—but didn't get something?"

"I'm sure there was the odd circumstance, probably," he suggested, his voice stiffening, "but that really didn't come into play."

"So, you say," she noted, "but someone always feels cheated in these things, leaving me to ask you, who would that have been in this case?"

"If there were such a person, I'm sure that some people would say that person would be me."

"And why is that?"

"Because I didn't get a restaurant or any early distribution of family money from my parents at all. At the time, even at twenty, I was doing very well with my own contracting business, so nobody thought I needed extra handouts. And I had spent enough time working at the restaurant in my teens to know that I was not cut out for that line of work and found my own passion instead. So my parents took over the restaurant supposedly intended for me. They just delayed their retirement until they found a suitable manager to run it."

"Which isn't the same thing, in my opinion, since that's almost like being penalized for being successful."

"That was part of the argument I used at the time. Just because I had some money didn't mean I couldn't use more. And just because I've been somewhat successful, that doesn't mean I'm not still a Burgon. The restaurants were to stay with a Burgon. Who knew that I wouldn't want one when I retired to oversee? So I'm not off the hook totally on that point because I still carry some resentment. However, my parents totally didn't see it that way."

"Interesting."

"Not really," he snapped, his tone sharp. "I didn't have a bone to pick with any of them. I have enough money."

"But you also stated you didn't have a ton of money."

"No, of course not," he said bitterly. "And given the state of the economy right now, we came here to help out, you know, and to see if we could do anything to build a life here. But don't worry, I'm not quite destitute yet."

"And Danny and his restaurant?" Doreen asked.

Zev chuckled. "Danny at least tried, which appeased our parents. His lazy wife even supposedly helped out. I doubt she was much help, and I bet it was mostly for show. Danny ended up selling his restaurant before a whole year had passed."

"You could have done that, then just sold the restaurant," Doreen pointed out.

"Nope. Not for me. Not even for one minute."

"What do you think about her husband?"

"Whose husband? If you're talking about Alice, I would say her husband is a lay-about who doesn't do anything," he snapped. "We don't get along, as I have told you already."

"Right," she noted. "So, how much money are we talking about, this early inheritance distribution?"

"I don't know precisely," he replied. "I think my parents bought all four restaurants for about one hundred thousand apiece."

"And you didn't get anything, whether restaurant or money?"

"No, I didn't get anything."

"I'm getting a headache just thinking about your family dynamics."

"Yeah, well, we've all been getting a headache from the family for a long time," he muttered.

"Do you think your sister in Alberta, Katie, was murdered for her inheritance?"

Zev sighed. "If she was, the only Burgon who stood to gain was Jillian. Well, and me."

"What about Katie's restaurant? Who got that one?"

"Jillian. She sold it, and that money went to pay the bills because apparently Katie wasn't doing as well as we all thought. So, a little bit of money was left from the sale, after paying off debts, but that went into the pot for Jillian."

"Okay, good," Doreen said. "How long was she with her fiancé?"

"They'd been together for a very long time, but I don't know how many years it was."

"So maybe since her mother was murdered?"

"Not exactly right then but not far off. Barry was a family friend at the time."

Doreen pondered that.

Zev added, "If you think Barry had anything to do with Katie's death, you're barking up the wrong tree. He was too young, just a teenager."

"I'm just trying to find anybody who had anything to do with anything."

"We've all racked our brains, and we haven't come up with anything in ten years. So I don't know what you think you can do," he muttered. "I should never have talked to you, but I was really worried about Jillian."

"And you should still be worried about Jillian," she shared. "Do you know if she and Barry had any issues?"

"You mean, as in breakup issues?" he asked. "No, I don't think so. As far as I'm concerned, there was none of that."

"Fine," she replied, noting Mack now held up his own phone and jiggled it. "Thanks for speaking to me. If I have any more questions, I'll call you."

Zev just groaned and disconnected.

Doreen looked over at Mack.

"I got called in on a case," he told her.

She gasped. "Another one?"

"Yes, but not a murder. I've got to go."

Doreen nodded. "I want to go home and go straight to bed anyway. I'm exhausted. My brain still wants to run around and do its thing, so I wonder just how much sleep I will get tonight."

"So you try to get some rest while it's running around, doing its thing, and, when it's done, you let me know what pops up." He drove her and her animals home. "Get some real food tonight, please."

"Will do," she muttered, as she clambered out of the truck, with her animals in tow, and they all walked inside her house with a wave goodbye to Mack. She grabbed a towel to try and dry furry feet before everyone took off to roam the house.

She hadn't been kidding. A hot bath and bed was about all she could manage tonight.

Chapter 22

DOREEN WOKE UP in the middle of the night and stared around the room. Mugs woke up and sniffed the air, but then he crashed back down again, completely unconcerned.

She relaxed into bed and murmured, "Now that is lovely. I'm so glad nothing is wrong. I don't know what got me so alert, but it just felt wrong."

She crashed soon afterward. When she woke up again during her usual morning hours, the case was running through her mind over and over again. She was missing something, and she knew it, but she didn't know what. She got up, grabbed her notepad, and started writing down the bits and pieces that she knew, and the bits and pieces that she didn't. Regardless, she still came up with no viable suspect—outside of Alice's husband. Then again, the husband had an alibi, according to Mack. Although he would talk to Randol again, that alibi would probably still hold up.

The fact that she disliked Randol didn't mean that he *didn't* have something to do with his wife's murder. Doreen wanted it to be Randol just because he hated animals and had threatened to shoot Mugs. Doreen always tried to be fair, except when people were killing people and were threatening to kill her animals. Then it wasn't about fair at all.

Groaning, she made herself some coffee and sat down in the living room with her notepad.

When Nan called her soon afterward, she asked her, "How are you doing, child?"

"Ah, everything on this case is going around in my head but not making sense. My head is spinning."

"You know what the answer for that is then."

"What's that?" she asked.

"You have to go back to the beginning. Forget all the hypotheses you have come up with. Forget about everything. Go back to the beginning and start fresh, as if you don't know anything, and I bet you'll come up with the answers." And, with that, Nan ended the call.

Doreen stared at her phone. "Easy for you to say, Nan."

But, in a way, her grandmother was right. Doreen had gone in multiple convoluted directions but had yet to come up with anything that worked. So far, nothing made any sense. Basically, she needed to eliminate everybody, and whoever was left had to somehow be the guilty party. And then it would be up to her at that point to prove it. Maybe that was an impossibility. She didn't know, but right now she wasn't getting anywhere. So why not try Nan's suggestion?

With Nan's advice in mind, Doreen went over to her laptop, opened up a blank page, and started with what she knew about the murder of Katie, Jillian's mother, from ten years ago in Alberta. Then Doreen followed that up with what she knew about the murder of Barry, Jillian's fiancé.

And finally she added the murder of Alice, Jillian's aunt. Doreen frowned. All were close to Jillian. With a shake of her head, Doreen went back to the first murder.

As she sat here thinking about it for a long time, writing off why it couldn't be each one of her usual suspects, Doreen realized, as she got to the end of the page, how she didn't really have very many choices left for suspects. And she didn't know how she'd done it, but somehow the person at the top of her list for Katie was at the top of the list for Barry and again for Alice.

So that one suspect must have been the killer of all three. But still, Doreen would have to prove it. No way Mack would just accept what she had to say if she didn't have something for him to go on, something for him to convince a courtroom and a jury. And, just in case she was wrong, she went back over her reasons for tossing out every other suspect, and it always came back to this one person.

But what she didn't have was the motive, and that was troublesome. As she sat here thinking about what she could do to figure it out, Jillian called her.

"Hey," she greeted Doreen, sniffing. "Any chance you can find out when my fiancé's body can be released?"

"Sure, I can do that for you, but I'm pretty sure they'll say it won't be soon."

First came silence, and then Jillian groaned. "Of course they will."

"It really depends on whether or not they have done all the tests they need to do," Doreen explained. "They will do their best to release him for burial as soon as they can."

"I hope so," she muttered. "I'm heading back to Alberta as soon as this nightmare is over."

"I'm sorry. I understand it's been a really rough time for you."

"It's been more than a rough time. All I do is cry and stare at the walls—oh, and answer your phone calls," she quipped on a dry note.

"Jillian, sometimes all I can do is ask questions and hope that I shake something loose."

"Yet you haven't shaken anything loose in my brain. I'm still confused, exhausted, and don't understand why anybody would want to murder such a beautiful man as Barry. He was a gentle soul," she muttered.

"Did you guys set a wedding date?"

"No, we didn't. We were, you know, waiting to confirm that this was where we wanted to be," she shared. "Of course, now I wish I had set a date."

"Of course," Doreen agreed. "Would you have invited your aunt?"

"Yeah, I would have invited them all. Family was important to me, and it still is."

"What about your uncle Zev? Would he move back with you?"

"I don't know. I'm not sure what his plans are," she replied. "We were really close, and then, when I hooked up with Barry, some of that closeness dissipated, which is normal and natural, I guess. However, when we had so much trouble in Alberta, we decided we needed to go somewhere else. Uncle Zev was the one who opted for Kelowna and suggested that we come along, since my Aunt Alice had the restaurant and would give me and Barry a job, and we could hit the ground running."

"And that was a really good plan," Doreen noted.

"I know. I know that. It's just so hard."

"I get it," Doreen said. "Anyway, let me contact the detective and see if we can get an answer for you. Actually I'll just contact the coroner myself. Give me a few minutes." She ended the call and phoned Elizabeth, sharing that she had just spoken to the family and that they were wondering when the body could be released.

"Give me a couple days, maybe even by tomorrow. I'll contact them directly, so they can make plans for the funeral."

"I think they're already deciding on the process." Doreen spoke with her for a few more minutes.

Then Elizabeth suggested, "Anytime you want to come down and have an in-depth look at what happens in my corner, you are welcome."

"I would love to," Doreen exclaimed.

"Really?" Elizabeth asked.

"Yes, I've never seen an autopsy, never seen the tools or anything. If nothing else, it might help me sort out some of the problems I have with these cold cases sometimes."

"I don't know how it can," Elizabeth replied, "but we can set it up in a week or two, if you want."

"Sure," Doreen said, "maybe when we get back from Vancouver."

"Vancouver?"

"Yeah, I've got to go down and sort out my ex's houses," she explained, with a sigh.

"Wow, at least you have houses to sort out." Elizabeth laughed. "That's … not a bad way to be left."

"No, it's not a bad way," Doreen conceded. "With most of the murder cases I've seen, they're all about gain, one way or the other. It's always about power, revenge, or love."

"*Nah*, I would say money is the biggest of them all," Elizabeth countered.

"I'm afraid you're right." Doreen sighed. "I wouldn't be

surprised if that's what this one is about too."

"Yeah, but they were just broken-down restaurants, right?" Elizabeth asked. "So where's the money in that?"

Doreen snorted. "And you also know that people would kill each other for a cup of coffee. It's all about priorities."

"If it isn't about money, what else could it be?"

Then it hit her. Doreen sat back and grinned. "Thank you very much, Elizabeth. You may have just solved it."

"Solved what?" she asked, with lively curiosity.

"Got to go." With that, Doreen ended the call with Elizabeth.

Doreen shook her head. She wondered if she had really gotten it so wrong right off the bat. She thought maybe she had, but once again she still had to have some answers for it all.

When her phone rang again, she didn't recognize the number. She sighed, picked up her phone, and answered it. It was Danny Burgon.

"I have the painting nearly done," he announced. "I think you should come and take a look and see if it's what you were wanting. I guess I'm worried that you won't like it."

"I'll be happy to come," she replied in a delighted tone. "Do you want me to bring the animals in case you need more pictures?"

"I would love to see them anyway," he stated in a mild tone. "So, sure, bring them along. When do you want to come?"

They set up to meet in a couple hours, and Doreen added, "I'm looking forward to it."

"I hope so."

Just enough nervousness filled his tone that she sighed.

"You don't do this very often, do you?"

"No, I sure don't," he admitted, with a snort. "Most people don't want to pay for commissioned work."

"I guess there can be a negative connotation on a commission too, isn't there?"

"Not really, most of us have had to do commissions in order to pay for bread and butter in our world," he explained, "but it's not always that easy. You have to do whatever it is that the client wants you to do, instead of what you want to do yourself."

By the time she got off the call, she was a little less struck by her current solution to the three murders problem. But it was still something she couldn't let go of. Letting it walk around in her mind, she got up and tried to turn her attention to some mundane chores, like putting on laundry and feeding the animals. She filled the time with tasks until she could leave to see the painting.

She also hadn't really heard about a party for Nan. She wasn't sure what Richie may have been planning or what Nan may want done.

By the time Doreen left for Danny's house, she was nervous, anxious, and excited. After a drive that seemed to take forever, she and the animals finally pulled into the driveway. As she got out, she was surprised to see Zev there.

He looked at her and shook his head. "Don't go bothering Danny now too. He didn't do anything. I don't know why I'm surprised you are here. It didn't take you long to show up on Danny's doorstep."

She smiled. "I've been dealing with him anyway on a portrait."

"Interesting," he muttered.

Doreen looked at the front of the house and found

Danny's wife inside, standing at a window, waving at Doreen with a big smile on her face. "That's the first time I've ever seen a smile from her."

Zev nodded. "She hasn't had a very happy life."

Doreen heard an odd note in his tone. "Is something between the two of you?"

"No, not anymore," he admitted. "There was originally, but she ended up marrying Danny instead."

"Ah, that's not an easy thing either."

"No, it sure isn't." He tried to smile, then looked at her and added, "It was a long time ago."

"Doesn't seem like it's died away."

"Doesn't matter. It's not as if I'll take away the wife of somebody who's in a wheelchair," he declared, with a shrug. "She made that decision a long time ago."

But even after that statement, Zev stood here and stared at the window for a shade too long.

Doreen sighed. "Still, if people are married and miserable, it's better to be divorced and happy, than to go through life just wishing you had done something different."

He stared at her, looked back at the window, and shrugged. "I don't think she would have me now."

"And why is that?"

"I don't have a fortune for her."

"She sure doesn't have a fortune here," Doreen pointed out.

He nodded. "But now they should get Alice's restaurant."

"What about Alice's husband?"

"No, he doesn't get the restaurant. I told you that, remember?"

"Right, just family. ... So, if Danny doesn't get the restaurant, or if he didn't want the restaurant, would it go to you?"

He looked at her and then slowly nodded. "I guess it would. Or maybe to Jillian, if she still wanted it."

"If you ran it, you could make a fortune off it, couldn't you?"

"I would hire my niece to run it," he said, followed by a laugh. "I think she could make a go of it. I doubt there's a fortune to be made though. Times are tough for restaurants right now."

"Is she that good?"

"Oh, you have absolutely no idea. She's very good and quite talented in the kitchen."

"What about her fiancé?"

"Much less so," he replied, "and it was a bone of contention between them. She wanted to be a chef, but he wanted to be their chef."

"Ah, do you think they would have made it?"

"No, I'm not so sure they would have in the long run," he shared. "My niece is fairly dominant, and he was much less so. But he did want to be top dog in the kitchen, and I think that would have broken them up in the end."

She nodded. "Do you think Jillian could have killed Barry?" Startled, Zev turned and glared at her. She went on. "You've had time to think about it," she pointed out, "and I know it's your niece, and you love her dearly, but it's just a question."

"What are you really asking me?"

"Do you think she could have done it?"

"*Could* she have? Yes. *Would* she have killed her own fiancé? No. She's not killer material."

"News flash," Doreen replied. "Everybody is killer material." When he looked at her, startled, Doreen explained, "There is always an instance where everybody will kill, so don't let yourself think that isn't true."

"Let me just repeat that I don't believe Jillian would do that."

"And you've never had your doubts over it?"

"No, never," he declared.

She nodded. "Good to know. Just in case, … watch your back." Startled, he stopped to frown at her, and she added, "You could be the only one standing between her and the restaurant now."

"Don't say that," he snapped. "Jillian would never do such a thing. Besides it's not coming to me. It should go to Danny."

"What about this one?" She pointed casually where the wife had been standing in the window. "Since her husband is also the only one standing between her and the restaurant, could she have done it?"

"She was not born a Burgon. So, she can't get a Burgon family restaurant," he stated once again, as he turned to look up at the window. Doreen twisted to look too. But the woman had disappeared. Zev shuddered. "I don't like the way your mind works."

"I'm sure you don't. Neither do I at times," she admitted. "Yet I can tell you that, more often than not, though everyone may not like what comes out of my mind, so often it proves to be correct," she murmured. "Just think about the people around you."

"Why do I have to do that?" he snapped. "Why should I?"

"Because somebody killed your sisters, both of them. The question is, who?"

"By that same reasoning," he pointed out, "I should also be a suspect."

She smiled brightly at him and replied, "Who said you aren't?" And, with that, she walked up to the front door.

Chapter 23

DOREEN WAS LET in by Danny's wife, who pointed down the hallway.

"He's in the studio. You can go back there on your own." As the animals passed her by, her lips curled.

Doreen nodded. "I guess you're on the same page with your brother-in-law."

She looked at her, startled. "What?" she asked, her gaze going outside, then back at her.

"Not that brother-in-law," Doreen clarified. "The husband of your murdered sister-in-law, Alice. Randol hates animals too."

She nodded. "That's right. He does. He was bitten as a child. To hide his fear, he tends to snap first," she explained, "though he's really not very dangerous. He looks rough, and he talks a big game, but he's really not that bad."

"Really?" Doreen asked, frowning at her.

She nodded. "He likes to give that impression, but he's really more of a teddy bear."

"And a blackmailer."

She snorted. "He's lazy as all get out," she muttered. "Alice really struggled with that. He always wanted money,

money, and more money."

"I think he still does, and I think he was there that night, looking for money."

"That would be him. They had some arrangement, but he wouldn't stick to it and was forever going back after more money."

"Would he have killed Alice for it?"

She stared at her and shook her head. "Oh, God no. That would be like killing the golden goose for him. Even now, I'm sure he's panicking."

"And the restaurant, shouldn't it come to your husband now, after Alice's death?"

"Maybe, though I don't really know. You can't really trust that woman either. She was a viper."

"Your sister-in-law? Alice?"

"Yeah." She nodded. "She was all about the business, all about money, all about everything except being nice."

"I'm sorry. That makes it tough if you don't have anyone you can count on, not even family."

"There is nobody for me," she stated, with a sharp look in Doreen's direction. "Nobody you can count on in this family. Just a word of warning."

"Got it," Doreen said, as she headed toward the studio. "You do realize nobody has anything good to say about you either."

The woman looked at her in astonishment and then shrugged. "I'm sure they don't, but the difference between me and them is that I really don't care." Then she turned and slammed the front door. Doreen quickly headed to the studio, and, as soon as she stepped inside, the animals raced over to say hi to the painter. He bent down as much as he could and cuddled them.

"You are truly blessed to have them," Danny said, with a bright smile.

"I know," she murmured. "They have been a blessing all around."

"And that's why I'm a little worried that I may not have done them justice." He frowned as he looked down at them. "It would really be hard to not have their personalities shine through."

"Let's see what you've got."

"It's not quite finished."

"I understand. Let me see anyway. … I doubt it's as bad as you seem to think it is."

"Maybe so, I don't know," he muttered. "I absolutely enjoyed doing it, but, … well, you'll just have to see what you think." Then he rolled over to where the canvas was and pulled back the cover.

Doreen gasped in shock and in absolute delight because he had captured the animals in a way that she hadn't even imagined possible.

Danny didn't even look at the canvas. He just watched her face. "You really do like it, don't you?"

"It's beautiful," she cried out, as she walked closer to study the details. He had literally captured Thaddeus standing on Mugs's head, as if he were king of the castle, and Goliath snuggled alongside Mugs. "You've done a fabulous job."

She heard the sigh in his voice. "Thank you. I've lost my confidence in my artwork."

"And why is that?"

"Because nobody likes it, and everybody, *every*body, tells me that I should just give it up."

"Oh, please don't," she replied, studying the picture.

"You really are gifted, and this? … This is fabulous." She laughed as she took in more and more of the details and the colors and whispered, "This is truly wonderful. Are you sure it's not done?"

"It's not quite finished yet, but I should have it done in another day or so."

"That would be lovely," she said, staring back at the portrait, "but, to me, it looks to be done already."

"No, it's not," he insisted, followed by a sigh. "I also wanted to ask, do you have any answers on my sister's murder?"

"No, I don't yet," she shared, "and you're about the only one who hasn't talked to me about it." He glanced at the door, and Doreen nodded. "Your wife's upset with me already."

"That's par for the course, and, when you poke your nose into the business around here, she can get pretty upset."

"I heard that she doesn't contribute very much."

"No, and I think she was always very disappointed that I wasn't part of the restaurant. I think maybe she saw herself as the hostess of the evening, you know, coming in every night, talking among the patrons, drifting her way through in fancy gowns," he described, followed by a laugh. "But the reality is so much different."

"Of course it is. Did you ever have anything to do with the restaurant?"

"Oh, I did early on. But, after my accident, not very much at all. I just hole up here and play with my paints."

She smiled and pointed a finger his way. "You need to get rid of that attitude very quickly. You aren't *playing with your paints* here," she declared, as she faced the portrait beside him. "You're creating a masterpiece. In fact, I should take this home right now. I'm worried about somebody ruining it before I can get it."

"That won't happen."

"Are you sure? You should know that I'm upsetting a lot of the family right now. I don't want anybody to see this, realize it's for me, then have them come in here and destroy it."

He stared at her in shock. "Oh, good God, that would break my heart."

"And mine," she added, with a long look at the painting. "And," she said, now staring at Danny, "while we're at it, … do you have any suspects in your head as to who would have killed your sister?"

"Her husband, for one."

"Why would you think that?"

"Because he's a greedy lowlife."

"And I understand your wife and Zev have also known each other a long time."

He snorted. "I'm surprised she didn't leave me for him years ago. He moved to Alberta after we were married, and it's only recently that he's come back to Kelowna. … I've wondered if it would start up again."

"Was there an actual affair?"

"Yeah, there sure was," he confirmed. "Just after my accident. I think she was planning on leaving me then, and Zev was upset about it. Anyway he took off without her, and I think that devastated her."

"I presume, in her mind, she didn't sign up for this," Doreen suggested, as she motioned at the wheelchair.

"No, in her world she didn't sign up for any of this. Neither did I. It's just silly fools like me who get caught up in a wheelchair and never amount to anything," he said sadly.

"Which, as we both know very well, is absolutely incorrect," Doreen declared, "because *this* is *not nothing*." She pointed at the portrait he had done for her and Nan.

He looked at it and smiled and asked, "Do you really think it's okay?"

"Oh, it's so much more than okay," she replied. "It's absolutely brilliant. A lot of people will see this."

"Will they though? Your grandmother lives in a retirement home, doesn't she?"

"Ah, you've heard about her, have you?"

"Of course. I searched for you on Google, and she came up as part of Doreen's Devils, or whatever the heck their name is," he shared, with a laugh.

"Doreen's Deputies. They are also devils for sure, but they're also very beloved," Doreen replied, "and they have been a big help trying to solve some of the cold cases that I've worked on."

"Of course, and anything that keeps that generation happy and engaged is amazing."

She smiled and nodded. "Now, how much longer do you really need, because I want to take this home with me today."

He looked at her. "Really?"

She nodded. "Really. I don't want to risk having anything happen to it."

He frowned at that.

She turned to him and added, "When three members of this family have already been murdered, I can only advise you to please take care of yourself."

He winced and nodded. "I did consider that already."

"And, if you did, who is it that you think would be the one to kill you?"

"I know my wife hates me," he said softly, "and that's a very hard thing to admit. Yet I don't think she would kill me."

"And yet, if the restaurant comes to you, and you are out of the picture …"

He nodded. "She might think it would go to her. However, it only goes to anyone born a Burgon."

"Even if she somehow got the restaurant, would that make her happy?"

"Only if she has somebody to run it."

"And who would that be?"

"Maybe my niece Jillian. I don't know. According to Zev, the girl is quite gifted."

"I've heard that," Doreen agreed. "The trouble is, I have too many suspects. And, of course, Zev's one of them."

He turned to her and asked, "Why?"

She shrugged. "He happened to be in place every time. He was in Alberta when your sister Katie was killed. I'm not saying he was at the restaurant the night your sister Alice was killed, but he was here in Kelowna."

"But he was there."

She turned slowly to face him. "He was?"

"He was. He stopped in, had an argument with Alice, and took off, but definitely some words were exchanged. Of course, it was earlier that day, not exactly the time she was killed." He frowned and added, "I'm not even sure which night it was now."

"Good to know," she muttered, staring at him. "That is something I don't think Zev has admitted to anybody."

"Nobody'll admit anything in a murder investigation, will they? They want to keep everything quiet and try to keep themselves out of the limelight."

Doreen nodded. "But, at some point, that doesn't work out so well."

"No, it sure doesn't." He smiled, looked over at the painting, and added, "The good news is, I had nothing to do with it. I can't even get out of the wheelchair for very long," he told her. "I have home care come in and help me three times a week—something else that my wife can't stand."

"It sounds as if a divorce would make you happier."

"It would make her happier. I don't have a whole lot to do with her anyway," he noted.

"So why don't you give her a divorce? Why don't you offer it to her? You can just let her off the hook," Doreen suggested, studying him. "Just think of how much painting you can do without all that interference."

He burst out laughing. "I'll consider it, though I don't know. I'm not sure I'm ready to be on my own."

"Nobody said you had to be on your own," Doreen pointed out. "And maybe you want to be part of the restaurant world again."

"No, I do not want to be part of the restaurant world," he stated. "I was part of the restaurant world before. How do you think I wound up in his wheelchair?"

She frowned at him and said, "Maybe you should tell me how you had that accident."

"It was Alice. We had an argument, and, as I turned to stride away, I swear to God, she pushed me, but I don't have any way to prove it," he admitted. "One minute I was walking away from her, and the next I was headed down the stairs to the storeroom and fell. Broke my back. Such a simple thing."

She stared at him for a long moment.

Danny nodded. "So, yeah, do I think she could have

been involved in killing someone? Heck yeah, but, since she's the one who was killed, maybe not."

"Oh Lord," Doreen muttered. "The tangled webs we weave."

"I know," he acknowledged. "Believe me that I've spent a lot of time thinking about it, wondering if she did it on purpose. Nobody else was around, so it was her or no one," he shared. "I just don't have any way to prove it."

"I'm so sorry. That's not how we want life to be."

He laughed. "No, you may not want it to be that way, but it seems to be the way life always is."

"No, not always," she countered. "Did Alice suggest to your wife that she marry you?"

"Yes, she did, but I think that was because Alice convinced my wife that she was also supposed to get some of the restaurant money, or maybe Alice was just trying to lock me up with somebody."

"I don't understand."

"It's just old family stuff."

"It may be just old family stuff, but sometimes the same old stuff comes back around with some really ugly updates."

He looked at her and then slowly nodded. "You could be right, but I would hate to think that what happened to me has anything to do with any of this."

"But I won't know if you don't tell me these things," Doreen pointed out, frowning at him. "So, what happened to you? Obviously you fell down the stairs, but do you really think Alice did it on purpose?"

"In my mind, and I've gone over it a million times," he explained, "that's the only conclusion I can come up with."

"Was it an accident? Was Alice sorry afterward?"

"She's always denied having anything to do with it."

"So, you did talk to her about it?"

"I did."

"And you're sure nobody else was at the restaurant at the time?"

"Nobody else was at the restaurant," he confirmed. "It was just her. From her viewpoint, I fell because I was angry. I tripped and fell down the stairs, and she didn't find me for a while. Apparently, whether I believe that or not, I don't know, but the bottom line is, I ended up in a wheelchair."

"And you were already married, right?"

"Yes."

She sighed. "I'm so sorry."

"That's okay."

"So, I've got another question for you," she began, "and this one is a little bit uglier."

He stared at her. "How can you look so nice and have so many ugly questions?" he muttered.

"Would your wife have killed your sister Alice?"

"Why?" he asked, looking at her in surprise. "What would that possibly gain her?"

"If Alice was responsible for putting you in a wheelchair, maybe your wife finally decided to get revenge."

"But why now? Why all these years later? What would it get her now? I mean, she's had lots of time to do it. There wouldn't have been any particular reason to do it now. It would make more sense for my wife to kill me, if she thinks she's getting some money out of Alice's restaurant."

Doreen frowned. "Maybe, maybe not," Doreen conceded, with a nod. "Still, I had to ask."

"And I appreciate your thinking about it," he replied. "Yet the more I think about it, maybe you're right. Maybe it is time for a divorce."

"It's certainly worth some honest consideration, though, if she wants to hook up with Zev again, they may be looking at going back to Alberta after this."

"Maybe," he said, looking away from her. "I was wondering about getting my niece Jillian to run the restaurant."

"And that could be a good idea too. However, it also would be very painful for her, as she just lost her partner there as well."

"I wasn't thinking about that, but you're right. It would be rough, wouldn't it?"

"Probably rougher than anybody would really want to think about," Doreen replied, "but you'll have to look at your options. Of course you have to get through Alice's will to see if you even end up with it. Maybe it goes to both you and Zev."

Danny shook his head. "Zev made that decision long ago. So I don't think Alice had a choice to give it to anybody else but me, unless she gave it directly to Jillian."

"No matter who gets it, you may want to consider taking good care of yourself over the next few days. Somebody is pretty interested in the Burgon family. I've been told the restaurants are to stay in the Burgon family line, but is there any scenario where it could go to your wife in the case of your demise?"

He froze. "You really, *really* don't mind saying awful things, do you?"

"No," she admitted, "but I also really, *really* love your artwork, and I would absolutely hate it if something happened to you."

"Good God," he whispered, stars in his eyes. "You really do like it, don't you?"

"I do," she declared. "How can you not look at that and

see the talent just coming out of your pores?"

"Probably because I've spent a lifetime not believing I had any talent," he replied, with a self-deprecating chuckle.

"Now you've got a chance to change that," she reminded him.

"Are you sure you want to take it right now?" he asked again.

"I'm sure," she stated. "I can't imagine what it is you think you could do to make it better. This is absolutely amazing."

"Let me just … No. It is finished. I just keep thinking I can improve it and was so worried you wouldn't like it."

"No, you can't improve it." She pulled out her purse and handed him five crisp one-hundred-dollar bills.

"No, no, no," he said. "The total was five hundred, and you already gave me half, remember?"

"I do remember," she confirmed, "but I'm paying you five hundred on top of the deposit, and this painting is likely worth far more than that."

"Seriously?" He stared at her in shock.

"Yes, seriously."

He looked down at the money, then up at her, and one of the most incredibly beautiful smiles crossed his face. "Thank you. It's not even about the money. It's just the fact that you are willing to pay more for my work."

"I would pay a lot more now that I know how amazing you are. And, rest assured, I'll be telling people about you. So, whether you like to do commissions or not, you better get ready."

He laughed at that. "Come on. I'll show you out." She gently picked up the painting, and Danny rolled with her toward the door. The animals stayed awkwardly at her side, yet kept getting in the way of his wheels.

"They really aren't used to wheelchairs, are they?" Danny asked.

"You would think they would be since we're down at the home all the time, but they seem to be all over you for some reason," She frowned, then looked at him. "They're very protective of people they know and love."

He looked at her, surprised, then looked down at them. "I'm fine." Yet a frown crossed his face. "I promise that I'll keep your warning in mind."

She nodded. "You do that, please."

And, with that, she finally managed to get her wiggling crew out to the vehicle, where she very gently put the canvas on the back seat and insisted that all the animals ride in the front seat. She was paranoid that anything would happen to the painting.

With a wave, she headed back out and drove very carefully home. As soon as she got there, she took the canvas out of the back seat, carried it into the kitchen, and propped it up on the kitchen table, then immediately tried a different location. Her concern was that Thaddeus might peck at it.

She spied a couple nails in the walls in the living room that she hadn't ever bothered to pull out after removing the other paintings located here. So she hung this painting on one of those. At least it was out of everybody's reach. There she stood and admired it for a few minutes, then took out her camera and snapped several photos, sending one to Mack.

He called her a little bit later and asked, "What is that?"

"Oh my gosh," she cried out, "you won't believe it. That is Nan's birthday present. It's absolutely perfect. It's such a ..." And she told him all about it.

"That is fabulous," Mack agreed, "and what an amazing and lovely gift."

"I thought so too. As you know, I'm still really new to this whole gift-giving thing. I had no idea what to do, and then … I even surprised myself with this idea."

He burst out laughing. "You continuously surprise me with how well you're doing, so give yourself credit. That is really nice, and I can't wait to see it in person."

"I'm really worried about him too."

"Who? The artist? Why is that?"

"Because Alice's restaurant may now be his. In my understanding, it can't be passed down to Alice's husband because it has to stay in the family, in the Burgon bloodline family. The husband was already getting money every month from Alice, so harming her would be killing his golden goose. Then there is Danny's wife, who is extremely unhappy about everything, and she apparently had a prior history of cheating on him with his own brother, none other than Jillian's uncle Zev."

"Good God," Mack muttered. "Why does everything have to be so convoluted?"

"It's just family issues," she noted, "and family is messy."

He burst out laughing. "You're right. Family is messy," he confirmed. "Look. You work it out in your head, and I'll come by—hopefully in another forty minutes, if I can get out of this place. We can talk then."

"Good enough," she said. "That's two people whom I've now warned to stay safe, and one of them was more or less just left …"

Mack interrupted her, "Hang on. I've got to call you back." And he ended the call.

She groaned and waited, but, when he didn't get back to

her very quickly, she wasn't sure what was going on. She just hoped that it wasn't anything bad again. She kept admiring the painting, absolutely loving it. Before too long, she realized that she had to hide it before Nan accidentally saw it before her birthday. So, with that in her mind, Doreen picked it up and carried it upstairs to her bedroom, where she hid it in the closet.

Even as she was coming downstairs, Nan called. "I've decided to have a birthday party," she announced. "I didn't want anybody to plan a surprise party, so I've just decided we'll have a party."

Doreen laughed. "That sounds good. When and where and who?"

"Everybody," she declared, "at least everybody here, plus you and Mack, of course. I don't know about anybody else," Nan added, "but that seems to be enough people already."

"It's definitely a lot of people," Doreen agreed, with a smile. "But it's only enough people if it's enough for you."

"It's enough," Nan stated, with a snort. "The last thing I want is a big party, with all of them fussing over me."

"You'll get it anyway."

"Maybe so. Anyway, it'll be in two days, if that's okay."

"You left that up to the last minute."

"No, I didn't," she declared. "I just didn't want anybody making a fuss."

"Or you decided that nobody would make a fuss, so you chose to take the reins in your own hands and do it yourself?"

Nan went silent for a moment, then muttered, "Maybe, but I won't admit to that now. Anyway, please come."

"Of course I'll come," Doreen stated. "I only just now picked up your birthday gift."

"What did you get me?" she cried out.

"Ha, I'm not telling you. You'll find out on your birthday and not one moment before."

"Oh, that's just mean. That is just mean, child."

Doreen chuckled. "Nope, it's not mean," she argued. "It's all about anticipation." And, with that, she ended the call.

She turned to her animals. "Now, back to the case. My question is, *Who will be next?*"

They all froze, and she nodded. "You know somebody will be. The only question is who."

She had two in mind, but what she didn't know was whether there would be a third, and the third one she needed to worry about because, honestly, the third one was her.

Chapter 24

GETTING INTO BED that night, Doreen had to admit her nerves were wearing on her. She had to remind herself that she could easily be that next victim. And, with that worrisome thought in mind, she double-checked the security system, then wrote Mack a handwritten note, just in case. The fact that she was even doing this was silly.

She groaned, knowing how angry he would be if he found her the next morning. So, she phoned him, and when there wasn't an answer, she phoned the captain.

The captain answered and explained, "We've got an incident downtown. That's where he is."

"Okay. Not in the restaurant district at all, was it?"

"It is actually. A break-in at that Rocking Horse restaurant."

"Why was Mack sent?"

"He just happened to be on the roster," the captain noted. "Don't worry. Everybody is pitching in because we're so short-staffed."

"And because it was that location."

"Of course."

"I still think there's likely to be another murder."

"For what though?" he asked in confusion. "The place has shut down. Nobody was there working, so it's not as if anybody will be hurting anything."

"Maybe not."

"Doreen, what are you thinking?" he asked in a warning tone.

"I don't really want to say, just in case it sounds foolish."

"And, if you sound foolish, you know that I'll tell you."

"I've already warned two people about being the next victims."

"Good God," he muttered. "What do you mean, the next victims?"

"I believe two other people in this scenario could end up dead," she replied, "and I suspect it will be sooner than later."

"And who are these two?"

After she quickly explained the two, he took a moment to write down the information.

Doreen sighed. "There is a third possible victim as well."

"So, who is the third potential victim?" When she hesitated, he growled. "*Doreen*," and there was that all-too-familiar warning in his tone.

"Me," she admitted.

"Oh boy," he muttered. "You're thinking that one of them is coming after you?"

"Yep, I sure am," she said.

"I'm calling Mack. You stay right where you are and keep your doors locked."

"Yeah, that's why I was trying to get a hold of him. ... He'll be pretty mad at me."

"Ya think?" the captain roared into the phone. "Don't you move." And, with that, he ended the call.

When Mack called her a minute later, he yelled, "What the heck?"

"I'm fine," she said. "I'm totally fine."

"The captain doesn't seem to think that you'll stay that way."

"I may have given him the wrong impression."

"I don't think so," Mack growled in that same warning tone that the captain had just used. "I got a bit of a garbled message from him."

"Yeah, the whole mess is garbled anyway," she noted, "but I did warn some people that they could be next, and then realized that, if I'm right, I could be on that list as well."

"Jesus," he snapped. "I'm on the way."

"You didn't want to work that case anyway?"

"No, I didn't," he admitted, "but neither do I want to have nightmares about somebody coming after you again. Just tell me that you're locked in?"

"I'm locked in. It's fine."

"Really? We've seen any number of people get around security systems, and yours isn't as good as I would like it to be. I swear to God, we'll fix that after this."

"As soon as I get money."

He snapped, "You've got money." Doreen heard his thumping footsteps audible in the background. "We're fixing it no matter what."

She smiled. "So, you're coming?"

"Yes, I'm coming, but you knew I would be."

"No, I didn't know you would be," she argued. "I've been trying to get a hold of you for a while."

"I know. I'm sorry. It's been crazy. Is that why you've been calling me?"

"Yes."

"I'm already on the way."

"Good. … By the way, when you drive up, keep an eye out."

"For what?"

"For somebody, anybody."

"You want to tell me who?"

"No, it will probably be better if you just come."

"I'm already in the vehicle," he snapped, his tone deepening with both fear and anger. "But if you don't tell me what I'm walking into …"

"I don't know what you're walking into," she stated. "That's why I'm warning you ahead of time." It made perfect sense to her, but, to him, it seemed as if she was just trying to irritate him. "I'm really not, you know."

"Not what?" he roared.

"Trying to irritate you."

"You could have fooled me," he snapped, "because, honest to God, it seems as if that's exactly what you're doing."

"I'm not," she snapped back. "I'm really not."

"Good, I'm glad to hear that," he yelled, "because you're not making any sense."

"Where are you now?" she asked, as she walked around her bedroom, looking out the window.

"What difference does it make?" he asked. "I'm on the way to you."

"I just wondered how long until you get here."

"You're really worried, aren't you?"

"Maybe. … It just hit me."

"Are you okay? Are you sure?"

"Yes, I'm sure. Anyway, I'll wait until you get here."

"No, you'll stay on the phone."

She looked out the window and could have sworn she saw a shadow walking by the creek. "Looks as if people are out on the creek," she muttered.

"It is 11:30 at night, Doreen. There shouldn't be anybody down at the creek."

"Yeah, but it looks to me as if people *are* at the creek."

"You mean, having a party?" he asked hopefully.

"I don't think so."

"Of course not," he muttered. "Doreen, you sure do know how to get a fire lit under people."

"We just weren't getting anywhere," she muttered.

"I know we weren't getting anywhere, but that doesn't mean you nudge people in order to get things to happen."

"But, if I don't do that, nothing seems to go anywhere."

He groaned. "We'll talk about it when I get there."

"Probably not," she said cheerfully. "Chances are, you'll be a little busy."

"Do you see somebody?"

"No, not yet. I'm thinking it won't be long."

"For crying out loud," he muttered, "why won't you tell me who?"

"Because I don't want to put a jinx on it."

"A jinx?" he repeated. "You've got me racing toward you at warp speed because you're thinking that you'll get attacked, yet you won't tell me who to look for?"

"No, because I'm really not sure."

"Yes, you are. You're sure, and you know it. You're just hoping you're wrong."

She sighed loudly. "I just really don't like it when people act like jerks."

"Ya think?" he snapped. "But the fact is that they're mean, and they will still be problems. You can't fix that."

"I know. I was just trying to fix some things before it all blew up."

"Fixing some things often means everything else goes to pot."

"Yeah, ... probably so," she muttered. Just then the shadow became visible, creeping up along the trees. "How far out are you?"

"I'm coming very quickly, maybe about four minutes."

"*Hmm.* Yeah, you should meet him just right then."

"Are you telling me that he's out there?"

"Somebody coming up along the tree line from the river," she shared.

"How did they find out where you live?"

"It's not that hard. We're even on the blooming tour bus for the gardening and tourist spots now, remember?"

"Right," he noted bitterly. "How could I possibly forget that detail?"

"The shadow has just detached from the back," she added, striving for disinterest, aware that her heart was slamming against her chest. "And he's coming up to the front, so maybe turn off your engine lights and sneak up the driveway."

"Good God," he muttered, but he did just as she asked. "Done."

"Now, he should be checking out the front door."

"You put the security on?" he asked.

"Yes, I did, but as you mentioned,"—she sighed—"he's inside now."

Mack sighed. "I'm right at the house, and I'm racing inside."

"Yeah, good luck with that. I'm about to head downstairs, and I'll meet you at the front door."

"You stay where you are, for crying out loud," he muttered. "You just said somebody entered your house."

"Yep, they sure did, and they won't make it easy on us."

"They'll never make it easy on us, honey. I know you want to believe in people, but, at the end of the day, they are really just trying to save themselves."

"I know. … I was really hoping I was wrong."

"No, you thought you were right the whole time," he muttered, "and, one of these days, we'll have to talk about you sharing that information with me *before* we get to this point."

"You wouldn't believe me without any proof," she replied in a reasonable tone. "I had to get you proof somehow."

He groaned. "Where are you?" he whispered.

"At the top of the stairs," she whispered back.

"I'm at the bottom of the stairs, and I don't see anybody."

"No, but you know the security was off, right?"

"Yep, it was off," he confirmed in a very soft whisper.

"I'm coming down the stairs, so I'm hanging up now."

She quickly disconnected from the phone and crept down the stairs, and there was Mack—big, solid, steady Mack at the bottom of the stairs. She reached out a hand to grab his, then she smiled at him and whispered, "Kitchen."

"Why?" He raised an eyebrow, and they tiptoed into the kitchen.

She held Mugs back and then turned on the big overhead light.

And there before them was Uncle Zev. He stared at her in shock, then turned to look at Mack and frowned.

"Did you get into the wrong house somehow?" Mack

asked, crossing his arms over his chest.

Doreen looked at him. "I'm so sorry, Zev. I so hoped it wasn't you. I really did."

"I don't know what you're talking about," he replied stiffly. "You weren't sharing any information, so I just couldn't resist. I had to come in and see."

"Of course you did," she said, with a smile, and then pointed to his side. "So, there doesn't happen to be a kitchen knife in your pocket, does there?"

He paled ever-so-slightly.

She nodded. "I'm afraid I'll have to ask you to put that down. I'm not really interested in facing off against someone wielding a kitchen knife."

"How did you know?" he asked, staring at her.

"Because of all the reasons for you to do this, it was the motive that got me. I just couldn't figure it out. But then, Danny, your painter sibling, more or less confirmed what I was dealing with."

"What are you talking about? He's a useless painter, and what's that got to do with anything?"

"He's a very talented artist," she countered, "but he pointed out how his wife really wanted to be with you, but, with you going back to Alberta, that wouldn't happen."

"You think she killed everybody?" Zev asked, staring at her.

But Doreen caught that gleam in his eyes. "No, I'm pretty sure I know exactly who killed whom. I'm still a little murky on motive, but that's okay. I'm sure the cops will figure it out."

"I didn't have anything to do with that," he pointed out.

"Yes, you did," she stated. "Not only did you kill Jillian's mother ten years ago, but you also killed her fiancé, Barry."

He blanched. "What?"

"Yeah, and then you killed Alice, your other sister. I'm also pretty sure you're about to make a deal with your brother, Danny, for the restaurant, maybe even buy it, since they have no family for it to go to afterward. So, this way it could become your niece's, but here's the best part, right, Zev? She's not your niece, is she?"

He was shocked into silence.

Mack turned and looked at her and asked, "What?"

"Jillian's his biological daughter," Doreen stated. "You must have had some agreement in place, even after all these years, to never tell Jillian that you were her biological father."

Zev shrugged. "Katie wanted children but couldn't have any. My long-term girlfriend was pregnant but didn't want to keep the baby. She was much younger than me and wasn't ready to settle down. So I made a deal with her and with Katie, and we agreed to a private adoption. Part of the terms were that Jillian could never know the truth. But Katie wanted to break that agreement. I couldn't let her tell Jillian. My daughter would hate me. So I did what I had to do. And now, when Barry and Jillian's long friendship developed into an engagement, I realized that I would lose her to Barry, who would take her away from me."

Doreen sighed. "They were going somewhere else, weren't they? Things weren't going that well here in Kelowna. Jillian wanted to stay, but Barry didn't. Yet Jillian was in love with Barry, and she would have gone with him. You would have lost her, even after you spent all these years staying nearby to remain in Jillian's life. You didn't want to lose her."

Zev stated, "She is everything to me. You don't understand."

"I do understand because it's all about family." She turned to Mack and added, "As we know all too well, families are messy."

"So messy," Mack agreed, with a sigh. "Did you really have to kill them though?"

Zev stared at Mack. "Sometimes it's the only option, when nobody would listen to reason."

"Maybe nobody would listen to reason," Doreen acknowledged, "but generally nobody thinks to commit murder afterward."

He stared at her, and, instead of a knife, he pulled out a small snub-nose revolver.

She sighed again. "Of course. That makes sense, doesn't it? You can't knife me to death or it'll just link my murder instantly to Barry's and Alice's and even Katie's, right?"

"It would. I'm so sorry." He looked at Mack. "I'm sorry for you too because I can't let either of you live."

Doreen snorted. "I'm afraid you'll be the one who's sorry." She looked behind him where Thaddeus was now wide awake on the kitchen table, and she asked, "Right, Thaddeus?"

Zev turned around, expecting somebody to come up behind him, just as Thaddeus flew into his face, beating his wings at him. Mack moved forward as well. And Goliath was already there, jumping onto Zev's shoulders, letting his weight carry him down the man's chest, the cat's claws digging deep. Meanwhile, not to be outdone, Mugs hit Zev in the back of the knee, and he fell like a huge tree and landed on the kitchen floor. Mack quickly took control of the gun and secured Zev on the floor.

She looked at Mack and nodded. "Families are messy."

He burst into laughter, then asked, "You knew, didn't you?"

"Yeah, I knew," she muttered. "I really hoped I was wrong, but I wasn't." With a smile, she asked, "Now can we plan that Vancouver trip? I really need a holiday."

Epilogue

NAN'S BIRTHDAY PARTY at Rosemoor the week before had been wonderful. Mack had driven to Doreen's house to retrieve Nan's special birthday gift. Mack had placed it carefully in his truck bed before peeking under the wrapping. His face had been wonderful to see as had been his whistle reaction. "Wow. She's going to love this."

And she had. So had everyone else. It had given Doreen such joy to see her grandmother's face. She loved her furry and feathered family as much as she did.

Now however the weekend and the party were already a warm memory and the long drive to Vancouver was almost over. He pulled up into the long fancy driveway, staring in shock at Doreen's former home.

"I know," Doreen muttered. "Even looking at it now, it's hard to believe I lived here for so many years."

"And yet it wasn't your home."

"Right," she agreed, giving him a bright smile. "It really wasn't. It was a cage, but it's still hard to go back in time and face how long it was and what my life was like here."

Mack just waited in the truck as she dealt with all these memories, with all these emotions.

Finally she shrugged. "It's fine." She opened the passenger door and stepped out. "I can't believe we're here. It was a decently long drive."

"You were looking at flying down," he reminded her. "Then changed your mind."

She nodded and smiled. "If we flew down, then we couldn't have brought the animals." She let Mugs out. He raced around, sniffing.

Mack smiled. "I guess this was home for him too, wasn't it?"

"He certainly spent some years of his life here, yes," she agreed, "but it's not as if he cares. If he's with us, that's what's important."

And, sure enough, even as Goliath got out, he sat right next to the tire and stared, as if not believing what kind of place they had brought him to.

"What's the matter, Goliath?" she asked. "I would have thought this would be right up your alley," she said, with a snicker. "After all, it is fit for a king."

Mack shook his head. "It really is, isn't it? Good God."

Another vehicle pulled up behind them, and Mack turned and smiled as Nick Moreau got out.

Nick took one look and whistled.

"*Right*," she muttered. Still, she walked over and gave him a hug.

"Hey, my almost sister-in-law. How're you doing?"

"Since we stopped at Merritt and had lunch together," she shared, with a chuckle, "I think I'm doing just fine."

"Good." Nick nodded. "I wasn't sure how this trip would go for you."

"I'm fine. Besides, I brought Mack for support."

Mack chuckled. "That's me. I'm just here for support."

"That's a good thing too," Nick noted, "because, on the way down, I did get a call from the Vancouver police."

"Really?" she asked, turning to him. "What about?"

"Apparently you had some break-ins in the garden area. They couldn't find any damage to the house or any entry points, but the greenhouse was broken into."

She stopped and stared at him. "Seriously? Drat. That was my little corner," she muttered, her heart sinking. "Wow, I hadn't really expected to feel that."

"Hey, it's okay," Nick told her, patting her shoulder. "Let's take you into the house, and we can look around while we're here. The police do want me to contact them about it as soon as we have some answers for them."

"Answers for them?" she asked, turning to stare at him. "How are we supposed to have answers for them?"

He chuckled. "It's vandalism, and it's an empty house. I'm pretty sure they aren't too bothered."

"Right," she muttered, raising both hands. "Why would they care?"

"You have to understand," Nick explained, "that this is a massive city down here and that you are in a very wealthy area to boot. So they do want to touch base at least."

She looked back at the palatial mansion. She slowly walked up to the front door. "It still doesn't feel real."

"Of course not," Nick agreed. "How long has it been?"

"I stayed nearby for a few months before I moved to Kelowna. So it may be more than a year now since I was booted out of this house," she muttered.

Nick nodded. "And look at how much your life has changed."

At that, Mack put a gentle hand on her shoulders. "Do you want to go in alone?"

She faced him and frowned. "Heck no," she muttered. "I still half expect Mathew to jump out of the woodwork at me."

"Even though he's dead and gone?"

"He may be dead and gone, but some things never die," she declared. "I was a ghost of the person you know now while I was in this house, and I really don't want to go back to that timid existence."

"And you won't," he declared cheerfully. "We're here to take care of the business end of what we have to deal with here. That's it. And, if you want to keep anything, we brought the truck, so you can take whatever you want back with you."

Thaddeus poked his head out from under her hair and gave a massive whistle.

"*Right*," she quipped. "Could have been yours too, you know," she told him and then laughed. "No, it couldn't. Mathew would never have allowed a bird in the house. Poor Mugs had a hard-enough time here."

"Why?"

"He had to be perfectly groomed all the time. The maids were instructed to wash his feet each time he came inside from the yard. No jumping around or onto people. He was shut up in a room when we had guests over. No begging for food at the table. No treats, except for those the staff and I snuck over to him. And, if he so much as passed wind, believe me that Mathew had him kicked out of the room immediately."

Mack chuckled. "Mugs is much better off where he is now. It's not as if a dog can control that."

"No, but I've got to tell you that it seemed as if Mugs had this instinctive knack for doing it on purpose, whenever

Mathew showed up."

"Maybe it was his way of getting kicked out, so he didn't have to deal with Mathew," Nick suggested, chuckling. He handed over the keys. "I'll let you do the honors."

She stared down at them, made a face, and then turned to the front door. Putting the key in, she unlocked it. Pushing it open, she stepped in cautiously. Mugs raced past her, Goliath on his heels, and went streaming down the hallway. He knew exactly where to go. "He's heading for the kitchen," Doreen shared, "in case you are wondering."

"He's not really expecting there to be food, is he?" Nick asked.

"There was always a stash of treats for him in one of the bottom drawers," she explained, as she headed in that direction.

She knew that the others were more or less following her, but their gazes were shocked as they stared around. She turned to them and admitted, "I know. It's a little over-the-top."

"A little?" Mack repeated, staring at her. "This is how you lived?"

"No, this is how I was caged, remember? Language is everything."

He smiled at her. "You know ..."

"Don't even say it," she muttered. "If I wanted this life, I would have stayed. I don't want it, don't want anything to do with it."

In the kitchen, she headed to the cupboard that was always full of Mugs's treats. She opened it, and, sure enough, dog treats were right there. "I'm surprised they didn't get rid of these."

She pulled out a few and tossed a couple on the floor for

him. He sat down and dug in. Goliath sat beside him, sniffing every once in a while, wondering what the heck he was chewing on but completely disinterested.

Catching sight of the greenhouse out the kitchen window, Doreen walked over to the ten-foot-tall double French doors and pushed them open, stepping outside into the fresh air.

Seeing the damage on one side, she cried out and raced over toward it. "Why would they damage the greenhouse?" she asked in shock.

"Depending on who it was and why," Nick suggested, coming up behind her, "it could have just been maliciousness. A lot of people just want to destroy things."

"But that's so sad," she whispered, as she stepped farther into the greenhouse and looked around. "It's such a beautiful space."

"This is a greenhouse?" Mack asked from behind her. "No way. This is huge."

She sighed. "I guess most people here would call it a conservatory."

"Yeah, ya think?" he muttered, clearly astonished.

It was obvious to Doreen that he was really struggling with what she had as her former home. She added, "Remember that none of this even matters to me."

"I'm working on remembering that," he conceded, "but I have to admit, … it's a shock."

Still, it wasn't anything that she wanted him to feel bad about. As she walked through the greenhouse, conservatory, or whatever Mack wanted to call it, she looked around, and her heart broke to see the damage. It was all fixable, yet it was senseless, and there was no need to hurt plants like this. She sighed. "We certainly have to put this to rights before we can sell it," she muttered.

Nick looked over at her. "Do you think it'll make a difference?"

"A conservatory like this should be in its prime," she stated, "and obviously it's not."

"That's true," he agreed. "Depending on how much it costs, it is something to take into consideration."

"I would like it brought back to the way that it was meant to be," she explained. "This was my space, Nick."

"And maybe that's why it was damaged," he suggested, turning to her.

She stared at him in surprise. "If it was, … that would imply it was somebody who knew me." She frowned, shaking her head. "I don't even know anybody here anymore." She looked around and sighed. "It is sad, but …" Then she walked over to where the worst of the damage was, planted her hands on her hips, and stared.

Mack came up behind her. "Problems?" he asked her.

She turned to him. "I had Vidalia onions here. I kept them growing all year-round, so we always had fresh onions. I know it sounds silly, … but it was just one thing that I could do myself, and it was always a fun hobby."

"Okay," Mack replied. "So, what's the problem?"

"This is where the worst damage is, and it's this particular bed, and that makes no sense."

"Why not?" he asked.

She frowned, then looked at him, and her eyes lit up, as a tickle of amusement slipped through her. "On the other hand," she began, "I get that this is not exactly a *case*-case, right?"

"No, not a case, just vandalism."

"But maybe," she began, chuckling again.

"What is it that's making you laugh about this?" Mack asked, perplexed.

She snickered. "*Vandals in the Vidalias.*"

"Hopefully that's all that is going on here," Mack noted.

And then Doreen looked around the bed again, gasping as she pointed. "Maybe not."

He turned, and there—sticking out the far end of the garden bed—was something that didn't belong there. He leaned forward to get a better look.

She whispered, "Is that a nose?"

He frowned, turned back to her, with his gaze finally going to Nick, and Mack nodded.

"Yes, it is."

This concludes Book 4 of Lovely Lethal Gardens Rewind: Weapon in the Watermelon.

Read about Vandals in the Vidalias: Lovely Lethal Gardens Rewind, Book 5

Lovely Lethal Gardens Rewind: Vandals in the Vidalias (Book 5)

Doreen eagerly anticipates her escape to the coast, leaving behind the wintery blues of Kelowna. However, the trip means returning to her old home—back when she was married to Mathew—stirring up a whirlwind of memories. She hopes for a peaceful journey, but, as soon as she steps into the conservatory, she realizes her hobby has unexpectedly followed her here.

Mack takes a few days off work to assist Doreen in sorting through Mathew's belongings, aware of the emotional challenges she faces when revisiting her former life. His curiosity about her past is piqued, yet what he discovers is both unsettling and intriguing.

Amid this visit, a perplexing mystery unfolds. Why is a victim in the Vidalia patch, Doreen's cherished garden bed? Could this be connected to Doreen herself? Or is she just unlucky again—or rather is she in the right place at the right time … again?

Find Vandals in the Vidalias here!
To find out more visit Dale Mayer's website.
https://geni.us/DMSVandals

Author's Note

Thank you for reading Weapon in the Watermelon: Lovely Lethal Gardens Rewind, Book 4! If you enjoyed the book, please take a moment and leave a short review.

Dear reader,

I love to hear from readers, and you can contact me at my website: www.dalemayer.com or at my Facebook author page. To be informed of new releases and special offers, sign up for my newsletter or follow me on BookBub. And if you are interested in joining Dale Mayer's Reader Group, here is the Facebook sign up page.
http://geni.us/DaleMayerFBGroup

Cheers,
Dale Mayer

About the Author

Dale Mayer is a *USA Today* best-selling author, best known for her SEALs military romances, her Psychic Visions series, and her Lovely Lethal Garden cozy series. Her contemporary romances are raw and full of passion and emotion (Broken But … Mending, Hathaway House series). Her thrillers will keep you guessing (Kate Morgan, By Death series), and her romantic comedies will keep you giggling (*It's a Dog's Life*, a stand-alone novella; and the Broken Protocols series, starring Charming Marvin, the cat).

Dale honors the stories that come to her—and some of them are crazy, break all the rules and cross multiple genres!

To go with her fiction, she also writes nonfiction in many different fields, with books available on résumé writing, companion gardening, and the US mortgage system. All her books are available in print and ebook format.

Connect with Dale Mayer Online

Dale's Website – www.dalemayer.com
Twitter – @DaleMayer
Facebook Page – geni.us/DaleMayerFBFanPage
Facebook Group – geni.us/DaleMayerFBGroup
BookBub – geni.us/DaleMayerBookbub
Instagram – geni.us/DaleMayerInstagram
Goodreads – geni.us/DaleMayerGoodreads
Newsletter – geni.us/DaleNews